DRAWN TOGETHER

LAUREN DANE

BERKLEY BOOKS, NEW YORK

THE BERKLEY PUBLISHING GROUP
Published by the Penguin Group
Penguin Group (USA) LLC.
375 Hudson Street, New York, New York 10014, USA

USA | Canada | UK | Ireland | Australia | New Zealand | India | South Africa | China

Penguin Books Ltd., Registered Offices: 80 Strand, London WC2R 0RL, England
For more information about the Penguin Group, visit penguin.com.

This book is an original publication of The Berkley Publishing Group.

Library of Congress Cataloging-in-Publication Data

Dane, Lauren.
Drawn together / Lauren Dane.—Berkley trade paperback edition.
pages cm
ISBN 978-0-425-25609-1
1. Women tattoo artists—Fiction. 2. Erotic fiction. I. Title.
PS3604.A5D73 2013
813'.6—dc23
2013006287

PUBLISHING HISTORY
Berkley trade paperback edition / October 2013

PRINTED IN THE UNITED STATES OF AMERICA

10 9 8 7 6 5 4 3 2 1

Cover art by Tony Mauro.
Cover design by Rita Frangie.
Text design by Laura K. Corless.

Praise for the Brown Family novels of Lauren Dane
LAID BARE

"[*Laid Bare*] moves and surprises you in all the best ways. I loved this book!"
—Sylvia Day, #1 *New York Times* bestselling author of *Entwined with You*

"The sex is sizzling, the emotions are raw . . . *Laid Bare*, quite simply, *rocks*!" —Megan Hart, national bestselling author of *Switch*

"The hottest thing since Prometheus gave us fire. Don't miss this book." —Ann Aguirre, national bestselling author of *Agave Kiss*

"Each and every love scene pushes the boundaries." —*Joyfully Reviewed*

"*Laid Bare* lives up to its title." —*The Best Reviews*

"A highly erotic read." —*Fiction Vixen*

"*Laid Bare* is proof that it's sometimes worth reading outside your comfort zone. This book is a gem and I can highly recommend it."
—*Monkey Bear Reviews*

"This book was just wow! Yeah, I know I should have known after reading so many great reviews, but seriously, I never imagined it to be so good." —*The Geeky Bookworm*

"Amazing! . . . This is the best book I have read this year."
—*The Book Girl*

"*Laid Bare* is a fantastic read on many different levels, but it's the way the story speaks to your heart that cements it as a must-read title."
—*Romance Junkies*, 5 Blue Ribbons

continued . . .

"*Laid Bare* puts the emotions of the characters right out in the open, nothing hidden." —*Manic Readers*

"In a word, this book is amazing. All three characters are magnetic and thoroughly realistic . . . With ménage and some mild M/M scenes, this is Dane's best story yet!" —*RT Book Reviews*

"If you like steamy sex scenes featuring dirty men and their dominating ways, you will not want to miss *Laid Bare*." —GeekVixen.com

INSIDE OUT

"*Inside Out* is tender, romantic and unapologetically sexy. Lauren Dane writes with an emotional depth and authenticity that always leaves me breathless." —Lara Adrian, *New York Times* bestselling author

NEVER ENOUGH

"If you even slightly enjoy a dirty-talking hero and a confident heroine who knows how to let loose behind closed doors all wrapped in an interesting and sometimes heart-tugging story, you must read this book!" —*Fiction Vixen*

Ever since Erin first came onto the page in *Laid Bare,*
I've had so much love for this group of family—
intentional and biological.
The Brown Family novels have been a joy to
write and I'm very grateful readers have enjoyed them so much.

I'll be back at some point because I can't really imagine
being totally done with these folks.
After all, there's a whole new generation
of artists and rockers coming up.

In the meantime,
this one is for the readers who've made this series possible—
especially for those of you who've understood
that, despite her crusty exterior,
Raven was worthy of her happily ever after.

ACKNOWLEDGMENTS

As always, my thanks go first and foremost to my husband. Without the support and understanding from my family, this gig would be a lot harder. And without him it'd be a lot more difficult to write an alpha male!

My thanks always go to my friends, who are such a fabulous support system. To Megan Hart, for being so awesome. And to my delightful, brilliant hoors at the Loop That Shall Not Be Named.

More thanks:

My incredible friend and assistant Fatin, who truly makes my life so much easier.

Mary, who is a wonderful beta reader.

My editor, Leis Pederson, who is so wonderful to work with.

The Berkley art department and Tony Mauro, who have consistently created such fabulous covers for my books.

Laura Bradford, my agent.

And always, to the readers who make this all possible!

1

"So Levi tells me you're a tattoo artist."

Jonah Warner was beyond hot. He was on-fire sexy. Like panties on fire. Raven looked him over, imagining him naked. Imagining him over her, under her, whatever. Just naked and doing something sexy with her would do just fine.

He had a voice like smoke. Like caramel and other things made with heavy cream and possibly deep fried. He was whatever things that were a thousand calories that you ordered anyway because you *had* to consume them.

"I do okay."

He looked her over with slow perusal. As if he was wondering what she looked like naked too. Which was absolutely fine with her.

One corner of his mouth lifted and she licked her lips, imagining his taste.

"You do more than okay." He held a hand out. "I'm Jonah Warner. Levi's brother. I know we've seen each other in passing at various events but I don't think we've formally met. I'd have remembered."

She took the hand and he slid a thumb over her wrist as he shook it.

"I'm Raven."

He made her all tingly in the absolute best way. She wanted a bite of this man. Maybe a whole mouthful.

"Did you do Erin's ink?" He tipped his chin toward where Erin stood with her brother Adrian.

"Nope. That's all Brody Brown. I do okay. He's a genius. But I'm hotter."

Jonah laughed then and she had to fight the urge to step closer. Anywhere but this party and she might not have resisted. But she'd promised Erin to try her hardest to remember her manners.

"You are most assuredly hotter. He's not my type at all."

"Thank God for that. If you were gay, I'd be very disappointed."

"That so?"

She nodded. "I mean, it'd be nice if a gal could watch. But the loss of such a stunning specimen would make womankind very sad."

He cocked his head, leaning back against the wall. "Brody recommended you actually. For ink. I have a project."

"What are you thinking of?"

"Would you like a drink?"

She shrugged. "Sure."

He took her elbow and steered her to the small bar. The party was in honor of Mary Whaley and her new fiancé, Damien. He'd asked her to marry him in front of a crowd of tens of thousands and she'd said yes.

A mutual friend, Gillian, was hosting and had invited Raven. Anyone else and she might have said no. She wasn't much for engagement parties. But it was impossible to say no to Gillian, so Raven didn't try.

She liked the way he handled her. He didn't ask, but he gave her a moment and some space to pull away. But once she didn't he took over.

He looked her up and down as they waited for the bartender.

"Pear martini for the lady. Sidecar for me." He slid some bills into the tip cup and handed her the martini once it was finished.

"Interesting that you'd assume I wanted this."

He tapped his glass to hers as he steered her away. "I had one earlier. It's strong and yet fragile. It occurred to me that it was a lot like you."

"You don't know me well enough to make that assumption." He held a chair out and she sat.

"I don't know you well enough to know what sort of sushi you like. But a drink is another thing entirely. It's good, yes?"

Oh this one. He had trouble written all over him. Bossy. Dominant. She would normally have thrown her drink in his face and walked away from a man like him. But there she sat, sipping a really delicious martini.

"Tell me about your ink."

"I want a full back piece. A wolf."

"Why?" She'd done a dozen wolves. If he wanted a full back piece, it should mean something or he should realize that if it didn't, he'd be stuck with something that meant nothing to him for the rest of his life. A small tattoo you could cover up or even get removed. But she was a big believer in full disclosure about the commitment one made with a tattoo of that size.

"Why do you want to know?"

"A back piece will take a lot of time. Some pain. Money. And it'll be on your skin forever. Partly I want to know because it'll be important in my design. For instance, do you want a Norse-style wolf? A Celtic-style wolf? Pacific Northwest Native American? A face in tight? A wolf moving or running? In a pack? Are there other elements you want in it? How do you envision it sitting on your skin? Also, this is a big, permanent thing. Sometimes people think it doesn't matter if the tat has no meaning and for some people that might be true. But a tat that large? I like to make sure people understand that a tattoo isn't like a pair of pants or hair color. You can't just change something the size of a full back piece." She shrugged.

He raised a brow. "I understand. How long have you been doing tattoos?"

"Since I was nineteen."

"So for what? Four years?"

She laughed. "You're so full of it. You know how hot you are, you don't need the bullshit to get some tail."

"You're a beautiful woman. Is that better?"

"Infinitely."

"Wolves symbolize things I believe are important. Loyalty. Honor. Protection. As for style, would it be possible to have you give me a few ideas to choose from?"

"Yes. I can show you some of my work. I have a portfolio."

"All right. You come highly recommended but it can't hurt to see your work. Do you do house calls?"

"I do."

"Would you like to have a drink with me? At my place. After you show me your portfolio that is."

"Is the drink contingent on the portfolio?"

"No. I'd want to have a drink with you either way."

He was blunt. She liked blunt a great deal. She was bad at reading people and being coy. It took more energy than she normally had. Definitely more skill.

"All right." She pushed her phone his way. "Put your number in there and I'll call to schedule something."

He leaned across, placing a hand over hers. "What are you doing tonight after this?"

A rush of heat blew through her.

"I'm busy." She was. She'd promised Erin she'd come over to see Alexander, and as that sweet little boy owned part of her heart, she wouldn't consider bailing, not even for a superhot turn in between the sheets with Jonah Warner.

"Hm." He sat back looking her over. He took her phone and put his information in it, doing the same with her number in his phone while he was at it.

She got the feeling he thought she was playing a game. And if that was the case, he could suck it. She didn't play games. They were useless and a waste of her precious time. If she liked a person and wanted to pursue something physical, she said so. And she had.

"Call me when you get the chance and we'll set something up." He handed her the phone and she tucked it into her bag.

"All right."

He started to say more, leaning in again, but Gillian tapped a glass and began speaking, so they turned their attention to her.

"Mary was the first person I met when I moved here back when Miles was a tiny baby. She and her family took me under their wing from the start. Little treats, homemade baby food, that sort of thing would show up. She has been a very dear friend since the start. Jules, Daisy and I are so thrilled to host this party because no one deserves happiness more than Mary Whaley, who has taken care of us all for years. So even though Damien has taken her away and spirited her down to Oregon for most of every month, we'll allow him to have her because he makes her so happy."

Jules put an arm around Mary. "To Mary and Damien."

Raven raised her glass and drank. She liked Mary well enough. She made Gillian happy, and that was important. She was good to Poppy, Gillian and Adrian's baby daughter, as well.

Raven didn't have many people she'd give a kidney to. But Gillian was one of them. And because Gillian loved Mary, that was more than enough reason to raise her glass and mean it.

They milled around and Erin caught her eye. Wanting to go home, Raven knew, to Alexander.

She turned back to Jonah. "It was a pleasure to meet you, Jonah. I've got to go now."

He stood, walking with her to where Erin stood with Todd and Ben, both her men. One her legal husband, the other the husband of her and Todd's heart. They'd both loosened up around her, especially once they realized how much she loved their son.

"I need to get my bag, I'll be right back."

Erin went with her, leaning in to speak quietly. "Holy crap, Levi's brother is so freaking hot. You gonna nail him?"

Raven rolled her eyes at Erin. "You've got two dudes of your own to nail; why the prurient interest in my knickers?"

"Be quiet about that. He's hot. Naturally I'll need every last filthy detail."

"He wants me to do some ink. There's chemistry. Chances are—if he's lucky—there will be filthy nailing to tell you about like you're my pimp."

Erin laughed. "I just want to check in on Poppy before we leave. Miles said she's popping a tooth."

Poppy Brown was clearly her father's daughter. She had the Brown ebullience. Always freaking happy. Always making noise or music. She lit up when someone she loved came into view.

So when they came around the corner to find Miles—Gillian and Adrian's now-sixteen-year-old son—holding his sister, who held his cheeks, patting them as she babbled, Poppy's little face lit even brighter when she saw her aunt and Raven.

She held her arms out and Miles frowned, loath to give her up.

"Once Aunt Erin has her, I'll never get her back."

Raven swooped in and took her instead.

"Hey, Pop, what's shakin?"

Poppy gave her a gummy grin, grabbing a fistful of Raven's hair. "Oh, I see your tooth."

Erin crowded in. "There it is. You have a chomper, Ms. P. Whatcha going to eat with it? A steak?"

Poppy gave a gusty laugh as she kicked her legs.

"I should have known you'd be in here with the baby." Gillian came in. She moved to Miles, putting an arm around him. "Hello to you, my biggest child. Mary says she's put a tote full of food in the fridge for you."

"Awesome." He kissed Poppy's head and ran off.

"I'm chopped liver to the food goddess and the baby."

Raven snorted. "Yes, that's so obvious. No one loves you, Gillian. You may as well eat worms." She'd had to explain that line to Gillian back when they'd first met.

"Give me that baby. I'm her aunt."

"Fine. Jeez. I'll see you later, Pop." Raven kissed Poppy's head and handed her to Erin, who immediately began to dance around and sing to her.

"I'm so glad you came tonight." Gillian smiled. "I don't like it when you're gone for so long."

Raven had been in Los Angeles and then stopped off in Honolulu for a while. She liked to roam. But she had people to return to in Seattle and found herself there more and more these days. She used to be gone for six months at a time and now she limited it to no more than a month.

"I'll be around for a while. Brody is down two people so I'll be there for the foreseeable future anyway."

Gillian smiled. "Good."

She shrugged, not always sure what to do with that sort of positive attention.

But Gillian got it. Much like Erin did. Gillian was an outsider. Had been for most of her life. She never pressed or got up in Raven's face about anything. That sort of acceptance was . . . it was startling, and it filled something inside.

"You know you're welcome to come back any time to see Poppy. And me of course."

"All right. I'll call you."

Gillian took Raven's hand and gave it a squeeze. "See that you do."

"We've got to get going. Alexander knows Raven is coming over to give him a bath and read him a story. He'll be mad if we're late."

Gillian's mouth tipped up into a grin. "Everyone's so afraid of you.

But they don't know that underneath that bitchy exterior is all marsh-mallow."

"All that postpartum stuff has made you goofy. That and your prolonged exposure to the Browns."

Erin handed Poppy back to her mother. "Hasn't done that to you."

"My bitchiness is bone deep. Even you people can't change that."

Erin linked her arm through Raven's. "Let's go."

"Thank you both for coming. We'll walk you out."

Adrian had been talking with Todd and Ben and the ever-so-delicious Jonah. But when he caught sight of his wife and daughter, his entire demeanor changed. Raven had to admit—to herself anyway—that having Poppy had changed him nearly as much as being with Gillian. He'd softened, even toward Raven.

"I'll meet you all back at the house." Raven nodded at Erin, who waved. She turned and nearly bumped into Jonah.

"Don't forget to call me."

She smiled. "I won't."

She put an extra bit of sway into her walk as she left. Didn't hurt to show him what he wouldn't be having that night.

2

He looked at his phone and her number for a while before he finally called. He'd dreamed of her, the delicious Raven, the night before. All lush curves and cat's eyes.

Jonah knew there was an element of danger with a woman like her. There were shadows in her gaze. She wasn't an easy sort of person. He got that from the way some spoke about her.

Then again, he wasn't an easy sort of person either. He'd dated easy women. Both kinds. If he wanted that, it could be had without too much effort. But that had gotten him a broken marriage and single parenthood.

He'd taken the last several years off from complications. He'd put his energy into raising his daughter, Carrie. She'd needed to finish high school and get prepared to leave for college. Her mother wasn't any help.

Though it had been difficult and he hadn't had much time for more of a life than parenting and working, it had been good. Carrie was smart. Strong. She'd had her pick of schools and though he'd winced when she chose Harvard—across the country . . . and Ivy League was still across the country—he'd also been incredibly proud.

He'd gotten used to being with her every day. Of getting up and having breakfast with her before she went off to school and he'd gone to work. The house was quiet now. Carrie was in Italy for her senior year of high school, having scored a spot in a prestigious art program.

The answered phone brought his attention back.

"Hello?"

Her voice did things to him, low in his gut.

"Raven? This is Jonah Warner."

"Why hello, Jonah Warner. I've got some designs for you to look at."

"Already?"

"Of course. I said I would. I keep my promises."

He liked that quality.

"Would you like to come to my house tonight?" he asked. "I've got a pretty busy day at work, but I'll be home by seven. I can make you dinner as incentive."

"All right, that works."

He gave her directions and she hung up and he was still smiling when he walked into court twenty minutes later.

"What are you smiling about?" His mother sent him a raised brow.

"What isn't there to smile over? It's a nice day. I won in court not once, but twice today. My mother has shown up in the office unexpectedly. Spoke to Carrie earlier, she's having a great time."

Liesl Warner wasn't stupid. She narrowed her gaze but didn't say anything else about it.

"Did she mention if she'd received my package?"

"She said it arrived Friday and to thank you." His mother scared people routinely, as regularly as she breathed. But she loved her granddaughter and sent her care packages several times a month. It probably made them both feel better.

"She sent me one too, with photographs as well. She's got quite an eye."

Art was important in his family. They'd been raised to appreciate it. His mother collected it, as did Jonah and Levi. It was no surprise really that Carrie wanted to be a curator or go into museum and collection management.

"Daisy has been a great deal of help." That had been surprising as well. Levi's hot young fiancée the artist had won their mother over quite handily. And she'd been supportive of Carrie as well. "I wasn't sure about your brother for a while, but Daisy is entirely suitable. He's far better behaved since they've been together. Have you noticed that? Now if they'd only actually choose a date to get married. My heavens, Jonah, what sort of engagement is it that lasts so long without a date?"

Ha. He wasn't going to touch that one. Not for all the money in the world.

In fact, it was time for him to get out of there so he could stop at the grocery store on the way home. He promised dinner but realized he had an empty fridge.

"I've got to rush." He gathered up his things. "Is there something you needed?"

He kissed her cheek on his way past as he turned out his light.

"Your father and I are going to the symphony tonight. Would you like to join us for dinner?"

"Not tonight. I've got some things to do. Have a good time though."

She looked him over again but didn't say anything else.

"I'm out of here." Raven gathered her stuff up.

Brody Brown, her friend and the owner of Written On The Body, looked up from his place just across from hers. "Whatcha up to tonight?"

"Thanks to your recommendation, I'm meeting with Jonah Warner about a full back piece."

"Nice. I saw something between you at the engagement party. Did I imagine more than ink talk?"

Brody knew her in ways less than a handful of people did. There was once a time when she could have let herself love him, and probably did, but she'd fucked it up. He liked to tell her she did it on purpose. But he'd been married for several years at that point. He and his beautiful wife had two kids and it fit him perfectly. He was still her friend. Always that.

"There's some chemistry."

Brody laughed then and she paused, cocking her head. "What?"

"Oh, just that from what I've seen and heard, he's the kind of guy who likes what he likes, exactly how he likes it. Gonna be fun to watch you try to sidestep being owned by a guy like him."

"Pfft. No one owns me, Brody Brown. And I happen to like what I like exactly how I like it. So maybe we'll be perfect for each other." She sniffed. "But for now, it's just a nice piece of work to do to pay the bills."

She waved over her shoulder as she left.

She stopped home before heading out to Jonah's house. She never used to have a place in Seattle. Or anywhere for that matter. She liked to house-sit instead. Kept her from feeling trapped. She traded out time in L.A. and Seattle mostly, did a few stints in Hawaii as well.

But when Erin had gotten pregnant with Alexander she'd wanted to be there for her friend. She'd known how freaked out Erin was about having another baby after losing her daughter in such a tragic fashion. And then it had been a high-risk pregnancy. So Raven had bought a condo in Capitol Hill with a nice view of downtown and the Sound. Just a studio. It had a bed and her music and sketch pads and clothes and that was pretty much all she needed anyway.

She got to spend time with Alexander, who she adored like crazy.

She'd never been one for kids until he'd come along. And then she'd found herself really enjoying Brody's daughters as well. Rennie, the oldest, who only stopped talking long enough to take a breath, and Martine, who had burst into toddlerhood and cracked Raven up.

So she'd let herself put some roots down and it hadn't felt bad at all. It had felt . . . all right.

She checked her mail, finding little of interest, and recycled the junk before heading upstairs to change and get her sketches.

Raven didn't work from transfers. They felt constraining. But she did like to work from sketches. Row after row of neatly organized sketch pads lined her bookshelves and she found the one she needed to take over to Jonah's that evening. She'd done several different styles so he could choose whichever he preferred from those.

She took her hair down from the ponytail she'd had it in all day and brushed it out. Brushing her hair had been a soothing ritual for her for as long as she could remember. Every night, every morning, whenever she was stressed or scared.

The clothes she had on were good enough for a long day bent over people doing ink. But. Well, she wanted to wear something pretty and sexy. Not too much of either. She liked Jonah. She hoped they'd end up naked and sweaty too. In the meantime, it wasn't a crime to look good for a man of his caliber anyway.

She'd mapped out directions online to his place so she found it easily enough. A nice neighborhood near the arboretum. His driveway curved a little up to the front of the house. Brick exterior. Lots of windows. Big lawn. His front door had a pretty knocker dealie on it.

She only had to tap it a few times before he opened it and stole her breath. He'd been dressed up for the party, but this night he had on a worn T-shirt that hugged over a broad chest and Levi's with bare patches on the thigh and at the hem. No shoes.

His dark hair was a little tousled and he had a look. Oh my, that look. Like he was going to take a big bite.

"Please, come in." He stepped back and motioned her inside.

She hesitated in the entry. There was a woman's stamp on that entry. Interesting that the man bore no indication of a woman's stamp at all.

"Can I take your things?" Jonah indicated the sketchbook and her bag.

"Oh sure." She handed them over.

Contrary to popular belief, she did have filters. A few anyway. She'd been working on it. Which is why she didn't blurt out the question she was dying to have answered about who had decorated the entry.

She didn't get involved with married men. She didn't have a lot of rules about her sex life, but that was one of them. She did not break her personal rules.

"Come through. Would you like a beer or a glass of wine? I hope chicken is all right. I should have asked if you were a vegetarian."

She followed him, checking out that ass and the broad expanse of his back. He'd look mighty fine with ink.

"Do you have other tats?"

"I do. Three others."

"Beer, please." She sat at the large island in the kitchen, watching him pull the beer from the fridge and crack it open. He had nice hands. Big. He moved with ease in his space. Though she'd seen him at the party and he moved with ease there too.

Confident.

He handed it over once he poured it into a glass and then clinked it with his.

"Chicken is fine. Who did your other work?"

"Two of them I got in Boston. The other in San Diego. How many do you have?"

"Six. Brody did them all. He'd kill me if I got them from anyone else." She snorted. "We're territorial, you know. Tattoo artists."

"Don't report me then. We've got about half an hour until the food is ready. Want to go out back? I picked up some appetizer-type stuff. You can show me the sketches while we have our beer."

He took her elbow and steered her out, not really waiting for her answer. But it wasn't rude, it was more . . . in charge.

Out back was a gorgeous deck overlooking the water and the lake beyond. He indicated for her to sit on a couch so she did. "This is pretty swank."

He nodded. "I can't complain. We used to live on the Eastside, but Carrie, my daughter, wanted to go to a high school over this way. She liked being able to help me decorate this place. Our old house . . . well, it wasn't hard to move."

That answered her question about who'd put the female stamp on the entry. "The mother?"

He was quiet a while. She figured that if he didn't want to talk about it he wouldn't.

"Yes. It was a house I bought for my ex-wife as a wedding present."

"What's that story?"

She drank her beer and sat back, looking out over the yard and the view.

Jonah wasn't used to people asking him really personal questions like this. Sure, his nosy mother and his brothers, who really had no manners when it came to family stuff. But not strangers.

It was oddly freeing.

"She left." He shrugged. "It was okay for about eight years. We had some good times. But she wasn't happy after that."

"What about your daughter?"

"My ex wasn't happy as a mother either."

A look flashed over Raven's face. Rage. And then it was gone. "She walked away from her kid or did you take your daughter from her?"

He started. "Do I seem that type to you?"

"People are seldom what they appear to be."

"That's pretty jaded."

"That's pretty reality. I don't know you that well. You clearly have a lot of money and you're not used to hearing no. Would you be the first rich powerful dude in history to railroad the wife to snatch the kid just because he could?"

Put that way . . .

He blew out a breath. "I'm not an asshole. No. I didn't snatch my daughter. But I would have if I needed to. My ex is far happier with my money than our kid. She walked away. Carrie was twelve so she made the choice to stay out here. Her mother lives on the East Coast."

"She sounds swell. Your ex I mean."

He paused and then laughed. "She's missing out on the best thing in the world." Jonah shrugged. "I can't pretend I understand it. It used to make me mad."

"Why not relieved? I mean, I know people who've gone through hellish custody battles. It sucks she's a twat and doesn't give two shits about her kid. But it sounds to me like your kid is better off without her mom in her life. Just because someone gives birth to you doesn't mean they're your fucking mother. Being a mom, or a dad for that matter, is more than biology."

"There's a story."

"Everyone has a story." She pulled a big pad out. "Here are some of the designs I worked up for you."

"I'd rather hear your story."

She sent him a raised brow and he liked it. A lot.

"Fine. But as you noted, I don't like being told no."

Her smile sent a shiver through him. "You'll get used to it."

He took her hand, turning it to press a kiss at her wrist. She smelled good. Warm. He liked the pleased surprise on her face and the indrawn breath.

"Or maybe you could get used to telling me yes."

"You're going to be a handful, aren't you?"

He nodded. "I'm told it's a flaw. I'll try to be worth it." This woman was a challenge, yes. But one he had every intention of undertaking. He wanted in.

"Hm."

He grinned as he sat back, taking the sketchbook and opening it. "Wow. These are incredible."

And they were. Such a range of styles and designs.

She scooted closer. "This one." She pointed to a design with multiple wolves. "Could go from your lower back up to your shoulder. I'd need to see where your other tattoos are to figure out how to integrate if they're close to your back." She turned the page. "This one would fit nicely square in the center."

Stunning. Concentric circles of design that built to create the image of a wolf head.

"It's more Celtic. The first is more Nordic."

There were others, but his attention kept returning to those first two. "Which do you like best?"

"You're a big man. Imposing. Intense." One shoulder lifted. "I like to see the skin where the tat would go. What your musculature is like. A bold tattoo needs to sit just right."

"Are you trying to get me naked?"

She smirked. "I'm sure it'll be worth the wait."

He pulled the T-shirt off and she hummed. That hum was a caress. She stood. "I need you up so I can get a better look."

He obeyed, staying very close. She didn't move away. Instead she looked up into his face. "Goddamn."

As compliments went, it was a pretty good one.

She circled him, near enough to brush the heat of her body against his skin. Her palms smoothed over his shoulders, across his back, down his spine. She traced the tattoo on his right shoulder.

"Decent work. I can touch it up here." Her fingertips brushed a spot of sensitive skin.

"Does it need that?"

"Only if you want it to look nice."

He turned his head and she was so very close. A quick movement and his hand cupped the back of her neck as he took that mouth of hers in a kiss. Hard and fast.

Her taste rushed through his system like wildfire as she opened to him. Her tongue slid along his as he claimed, took, demanded.

She kissed like she meant it. Matching him move for move. He'd kissed women before. But this woman knew what she was about. Took her time, tasting him. A nip of his bottom lip sent a shiver through him. He hauled her close, the sweetness of her curves against him. He was hard. So fucking hard.

All from a kiss.

When he got this woman naked they were going to set shit on fire.

He eased back, taking her bottom lip between his teeth a moment. "That was as good as I imagined."

Her smile was the furthest thing from coy possible.

"Dinner should be finished soon."

"Where are the other two tattoos?" She didn't step back and he didn't let go, but he had to move to show her.

Reluctantly he pulled away and unbuttoned his fly enough to show her the star below his belly button.

"My." She licked her lips.

"Is that a good *my*?"

Her gaze locked with his. "You know it is."

He guessed he did. He worked hard on his body. It gave him somewhere to channel all his sexual energy after the divorce. When he'd discovered he liked things his ex never would have allowed. And then he got concerned it wasn't normal or healthy.

But he was far too old to worry about it any longer. All this time he'd dated on and off. Fucked when he could, around Carrie's schedule because she was his priority. He'd had tastes here and there, never wanting to go too far. Never fully trusting any of those women to give him what he needed, or to let go of all that dark desire he harbored. He had felt that it wasn't worth it to really go full out with someone unless he was going to be with her full time. What he wanted, what he liked, wasn't a game.

And it had been fine.

But with this woman it was different. She was not fragile or shy. She was not coy. She wore her sexuality openly. She was the kind of woman a man could be an equal with.

He liked that a great deal.

"Is the other tattoo on your cock?"

He barked a laugh. "Fuck no. I like my cock too much to let anyone jab it with a needle."

It was her turn to laugh. "Good. Cock tattoos are not hot. You, on the other hand are very, very hot."

"The other tattoo is on my thigh. A small one. I'm thinking of getting it covered."

"Your ex-wife's initials? Wedding anniversary?"

"Am I that transparent?"

"No. But you don't seem the type to get tweety bird on a weekend bender or whatever. So if you wanted to remove it or cover it, I figure it's something you don't want to be reminded of anymore."

"I nearly said it was Yosemite Sam. But then I didn't think I could keep a straight face. It's our wedding date. She got one too, though I imagine she's covered it. At first I left it there to remind me of my mistake. Now it's just numbers inked into my skin."

He put his shirt back on and she made a little disappointed sound that brought a smile again.

"What's the star for?"

"I liked it."

"I like stars." She pulled her shirt up and he saw the smattering of stars across her belly and up her side.

"I like yours better."

"Good to know."

The kitchen timer began to ding and with a sigh he turned. "Dinner's ready."

3

"You're a pretty good cook." Truth be told, she'd sort of expected him to have a cook who also cleaned and took care of him.

"Carrie and I learned a lot together. She's better than I am. Mainly because my mother insisted Carrie be taught to run a household." He snorted.

"You disagree?"

"My mother's perspective is that it's a woman's duty. Mine is, she should know because she's a person who will be an adult on her own."

He was a surprise. Not that she wasn't around men who would raise their daughters to be independent women, but he clearly came from an established, *moneyed* family. She knew through Erin that the family matriarch was all about position in the community and all that jazz. But her sons, the two eldest anyway, were pretty open.

She nodded. "She's going to college so she'll need to know how to cook."

"Only so much Cup o' Noodles she can eat."

It made her smile to imagine him eating from a little foam cup. "Was that your college mainstay?"

"I had a roommate whose dad owned a restaurant. The guy was pretty amazing in the kitchen. I have to admit I ate pretty well in college. Law school involved a lot of takeout and peanut butter sandwiches though." He watched her with greedy eyes. "Can you cook?"

She shrugged. "I do all right. I have my few go-to meals. Spaghetti, tacos, soup. Nothing overly complicated. Erin, now she can cook."

"But she can't do tattoos."

He was a flatterer, Jonah Warner. And he knew just exactly what to say to get to her. It wasn't calculated in any way. Which only made it more powerful.

"She can't. But the rock star, two husbands, great kid, lots of money part gets her through."

He laughed. "How long have you known her?"

"Erin? Fourteen, nearly fifteen years now."

"Where did you grow up? I keep getting a little bit of Southern from you."

She tried to remain relaxed. It wasn't as if she never spoke about her personal life. Within limits. "Arkansas."

"Really? Where?"

She'd told people about Happy Bend, but this man . . . well, he got under her skin. Telling him this thing gave him power of a sort. She wasn't altogether sure if she wanted that.

"Small town in the middle of nowhere. Anyway, now that I've seen your back I think either of the first two designs would work really well. The others all would with some editing. But the tattoo on your shoulder would impact how I'd wrap a few of them."

"You're mysterious."

She snorted. "Not so much."

"If not, then tell me the name of the town."

She raised a brow. "You really don't like to be thwarted, do you? The thing is, even though you're ridiculously handsome and you kiss like you'd be really good in bed, I'm not going to be goaded like I'm in grade school." Not that she'd ever been much of a normal grade-schooler anyway.

"And to think you said *I* was a handful."

"Well, we all have our crosses to bear."

"So tell me something. Anything."

He was so ridiculously charming she couldn't resist.

"My favorite color is purple."

"Mine is green."

"I bet it looks awesome on you."

"What makes you say that?"

"Your eyes and hair, the sort of tawny skin tone . . . it would work with a deep green."

"What color are your panties?"

She grinned as she took a sip of her beer. "Who says I'm wearing any?"

He choked.

"Black. Wearing underpants with trousers or jeans is sort of mandatory in my personal rule book."

"There you go, cutting into my fantasy."

"Are we pretending I won't make your fantasy reality?"

He got serious as he looked her over so closely she had to fight back a blush.

Her shrug aimed at nonchalance but most likely failed. "I don't play games when it comes to sex."

Usually she said it calmly, but just then he made her feel defensive. Well, no, *defensive* wasn't the right word. Like she needed to declare it with her chin jutted out. Or something.

"You don't? Well, there goes *that* fantasy."

She laughed, relaxing.

"Well, there are *games* and there are games. I like what I like. I'm an adult. I think it's a waste of time to pretend we aren't sexually attracted to each other when we are."

His gaze went hooded.

"All right. I can get on board with that. I want you."

Heat and cold washed over her. Which was silly. She wasn't a virgin by any stretch of the imagination. But this sort of desire left her breathless. Giddy. She wasn't used to this. A slow heat sure. She'd felt that with Brody Brown for a very long time. He was an attractive man who cared about her, and that had been comforting as well as exciting. But this man . . . well. He wasn't the long, slow dance that men like Brody Brown were. This man was intense. He stole her breath.

Being so out of sorts and off balance wasn't something she did well.

Then again, she had no intention of leaving, so to pretend otherwise was ridiculous.

"And I want the Celtic design one. Circles. I like that."

She would have chosen that one in his place as well. He was a warrior type. Big and braw. Smart. Good lord, she could see the intelligence and cunning in his gaze. Like a wolf, she supposed.

"Nice choice."

"I feel vindicated that you agree."

"It'll look good on you."

"Why do I get the feeling you'd never allow otherwise?"

"I like my work. I like my reputation. If I cut corners or got sloppy, I'd have neither."

"That . . . and I think you're a control freak. Have you ever given any thought to releasing that control?"

His voice had gone low and silky and it sent a shiver through her.

"Are you going to try to convert me now?"

He laughed, but there was more than simple amusement there. This was foreplay.

"I suppose I'd like to show you my idea of heaven."

Good lord.

"Do I have to read your pamphlet now? I like candy on Halloween. I like to dance. I particularly enjoy premarital sex."

He stood, stacking her empty plate on his before carrying them to the sink. "In my religion, you can have all the candy, dancing and sex with me that you can stand."

"Hm. Well, perhaps conversion is something worth considering."

"First things first. Tattoos."

He got such a smug expression she was torn between amusement and annoyance. Men. "It's probably going to take at least two sessions, maybe three. Your design has a lot of shading. Just the outlining alone will take several hours. I can do it here if you like. Or you can come to my place or the shop."

"The shop is near Green Lake, isn't it?"

"Yes. Near the zoo. The regular hours are eleven to ten. But I can work around that if you need."

"Oh, I do need. But not that. Where is your place?"

"Capitol Hill." Really only about ten minutes from his place.

"And you could do it here you said?"

"You'll need a comfortable chair or a table to lie on. It needs to be the right height so I can work and not be stooped over. I'll have all the sterilized equipment with me, no matter where I do it."

"I don't have a tattoo table. But, and you're going to think I'm such a rich asshole, I do have a massage table. In my defense, I had to get surgery on my knee several years ago and the physical therapy involved massages. Because my schedule is crazy, they came out here. It's in a closet, but would that work?"

She laughed. "You *are* a rich asshole. But it should, depending on how high it is. I can work back and forth between a chair and the table. It should keep you more comfortable too."

He glowered and then stomped over, pulling her into his arms to kiss her hard and fast.

"I have to warn you that if insulting you gets me kissed, this is a negative-association thing. I'll have to keep it up to get more."

His dark look faded, replaced by a smile. "I'm not an asshole."

"Hmm. I have a theory about this. Would you like to hear it?"

"Come with me." He tugged and she followed. "You can tell me on the way."

"Where are you taking me?"

"Anywhere you'll let me. Tell me your theory."

"My theory is about rich people in general. So you're multi-generational rich. Old money, established family."

"You seem to know a lot about me."

"Yes, when I set my plan to get pregnant and trap you into marriage so I could live it up, I had a dossier created about you. It was either that or, say, live in Seattle where you're in the paper. Oh, or be friends with people who know your brother and his girlfriend."

He paused, looking her up and down. "Ouch."

"Indeed. Anyway, back to my theory. Second- or third-gen wealth produces trust-fund assholes who think work is red carpet for so-called charity events in between long bouts of shopping and partying. Rehab is involved sometimes. Marrying older men from other rich families who are supposed to calm Ms. Trust Fund and have her start breeding for the cause. But then there are those families who believe in noblesse oblige. Those successive generations make their kids have jobs. Raise them with a sense of responsibility and gratitude for their situation. Those kids, like you and Levi, work their asses off. But there's no getting around the simple fact that having money changes your life. You're accustomed to things like shorter lines at the airport, better service, nicer hotel rooms, your clothes are made better, you eat better. All that stuff. So you're not an asshole like some who'd yell at the cleaning lady or the valet. You were raised better than that. But you have a sense of entitlement. Not like the trust-fund kids, but it's there. You were raised with it. You can't get around it. You don't like being told no. You don't like being refused things. You wouldn't have this house and your expensive wristwatch if you weren't an asshole in some sense. You work for it and you have to overcome what some in your community do to be taken seriously."

"You're pretty smart."

She frowned. "For a gal who grew up in Happy Bend, Arkansas?"

"Now see, there you are."

"Here I am?"

He continued to draw her upstairs. "Yes. Happy Bend. Sounds like a lovely small town. Also, working hard and coming from money doesn't make me an asshole."

"It's not Mayberry. It's a shithole filled with assholes, alcoholics and losers." She clamped her lips shut against the words. "Anyway, I explained to you the difference between the asshole who throws cell phones at the help and the asshole who works hard but has a sense of entitlement to the best things in life. For instance, do you know how often I get asked by people if I do house calls?"

"No, but I get the feeling you're going to smack me with the point and I'm going to have to admit you're right."

"You should always assume that. But in this case, people ask for me to come to their homes very rarely. Sometimes if someone is recovering from a health issue that makes it hard for them to get out. But mainly, it's mover-and-shaker types. Who are simply used to being catered to. Now, like I said, there's a difference between types of assholes. If there wasn't, I wouldn't be allowing you to get me into your bedroom."

"How do you know that's where I'm taking you?"

"Because you want to fuck me."

"And I get what I want, Raven."

"In this case you will, yes."

He pushed open double doors and she had a very difficult time not being impressed, so she let it happen. Art dominated the walls downstairs as well, but up here, it was a different sort of art. Sensual.

The impressive thing, other than the art and the giant four-postered bed, was the view. The view out three walls of windows with wrap-around decking just beyond. The view that took in the lake.

"Gorgeous."

He looked her up and down. "I'm thinking the exact same thing."

"I'm no view of the lake. This is stunning." Imagine waking up to this every day. She might never get out of bed if this was what she saw each day. She'd just sit and sketch her time away.

"This is what sold me on the house."

She ran fingertips up the smooth, carved curves of the poster she stood nearest to. And hoped fervently he never fucked his ex on this bed. Not normally anything she'd have cared about. But . . . she didn't want to be associated with memories of another woman.

"I found this bed four years ago. In San Diego of all places, so it had to be shipped."

Well, that answered her question. No ex in this bed. Not a wife anyway.

"It's a king's bed."

One corner of his mouth lifted. "Is that so?"

She nodded.

The way he looked at her gave her butterflies. Is this what Erin meant when she talked about how Todd made her feel at times? Interesting.

"I'd like to fuck you. Well, I'd like to do lots of things with you, including fucking. You down with that?"

She nodded. "I'm *so* down with that."

"The glass is treated. No one can see in. So you should get naked for me."

She slowly unbuttoned her blouse to reveal the lacy camisole she was very glad she'd worn.

He hummed low, watching, his gaze on her a weight.

She stepped from her shoes, placing them beneath a nearby chair. The sticks came from her hair easily enough, sending it down her back and loose around her shoulders. The camisole slid from her skin, leaving her in a bra. A black-and-purple bra.

Next, the zipper at the side of her trousers slid down, enabling her to step from them.

"Your panties match your bra. I like that."

She didn't know why, but the fact that he liked it made her . . . proud.

The bra and underpants took only moments and she stood before him, far more than her skin bared.

He stared, long and hard, not trusting his words. She was so beautiful.

Long dark hair with threads of deep blue shot through it. Large, high breasts, silver bars through each nipple. Her skin was pale, creamy, and covered with ink here and there. Her legs were long, her toenails a deep red. She was bold, the way she looked back at him. And yet there was a fragility to Raven that grabbed him and didn't let go. He was torn between a clawing desire and a need to cosset and spoil.

The stars she'd indicated earlier started at her left hip and scattered up her belly, across to her other hip and up her rib cage. Up each of her inner arms she had thorns and roses that wrapped around her biceps and shoulders.

"I see three tattoos. Where are the others?"

She turned, pulling her hair aside. Across her back spilled ivy and purple flowers.

"What are the flowers?"

"Forget-me-nots."

Her voice, threaded with tension, tugged at him, drawing him closer.

"Eula?" He traced over the word that had been woven into a knot of ivy.

"My great-grandmother."

Each time she told him something personal it felt like a victory. "Ah. This work is stunning."

On her back at each hip sat a triangle with swirls.

"What are the triangles?"

"Triquetra on each side. Same basic concept, but the right is based on the disc I used to put in my 45 singles back when I had a record player. The other, well, it's got personal meaning."

"Enlighten me."

"The nature of three. Mind, body, spirit. Maiden, mother, crone. The three levels of earth. That design is Celtic. Like I said earlier, Brody did all my work. He's an artist, isn't he?"

Jonah didn't want any other man's name on her lips. Even though he knew Brody Brown was a man who appeared to adore his wife and two daughters. Jonah knew too that Brody and Raven had once been involved.

"You're quite the canvas."

He noted the soft upturn of her lips. A pleased, touched smile. He wanted to see it again.

"Can I undress you?"

The two of them paused. Each seemingly surprised by the request.

"Yes."

She pulled his shirt off again, leaning in to press an openmouthed kiss against his chest.

"Your body is beautiful." She murmured it, nearly to herself.

He didn't stop himself from sliding his palms over her shoulders and down her back, drawing her closer as she pulled his pants open and then down, kneeling as she did.

He stepped from his pants and shorts and then she looked up his body, shocking him into utter stillness as he took in the sight of this woman on her knees before him.

It was more than kneeling to get at his cock. It was . . . more. So much more.

"I like the way you look there. On your knees before me."

"Do you?"

He nodded, sliding his fingers through her hair.

"I do. Very much. So much that I think you should suck my cock. Yes, yes, I think that's definitely what you should do."

She leaned in, brushing her cheek against the line of his cock until he nearly hissed. How such a small thing could feel so amazing he didn't know, but it did.

She licked up the line from his sac to the crown, around and around, before sucking him into the heat of her mouth. Hot and wet, she took him deep, so deep he grunted at how amazing it felt.

Over and over, the rhythm of her down and up, down and up, the heat cooling as she retreated, only to shock him again as she swallowed his cock. Her nails scored up the backs of his thighs, her hands flattening on his ass to pull him closer.

From his vantage point he could take in the color on her back as her hair moved. It was so good he had an inner quarrel with himself. He told himself he could stop her in just a bit because he wanted more of her mouth. Then he told himself he had great recovery time and if he came in her mouth—and that idea appealed quite a lot—that he could concentrate on making her come and then by the time he was ready again, he could fuck her.

So he could have both.

Yes, that was it.

What he really wanted was to grab that gorgeous hair, wrap it around his fists for purchase so he could fuck her face. Not dignified. But he wanted it with so much greed it clawed at him.

She pulled back and looked up at him. The sight of those eyes and the expression on her face shocked him to his toes.

"Is there a problem?" One brow rose.

He laughed, giving in enough to caress her face and head. "Only the wealth of options you present."

"Liar."

"I don't know you well enough yet."

"Hm. You know me well enough to put your cock in my mouth."

Put that way . . .

He licked his lips.

"I said I didn't play games when it came to sex and I meant it. I think you should do the same."

He didn't want to scare her off. God knew he wanted at this woman for a while to come. But she was right.

"Get back to work."

His tone changed, and then his expression did. It sent a shiver through her and there was nothing more she wanted than to do exactly as he'd asked. No. *Commanded.*

So she did.

She knew he'd been holding back. Could feel the fine muscle tension in his arms as he'd touched her.

And then he shoved his fingers through her hair and tugged hard enough to bring a gasp, which quickly turned into a moan. That did things to her; shivers ran riot over her skin as her control slipped.

He tugged. Using her hair. Bringing her mouth on him closer, sending his cock farther back into her mouth.

She hated it when men touched her head during a blow job. But this was . . . different. Like a whole different planet.

He groaned and thrust as he pulled her forward, using her hair.

She struggled to get her breathing right, fought back panic. But she could do this, damn it. She *wanted* to do it. Wanted to make him feel good. Got off on the way he handled her, taking what he wanted.

And in a minute or two, she found her rhythm, got her breathing regulated and relaxed.

She hummed and he snarled. The satisfaction of affecting him like that seemed to shoot straight to her nipples, which throbbed in time with her thundering heart.

"Goddamn, yes. Like that. Christ, you're so fucking hot."

She held on, breathing, licking and sucking until his taste filled her, the hot wet of him titillated as she took everything he had to give.

And when she pulled back and kissed him, he picked her up, raining kisses all over her face as he moved her to his bed and lay her there with so much care she had to open her eyes to look at him.

He was smiling. "Wow."

It made her laugh as he joined her, the heat of his body against hers.

"Thanks."

"Now it's my turn to get a taste."

He kissed her. Kissed her so long and slow and deep she thought she'd burst from her skin. She was pretty sure she hadn't kissed like this in fifteen years at least. There was sex now, and so the kiss got short shrift on the way to fucking, which was a certainty. Back in the days of the long make-out, sex was an oh-my-god-I-hope-she-lets-me thing.

But this man knew he'd fuck her. And he kissed her long and slow because he wanted to. It was disarming and the panic returned. She was a kiss-a-few-times, fuck-hard-and-fast-and-go-home sort of woman. It suited her. But this was soul-deep fucking. Jonah Warner got under her skin, saw into her heart, and there were things inside she didn't want anyone knowing.

But he wasn't one to be rushed.

She took his hand and put it on her breast. He twisted the bar until she gasped into his mouth. And then he slid that hand all along her arm, clasping her fingers with his. And kept kissing.

He nipped her bottom lip. So hard it sent ripples of pain through her body. And then he returned to lave the sting with such gentleness it cut through her.

He kissed her, licked her tongue, her lips, he nipped and laved, sucked and seduced her mouth until she'd have given him just about anything.

And he was only getting started.

Later, she'd realize this was probably the moment she'd gotten in over her head with this man. But she couldn't think straight. Not with his hands on her. Not with the way he made her feel singing through her veins. She was drunk with him.

He finally pulled back, his face still very close to hers. His lips swollen from those long, drugging kisses. "You taste so good."

She swallowed hard. She worked to reclaim her inner sex vixen, but he rendered her a lazy mess, like a kitten in a freaking patch of sunshine.

He kissed along her jawline. Back to the spot just below her ear. She hadn't realized what an erogenous zone it was until he put his mouth there, hot, and sent sensation straight to her clit. She was so wet right then, just from kisses, for god's sake. She should have been embarrassed. But really, she only wanted him to keep on doing whatever it was he wanted. So he could continue to make her feel.

Nibbling across her collarbone, he took his time. Tasting her. Teasing her senses. The edge of his teeth surprising her when he nipped or abraded her skin with them.

"You're a master at this," she managed to murmur, sounding like a drunk.

"It's all you." He kissed along her rib cage, down her side. Up her belly until at long last he got to her tits.

"Hallelujah."

He chuckled as he nibbled along the swell beneath her nipple.

"I love how this looks." Then he flicked his tongue over her nipple until it hardened, tugging on the bar, stealing her breath. She'd always found the bars to enhance nipple play. But this was—like the rest of Jonah—something else entirely.

He licked and then tugged on the bar with his teeth, wracking her system with pleasure so sharp she had to clench her teeth.

"Mmmm. You like that."

"Uh, yes. I'm voting yes on everything you've brought to the table so far."

"Good to know."

He moved to her other nipple and did the same magic there. Nipples were great and all, but she wasn't usually one of those women who could come just from nipple stimulation. But Jonah's mouth might prove that wrong.

The scratch of his scruff only made the experience hotter as he abraded her skin. He kissed down her belly, over to the hollow at each hip. She floated in a haze of pleasure. She might have begged him to get on with it, but it probably never actually got out of her mouth.

He ran his tongue through the seam where her thigh met her leg. On one side and then kissed over to the other.

Then—sweet baby Jesus, thank you—he finally pushed her thighs wide.

She was a feast.

That's really all there was to it. Raven was a lush bounty and he couldn't seem to stop himself from binging. Her mouth, dear god, that mouth, so delicious. It certainly didn't hurt that her lips were swollen from his cock. Her skin tasted just right. Like nothing he'd had before. But he wanted it. Wanted more. Those pierced nipples had done him in. So fucking hot.

And now he stared at the ring nestled between her labia.

"Your clit is pierced. Holy fuck."

"Not my clit. The hood."

Her words were slightly slurred, slow and lazy. Good.

His cock wanted him to be aware that it was just fine and ready to go again. He wanted inside that glistening cunt.

But first he was going to eat her until he made her come really, really hard.

He leaned in close and breathed her in. Then he licked. So. Fucking. Good.

Hot.

The appeal of the piercing wasn't something he could deny. He tugged gently at first. But her moans deepened when he increased pressure, so he tugged harder.

He reached down to grab her ankles, shoving her feet up and back, spreading her open wide and utterly at his mercy.

More of this woman's bounty to take.

And he did. Licking and sucking, fucking her with his tongue. He wanted this to last.

Her clit was swollen and hard. Each time he licked over the piercing she gave a long, shuddering sigh. Probably mimicking the one in his head. Over and over. She was so amazingly responsive to his touch. So he just kept touching.

It was the way he sucked her clit into his lips, licking the underside after he'd tugged on that damned ring, that finally pushed her over. Her back bowed, muscles seized and she groaned long and hard as her taste filled every part of him in a hot, slick rush.

He found the muscle control to reach for the nightstand.

She opened her eyes and stretched lazily, grabbing him with her thighs and holding on. "Where you goin'?"

He held the foil package up for her to see. "Just a quick intermission."

Her smile made him even harder.

"Roll over. Ass up. Head down."

She complied so easily he had to take a deep breath and count to ten before he touched his cock to put the condom on.

"Goddamn, you're like a work of art."

He lined up at the notch of her cunt and pressed in, the breath leaving him. So hot she scalded him through the latex. She pressed back, taking him in deep and he slapped her ass without thinking. Then he snatched his hand back, unable to tear his gaze from the rising, red handprint he'd created.

But she didn't punch him or recoil in horror. Instead her cunt gripped him tighter, so tight he nearly saw stars when he had to close his eyes to get his control back.

"I decide the pace."

"All right."

He rewarded her with a hard thrust and she gave him a moan that shot through his system.

Her skin was beautiful and pale. The mark he made only spiced the edge of his hunger. He wanted to see a bite mark, or the bruise from his thumb. Wanted to know she'd wear the evidence of the way he'd been in her, long after she'd left his house.

Greed for her seemed to rush through him. Desire so deep he struggled against it until he realized there was no way out and simply gave in. She'd been different from the first moment he'd spoken to her. Hell, even before that as he'd caught sight of her at the edges of the few events they'd both been part of.

He ran his hands over her curves, over the nip of her waist, the bumps of her vertebrae, the sweet flesh of her ass.

And he gave it another slap. Again, harder than he'd imagined.

It burned. The pain, for long moments, had roused her from that lazy pleasure at the way he'd felt when he'd worked his cock into her pussy. And then the burn spread. Slow and delicious. Tingling.

And then . . . he'd told her he controlled the pace. He'd ordered her around, and for the first time in her life, instead of reacting and pushing back, she let him. And it had been . . . really, really good.

So she let it be.

He'd given her an orgasm from his mouth that had pretty much devastated the memory of every other damned orgasm she'd ever had. And her sex life had been really healthy and awesome. So really, what was the point in arguing when he clearly delivered on the promise to make her feel good?

His cock was fat. Filling her just right. His hands had settled at her hips, fingers digging in to control her movement as he'd begun to fuck her in short, hard digs that sent her tits brushing against the blanket beneath her. Sending slow waves of pleasure through her when she'd just come moments before.

He had game all right.

Jonah fucked her at his pace. Just like he'd said. Slow and hard. A fairly irresistible combination. She'd fallen into a place, a dreamy sort of consciousness, floating on the pleasure, flattered—insanely so—that he so clearly found her desirable.

One hand let go and he got closer as he reached around her waist and down, finding her pussy. She sucked in a breath as he tugged the ring and then squeezed her clit. He played awhile, seemingly testing her to find what she liked best. And then he worked it, over and over and over, until she was coming again and he grunted a strained curse and pushed in deep.

They fell to the mattress. He disappeared for a few moments and came right back, putting an arm over her waist and then pulling her close.

"When I regain the ability to move again, I have ice cream in my freezer."

"You're going to propose some sort of Faustian bargain, aren't you?" She mumbled this into the hard muscle of his biceps. "I mean, awesome sex, great food and now ice cream? Will I have to give you my soul?"

He chuckled. "Maybe."

And she still didn't run.

4

He really couldn't have said why he found himself standing in front of Written On The Body just three days later.

Which was a total lie. The reason lay just inside. Jonah hadn't been able to get her off his mind. Her voice, the way she smelled. The feel of her body against his own. She'd lodged herself under his skin, drawing his attention. And he didn't care to fight it.

That night at his home he'd wanted her to stay over but she'd refused. Politely enough. But when he'd woken up alone and hard, it had only underlined how much more he craved from this woman.

She stood at the counter, grinning up at Brody Brown. Jonah frowned. Oh, he knew there was nothing romantic between them. Not anymore.

Just the evening before he'd seen Levi and Daisy at an art event in town and he'd opened himself up to so much trouble when he'd pumped Daisy for information about Raven. He'd never hear the end of it. From Daisy and from his brother.

He knew though that for a time, many, many years before, Raven and Brody had been a thing. That Brody had been in love with her, or had thought he was, and she'd never wanted to settle down and had been with someone else. Daisy had been careful to underline, though, that Raven, by all reports, had been clear with Brody that she wasn't monogamous. It had meant something to know she hadn't cheated.

But the two were close to this day. Daisy had indicated that there was trouble when Brody's wife, Elise, had first come onto the scene, but the two women had worked things out, and that she was extremely connected to Brody and Elise's daughters.

He knew she wasn't seeing anyone seriously. Again, Daisy had underlined her lack of *wanting* to see anyone seriously. Which Jonah thought was bullshit. If anyone deserved some seriously, it was Raven. She needed a man to cherish her. To anchor her. He was old enough to understand this thing he felt about her was way more than infatuation. There was a lot of getting to know each other to be done. But he knew what he wanted, and he got what he wanted.

He wanted Raven.

She turned her head at the sound of the bell at the door and her smile changed when she recognized him. She was touched. And he was doubly glad he'd come by.

"Hello, Jonah. What brings you here?" She moved around Brody to him and triumph heated his gut.

He took her hands, linking his fingers with hers, tugging her into a hug. She went willingly, kissing the side of his neck as she did.

"You bring me here. Are you free for lunch?"

"I have a piercing coming in in five minutes. After that I'm free for a few hours."

"You do piercings too?"

She smiled as he released her and she stepped back. "I do. Why? You got something you want me to pierce?"

"Maybe later."

She laughed.

"So how about I hang out for a few and we can head out when you finish? Is that all right?"

She shrugged. "Sure. Or you can pop over next door and grab a coffee or something and I'll collect you when I'm done."

"Can I watch you work? Or is it a piercing in a place I can't see?"

"It's an eyebrow piercing so you can watch from this chair here. My station is there." She pointed.

He grinned. "All right then."

Her client came in and he didn't fail to notice the more-than-friendly kiss the woman planted on Raven's mouth.

"An ex. But *really* ex." Brody stretched out in the chair next to Jonah.

"Am I that obvious?"

Brody laughed. "Nah."

"I know there are women in her past too. I'm not shocked or anything." If he couldn't hold her attention, it wasn't that he was male. He knew enough about their chemistry to understand it was more than that for her anyway.

Brody sucked in a breath and began to speak, but held back.

"What?"

"She's a lot more than she appears to be on the outside. I know you've been asking around about her. She's abrasive sometimes. Blunt. But she's not as tough as you might think."

"I'm not out to hurt her."

"That's good. Because she's had enough of that in her life. Just don't go thinking she's someone you can tame. That way lies madness. Heartache."

Well, Jonah tended to think that she'd find the right person one day. There was vulnerability there, just beneath her surface. That was the Raven that so fascinated him.

"I like her. She likes me. It's a good start. And how did you know I was asking around?"

Brody laughed. "I suppose I should let you know that nothing stays secret for long in our group. Gillian is very protective of Raven. She knows from Daisy, who is one of her besties. And then Erin found out and told Elise, who then told me. They wanted to know about you. If you fuck her over, it won't just be my foot in your ass. You'll have a gaggle of pissed-off women to be scared of."

Jonah knew enough of Daisy to truly understand that threat. The women who his brother's lady love surrounded herself with were strong and fierce as well as hot. "I thought she and your wife had a strained thing?"

Brody snorted. "At first, yes. But that was years ago. Raven is really special to me and Erin. She's good to my kids. She's good to my wife. Once she lets you in, there's a whole different side to her."

"And you?"

"Raven has repeatedly been there for me when I needed her to be. Without having to be asked. She moved up here more permanently after Alexander was born to be with Erin when Erin needed her. She is a friend in the deepest sense of the word. She's my family. And if you fuck her over, I will fuck you over right back."

Raven finished up and turned back, raising a brow when she caught him talking with Brody. She took payment and waved as her friend left.

"Whatever are you two talking about?" She came to stand in front of Jonah, holding her bag.

"I was telling him that you'd do a great job on his tattoo." Brody stood and Jonah did as well.

"Ready to go?" He held out an arm and Raven linked hers with it.

"Sure."

"Know any good places nearby?"

"The café next door is good. Erin owns it and still works there a few days a week."

"I won't have you to myself, will I?"

"Probably not. I'm totally irresistible, you see. Everyone loves me."

He put an arm around her shoulder to pull her closer. She wore snug jeans and boots with a really fantastic red sweater that hugged her curves. "I certainly think you're irresistible. And you smell really good."

"My goodness, I already let you see my boobies. You're being awfully nice."

"I'm a nice guy."

"You're pretty nice. And you eat pussy like a champion."

He paused, swinging her to face him. "It's a beautiful pussy." He kissed her quickly and released, pulling her back to his side as they kept walking.

"There's a little Thai place just ahead. I like it. The food is decent."

"Some tea would be good."

The place was packed, but after a five-minute wait they got a table and settled in.

He pulled her chair out and to his surprise, she allowed it. But when he sat, she put the napkin on his lap.

They ordered. She waited for him to lead, which . . . affected him and he wasn't entirely sure why.

But she was sure to order tea for them both and when it arrived she poured it out. "Do you take sugar?"

He took her hand instead, kissing her palm. "I like it that you're taking care of me. That you know I'm capable of it but you do it anyway."

She smiled. "Oh. Well. Thank you."

Shy fit her well. He loved her boldness, yes, but this side to her was alluring as well.

He let go. Reluctantly. Sipping his tea, he took her in.

"What?"

"Do I make you nervous, Raven?"

"You know you do when you do that look thing you're doing now." She sipped her tea. "And. You like it."

He laughed. "I guess I do. Are you having a good day?"

"Much better now that a handsome man swept into work and took me to lunch. How about you?"

"I had a hearing this morning. Went to a charity board meeting up here, that's why I was in the neighborhood."

"Which charity?"

"It's one of my mother's favorites. Created Families. A program that gives support to foster parents. It's a tough thing. Half a million kids are in the foster care system. They don't get the support they need and we've essentially just been writing off generations of kids. And the families who are in the program struggle. They have good intentions but often get lost in the system."

She stiffened and he put his cup down, concerned.

"Everything all right?"

She took a deep breath. "Yes. Fine."

"Liar. Is it the foster care stuff?"

"I am not opposed to foster care." She said it so carefully, so very stiff.

"You sure you didn't go to law school? That answer was pretty classic. These kids need help. There aren't enough homes for them. No one should have to spend their childhood bouncing from place to place."

"No, they shouldn't."

Then he got it. "You were in foster care?"

She looked down at her plate for long moments and he was sorry he'd followed up because while he wanted to know her, he didn't want to cause her heartache.

"I was, yes."

The food arrived and she busied herself dishing things up, asking him what he wanted and how much. It seemed to smooth them both a little.

"I'm sorry. I didn't mean to upset you."

She waved it away. "I was in and out of foster care from four to seventeen. So I know firsthand that kids shouldn't bounce around from place to place. It's nice that you're trying to help."

He wanted to say more but the look on her face told him she was done talking about the subject.

"So how about you come over Friday night? For the first tattoo installment. I promise you dinner and well-made martinis."

She pulled her phone out and checked her calendar. In some women he'd have suspected it was an affectation made to appear busy, but he saw plenty of things written down. And then got annoyed that she didn't say yes right away.

Which then annoyed him that he'd expect something like that.

"Friday works. I can come over at eight thirty."

"Good. Do you have days off?"

"Yes, usually one weekend day and one weekday. It gives Brody time with his family if I spot him on the weekends. Why?"

She used her chopsticks like an expert. He liked the grace with which she moved. And the way she seemed to step in and help her friends.

"Come spend the day with me. We can go see the leaves. Drive up north a bit, have a nice meal, drive back. Do you like jazz?"

"I like most kinds of music. Especially live."

"There's a place. In SODO. Big band jazz. We can stop off at the house and then go for a drink and some music."

Her face lit and he was glad he'd suggested it.

"Yes. I'd love that."

"All right then. I have some work Saturday, but I have Monday off."

"Okay then."

He wanted to push it a little. "You should wear red. I like you in red. And your hair down."

She looked him over as she ate for long moments. "All right."

Raven liked how he backed off after she'd told him about being in foster care. She liked how he'd opened her door and pulled out her chair. It had been . . . odd, yes, odd the way a thrill had rushed through her when he'd told her to wear red and leave her hair down.

If another man had said the same thing, in the same bossy tone he'd used, she'd have gotten up and left the restaurant. But he wasn't another man. And her pussy seemed to really like it when he got bossy with her.

Probably something she should get therapy for, like everything else in her life, but a girl needed a few issues, right?

He insisted on paying and she let him. It was thirty bucks anyway. He insisted on walking her back, her hand in his as he spoke about this or that, nothing serious or heavy.

He shielded her body with his own, walking on the outside, moving in front of her if a crowd came walking from the opposite direction. It was courtly. Gentlemanly.

No one treated her that way. But he did.

It shouldn't have mattered. It was just manners. But it did. And she wasn't sure if she wanted it not to matter more than she liked that it did.

At the door to the shop he paused, pulling her out of the doorway. He pulled her close and she wrapped her arms around his neck.

"Thanks for sharing your time with me."

"I'm glad you came out. I know it's not exactly near your office."

He shrugged. "My office is in the north part of downtown. It's really only about ten minutes away. And." He paused, bending down to kiss her, warmth rushing through her system at that contact. "I like seeing you."

"Like fried food."

Confusion washed over his features. "Hm?"

"I really like it. But it's super bad for me. And yet, I can't get enough. You're like egg rolls."

His confusion was replaced by a rather rakish grin. "I'm way less fattening."

"I'll keep that in mind. See you Friday at your place, then."

He let her go, hauling her back once more for another kiss before finally opening the door.

"Just gonna watch you walk away. Your ass is spectacular." He said it quietly, his breath brushing against her ear and sending a shiver through her.

5

Raven looked up from the client she'd just finished working on to catch sight of Erin coming through the door with Alexander on her hip.

When he saw Raven, his face lit up and he clapped. "Auntie!"

The thing about three-year-olds was that they didn't judge you. Oh well, they did, but for stuff like not having Goldfish crackers in your cabinets. So she always was sure to have Goldfish in her cabinets, because hello.

She'd never understood this about children before Alexander had been born. Raven had always tended to avoid them before that. But when he'd come along, she'd fallen in love nearly instantly.

Alexander, like his mother, was simply impossible not to love. And so she'd given up trying to keep any walls around her heart and it had been one of the best decisions she'd ever made.

Being with Alexander was always so awesome because he accepted her. The way she was. Not the way he thought she should be. There was something comforting in that.

She thanked her client, a guy she'd done work on for nearly ten years, and moved to where Brody had intercepted Alexander, swinging him up high and then bringing him in close for a hug.

He giggled, joy simply radiating from him. "Bo, Bo, Bo! Yo."

Raven laughed at what a big old softie Brody was.

Erin grinned up at her brother, watching the way Alexander crawled up that chest with absolutely no fear.

"He's going to give me a heart attack. He's not afraid of anything."

Brody snorted. "Welcome to my world. You and Adrian aged me at least fifteen years, and you're both still around today. Uncle Brody isn't going to drop this kiddo."

"No way, Bo!" Alexander kissed his uncle's chin, tugging his beard.

He wouldn't, Raven knew. He was just that sort of man.

"It's probably also that his dads are so gigantic he has no idea that's not the norm." Raven put her head on Erin's shoulder a moment as they watched Alexander.

"Could be. How are things?"

"Not bad at all. Seems to be my week for visits from people at the shop, so I can't complain. You?"

"Groovy. Want to come to Red Mill with me and the young master? He sat straight up in bed this morning and shouted, 'Rings!' I took that as a suggestion we come grab you for a lunch date."

Brody handed him over to Raven and he latched on, hugging her neck and giving her sloppy kisses. She squeezed him back, loving his weight and the way he trusted her to hold and not let go.

Erin kissed his elbow. "What say you, baby? Can Auntie come along for burgers and rings?"

He let go enough to lean back and look up into Raven's face. He grinned, showing a neat row of straight white teeth. "Sure. Yes!"

"Awesome. It's a date then." She swung him to her hip and he held on, playing with her hair as she checked her appointments. "I'm free for another few hours."

"I wish it wasn't so cold already or we could make a picnic of it."

"Ah well, it's always a picnic when we're together." She kissed Alexander's forehead.

They walked, as it wasn't raining and they weren't in a hurry. Once she put him down, Alexander held her hand on one side and his mom's on the other.

"How'd it go? With Jonah, I mean."

Raven rolled her eyes at Erin's failure to sound so casual when she was really just digging for info.

"He came in to take me to lunch yesterday. I'm starting his tat tomorrow night actually. You should see his house. View of the lake. Huge. Lots of art all over the place. He can cook pretty well too."

Well aware of Alexander's awesome ability to mimic and repeat any and all manner of things, Raven knew Erin was dying to ask about sexytimes but couldn't. This amused her greatly.

"Gillian says he asked about you. Through Daisy and Levi, of course. It was nice, don't get that look."

"He's the type who wants to know everything."

Erin laughed. "He's going to be so frustrated with you. Then again, I'm going to bet he finds the mystery hot."

"He's bossy. I'm sure he thinks it's simply his due to know everything about me."

Erin sent one raised brow as Raven opened the door at Red Mill.

"Rings. Rings. Rings!" Alexander did a little dance as they waited in line.

"I feel you, kid." She gave her order quickly and efficiently. They didn't mess around at Red Mill. You didn't talk on your cell phone when you got to the counter or they'd send you to the end of the line. They didn't have a twenty-eight-page menu. But everything they did, they did to perfection, including the green chili chicken sandwich and rings she was going to stuff down her gullet in just a few minutes.

It was late enough that they found a table and squeezed in. Alexander tapped and sang as Erin blew on the freshly made rings so he wouldn't burn his tongue.

Her friend was an awesome mother. Alexander would never have even a moment in his childhood when he doubted how much he was loved. It meant a lot to Raven to know that on his behalf. Meant a lot to know that Alexander would grow up to be an adult who lavished love and attention on his children too.

And it also meant a lot to Raven to know she could love this child and prove to herself that she wasn't so broken she was incapable of being a mother herself. If she ever wanted to, which she wasn't sure about.

But Alexander helped her put a lot of perspective between herself and her history.

"You're coming for Thanksgiving, right?"

Raven sighed. "I don't know, Erin. I usually travel at the holidays."

"But things have changed now." Erin tipped her chin in Alexander's direction.

"Will Adrian be there?"

"Gillian will. And Poppy. And Miles and Rennie and Martine. And Alexander."

Alexander waved an onion ring round. "I be there."

"That's always my favorite part, bud." She smiled his way before looking back to Erin. "You're really sneaky and underhanded." Erin knew Raven couldn't resist things if Alexander was part of them.

"I totally am. Which is ultimately part of my charm. Let's be real."

"It's sad you have such deep self-esteem problems. I'm not a holiday-with-the-family person. You know that."

"The people you were born to don't deserve you anyway. What I know is that *I'm* your family. And I love you and this monkey right here loves you and Gillian loves you. Brody loves you. Rennie adores you. Even Adrian has softened because that baby of his thinks you're the best thing ever. Please? You're often gone during the holiday season and I don't want you to be alone. I want you at my table eating turkey."

"You're not going to be satisfied until I agree, are you?" Not that Raven really wanted her to be disappointed. Knowing someone wanted her at their table meant something.

"Heck no." Erin's grin showed no guilt.

Alexander patted her hand. "Heck no. There's turkey!"

Raven kissed Alexander's temple and he shoved a piece of grilled cheese sandwich in his mouth.

"Fine."

"You need to always give in to my requests. Things would be so much easier that way."

Raven rolled her eyes and Alexander told her about his new preschool class before they finished up and walked back to the shop. Pausing for bird sightings and to take a few turns on the swings.

It had been a very nice two-hour break.

"It's good you have an in with the boss to take such long breaks." Erin winked at her as Alexander strolled over to watch his uncle work.

Erin owned the café next door so Alexander had spent a lot of his childhood not only there but in Written On The Body as well.

"Kid's got a fascination with ink." At least he knew people who'd give him great work when the time came. Or he'd end up a tattoo artist.

"He's lucky enough to be able to watch two of the very best in the world on a regular basis." Erin waggled her brows. "We need to get together for drinks so you can give me all the dirty details about Jonah," she added in an undertone. "You're coming to Delicious on Sunday, right?"

Raven shifted, uncomfortable. Mary, the woman who ran the supper club, came up once a month to host it for their friends and family. The food was wonderful, but it was exhausting to put out all the effort everyone expected of Raven.

Erin looked to Alexander, who had hopped up next to Brody, watching intently. "She asked if you were coming. Mary likes you. It's a fun adult thing and I so rarely get that. I want you there. I know it's selfish of me. But we can have some wine and you can tell me about Jonah."

"Or I can write you an e-mail or you can call."

Erin's expression told Raven that her friend wouldn't let up until she agreed. "Everyone is so nice. I'm not one of you."

"Stop pretending to be so hard. This is me you're talking to."

"It makes me really tired. With you I don't have to work so fucking hard. I'm just . . . anyway. Maybe I'll go."

Erin searched her features and Raven didn't want to be known so well right then. She craved the lonely—but under her control—space people made around her when they didn't get her.

And Erin made it worse by hugging her and speaking in her ear. "I love you, Raven. I love every part of you. I accept you because you always have loved every part of me. Thank you."

"Stop. Please. Not now." Tears threatened and she willed them away.

Erin brushed the hair back from Raven's face. "I'm sorry. I just like being around you and it's been so awesome having you here more since Alexander has come. I want other people to know you like Brody and I do."

"Yeah, well, not everyone finds my honesty refreshing." She stepped back, pulling herself together. "I have a client coming in a bit. I'll talk to you soon. I promise. And I love you too."

Brody had noted the exchange with a raised brow to Erin, but said nothing. Erin knew her brother would ask her later on just what had transpired between them.

Alexander patted the hand of the client getting the ink. "Nice going, dude." He hopped down as Brody laughed and kissed the top of his head. "Bye, Bo. See you later. Love you."

"Love you too, monkey."

Alexander ran back to his mom but stopped to get a hug from Raven, who'd knelt to get face-to-face with him.

"Love you, Auntie."

"You know I love you right back. Always and forever. But I like to say it anyway. Because you make me happy. "

Erin knew they weren't just words to Raven. Many people told kids stuff but didn't really think on the depth of commitment the words given came with. People said *I love you* with so much ease, but they didn't usually mean it. Not really.

The thing people did not understand about Raven, because they only saw her outside, was that she didn't say anything casually. Or easily. Though she was often blunt, it was her way of trying to connect on some level. But when it didn't work, it only pushed her further away.

She let very few people get close, but once she loved, she loved totally and forever. Alexander was lucky to have her in his life.

Even her men, who'd distrusted Raven at first, had come to realize just how fiercely Raven loved their son and through that, they'd come to know her better and even to like her.

She needed the details on this thing with Jonah Warner. For far too long, Raven had kept her dalliances shallow and only about the physical. A man like Jonah might only want a few fucks, but Raven was playing it close to the vest. Which was unusual.

"What are you up to tonight?"

"I have a late client here and after that I'm getting a massage."

"And tomorrow night is tattoo night with the bossy Mr. Warner. So then we obviously need to talk on Saturday. Come along with me. I need to get a new pair of boots and a birthday present for Ella. I'll pick you up at your place at noon. We can get lunch and go shopping after."

Raven eyed her suspiciously but nodded. "All right."

It'd give her more time to work on Raven about going to the supper club too. Win/win.

"Come on, monkey. We need to get bread and milk on the way home."

"'Kay." He tucked his hand into hers and squeezed, grinning up at her.

"What's going on in your life?"

Jonah had just signed on to a video chat with Carrie. She was so grown up, so far across the world, that for a moment the bittersweetness of it was a lump in his throat. This was his child. Only she wasn't a child anymore. She was nearly grown up. On the cusp of college. She looked a lot like her mother, but he knew she'd react to that beauty differently. And was grateful for it.

"Not much. I'm getting a tattoo on my back. The wolf idea we talked about before you left."

"Really? Good. Grandmother is going to freak. Please wait to share it with her until I get back so I can see it in person." She broke into giggles and he snorted.

"Your grandmother thinks you're such a proper young woman. I won't spoil it for her just yet. I miss you."

"I miss you too. I'm used to telling you everything every single night when you get home from work. Now I have to e-mail you everything. I went out on a date." She laughed again, most likely at the look on his face. "He's in the program here with me. He's nice, Dad."

It was really, really hard letting go. He knew he'd raised her right. With a sense of herself and her limits. He knew she'd make mistakes. Everyone did, especially when they were young. But still.

"Be aware I'll have to have anyone who hurts you killed." He shrugged. "I know people."

Carrie's delighted laugh soothed his suspicion of the phantom boy.

"Mom is going to be in Milan next month. She had her people contact me to see if I'd like to go to lunch and do some shopping."

He blew out a breath, trying to take cues from Carrie on how to react. He hoped his suspicion and derision didn't show. Most likely

Charlotte wanted an all-expense-paid weekend and would use their daughter to get that. But god knew he wasn't going to let that occur to Carrie if he could help it.

"All right. I can add money to your account and get you a ticket and arrange a hotel." That way he could control it somewhat.

"It's all right. I have a museum trip that weekend. I don't want to miss it."

He didn't know how to make it better. It tore him up.

"Tell me what you need."

"She walked away. I wish she hadn't. But she did. And I have you and everyone else at home. Maybe when I'm older I can do lunch with her and it'll be okay. But not now. Not for a while. Not here."

"You don't have to not see her because you're worried about how I'll feel. I want you to have a relationship with your mother, Carrie. She loves you."

"In her way. But it's all about her. And right now, here it's about me. She probably wants to see me to get you to give her more money anyway."

He scrubbed his hands over his face. That bitch he'd married had no right to manipulate their child to get more of anything from him. But she did it and he believed part of it was that she wanted to poke at him, knowing how much he hated it.

"I'm sorry you get put in the middle."

"I'm a big girl. Anyway, I don't want you to feel bad. I only told you in case you heard about it otherwise. I didn't want you to think I was hiding it. Let's change the subject now. Are *you* dating?"

"There's someone interesting. I don't know yet. Not dating. More like getting to know her first. If she's dating material, I'll tell you more."

"I'm not harboring any fantasies that you're going to get back with Mom or anything. You're a man in the prime of his life. I want you out there."

"I promise I'm not withering up and dying. I take my personal life seriously. I have a family and I'm not just going to bring random people into it. Not because I think you can't handle it. But because I respect my life and my daughter enough to make the right choices."

"You're so awesome. By the way, since I'm buttering you up and all, can I take a side trip to Paris with some of the other kids after Halloween? Just for four days. There'll be chaperones even."

"Hm. I want to hear from your program assistant about it. If it looks safe, yes. As long as you're home for Thanksgiving."

"Thanks, Dad. And yes, I'll definitely be home! I got the ticket and everything."

Things were changing. More than they had in a really long time. Since the divorce, when all the change had been positive but came from an extremely negative process.

But it was five years later. Seven, really, since things had deteriorated so badly between him and the ex. Carrie had blossomed as a teenager. Her grades had improved when Charlotte had left for New York and exited Carrie's life.

Carrie was moving on to the next step. Going to college in the fall. He missed that little girl he'd taught how to sail. But he knew she'd be a wonderful woman. Knew she was strong and intelligent and would succeed. He was proud of that. Proud of her.

And now he had time to think about himself again. Not as a father. Not as a son or a partner at work. But as a man.

Change was good.

6

"So let's try you sitting first. I'm going to get the outline started."

Raven had shown up with her hair tied away from her face, in an ages'-old Bikini Kill T-shirt and faded jeans. She was just as beautiful as she was more dressed up.

"How long will it take, do you think?"

"All told? A full back piece can take several sessions. This is mainly black and gray work, but there'll be lots of shading. That sort of detail is more time consuming than the larger sections of black." She shrugged. "It's not going to be a quick one."

Not like he was going to complain at getting her in his house one on one.

"Okay then. Dinner after?"

She gave him a raised brow. "You're not going to feel like making me dinner after I work on you for two hours."

"I know how to dial a phone. And I promised martinis."

She shrugged. "All right then."

He turned music on before pulling his shirt off and sitting, straddling the back of the chair as she rolled a nearby stool over.

"Step one is that I'm going to do a transfer of sorts of my design to your back. Mainly so you can see the position to be sure you like the placement. The detail I do as I go along. I like that part. It's organic. We gonna be all right with that?"

"Whatever are you trying to say?"

She snorted. "You're a control freak. This is my design. *I* make the choices. I'm quite bossy about that."

"I'm not sure you know me well enough yet to say I'm a control freak. Though you're right. There are areas I'm willing to cede to you. How the tattoo evolves is one of them. I've seen enough of your work to know you have a great aesthetic and one I click with."

"Hm."

She settled in behind him, touching him matter-of-factly for several moments before rolling back and putting a mirror in his hand. "Go look to be sure it's where you want it."

He did, liking where she'd put it.

"Good."

"It'll dominate your back, but in a good way."

He smiled her way and liked her startled response. Liked shaking her up for some reason. He felt like a predator around her.

"Sit down so I can get started."

He got back into position and so did she. He watched in the corner of his vision as she got her ink and stuff set up on a low table next to her stool. It wasn't long before the buzz of the needle machine filled the air and she got closer and began the outline.

Tattooing was a ritual for her. Some people lit candles or prayed. She loved the hum of the needle. Loved the feel of the skin under her hands and the beginning of a new design.

He was muscled. Not in a bodybuilder sense, but he was fit and he had wide shoulders and a strong back. The tat would look sexy on him and he was certainly bold enough to carry off a full back piece.

"Why did you decide to do tattoos?"

"It was a way to get away from sweeping up hair and doing shitty perms at the salon I worked at when I came out to L.A."

"Did you apprentice or go to school for it?"

"I got a job at a tattoo shop, cleaning up after hours. So I scrubbed toilets, and oh my god, let me say that was enough to get up the nerve to ask the owner if I could do ink work instead. He was a good guy and around my scrubbing and sweeping, he started to train me."

He'd been good to her. It had been hard for a good year not to suspect that he would use that kindness to get her into bed. But he never betrayed her that way. It had been the first real positive in years. A step into her new life. Where she was in control.

"The money was decent. I had benefits. The better I got and the better my reputation, the easier it was for me to move around and work here and there. Did you always want to be a lawyer?"

He lifted his shoulders. "It's the family business. My dad and his brother took over the firm their father started."

"Don't shrug."

"Sorry. You're bossy."

"I am about my ink."

"I have to say the pain and the hum of the needle sort of puts me in a trance. Having your hands on me isn't bad either."

"I'm the same way when I'm getting work done. I think it's fairly common. As for having my hands on you—it's not like you have to get a tattoo for that to happen."

"True."

"Back to the subject of the law. Do you like it? Or do you do it because you were expected to?"

"Do you just say whatever pops into your head?"

"Sometimes. If that was rude though, you'll have to explain why, because I can't see it."

"Not rude. Just . . . blunt, I guess. Most people don't say stuff like, 'Do you like your job or do you do it because your parents told you to?'"

"Well, one, I'm not most people, and two, I didn't say exactly that. Lots of people do things because they're expected to do them. Very few people do things because they love to do them."

She leaned around him to grab some tissues and that's when he saw the glasses she had to wear when she worked.

"You wear glasses?"

"When I'm doing close-up work, yes."

"I like them."

"Hm."

"I went to college because it was expected. I never had any intention of doing anything else. I'm the oldest, it's my duty. But I don't resent that. My family values education and it's absolutely true that my education has served me well, presented me with opportunities I'd never have had otherwise. As for law school? For a while I considered urban planning. I still love it, though I do it from a different angle."

"What about urban planning appeals to you so much?"

She liked to listen to him talk. Liked the easy way he had. So sure of himself, cocky, arrogant even, but not in a douchey way. He liked who he was.

"As you point out, I grew up with a lot. My parents raised us with the knowledge that we had a duty to give back because not everyone had what we did. My father and grandfather before him have always been involved in city planning issues. My grandfather is a master at getting people to pony up money and other resources to social services, for instance. My father and I sit on a committee of public and private representatives to deal with the scarcity of services for the homeless in the county."

"And how does planning affect that?"

"For instance, there are shelters, but the people in them can't come in until after six at night and must be out by seven in the morning. They don't always have the sort of facilities you'd need to land and then keep a job. So how do you then transition from homelessness to getting an apartment if you can't wash your clothes? If you have no ability to shower?"

You took shitty baths in sinks at gas stations. Your clothes smelled. She got that.

"So we helped raise money and get the neighborhood involved in the planning of a day center. There's a laundry where people can wash their clothing and their blankets if they stay on the streets. There are showers with donated soap. A few days a week we've got nurse practitioners who come in. It took a lot of people from a huge array of perspectives and interested groups to make it happen. Took us seven years from the first talks about ideas to getting it up and running."

"Wow. Congratulations, it sounds like a much-needed service." And it was a prime example of what she'd meant about how he was an asshole, but not an entitled one. He took his skills and his connections and he used them for good. "But you went into law instead of planning?"

"I did. I like the law. Levi and I are good at it. We have different practice areas of course, but it's a family business and I found my place in it. I do have a brother who is an architect, so clearly that runs in our genes too. I interned at my family's firm during the summers and realized that's what I wanted to do. I like the courtroom and not everyone does."

"So you're like one of those TV lawyers?"

He laughed as she smiled at her desired result. Of course she knew television lawyer shows were like the bane of actual lawyers, but she liked it when he laughed.

"Not so much. I do a lot of trial work. Appellate. I don't know if I'd love it as much if my practice was mainly motions and briefs. I like the people I deal with. Most of the time I like my clients."

"Appellate is what?"

"State supreme courts, United States Supreme Court, U.S. appellate courts."

She had him pegged as a mover and a shaker and he clearly was. She wasn't an expert on the legal system, but she knew enough to understand that if you argued before those courts you were a hotshot.

"I'm impressed."

"No, you're not."

Annoyance rankled her. She was being serious and he blew that off. "Don't tell me what I am or am not."

He turned his head, careful to keep his body in place. "I didn't mean to offend you."

"It's pretty difficult to offend me. But telling me what I think or feel is a way. I don't say things I don't mean. And if I'm wrong, I'll say so."

"I apologize. And thank you for the compliment."

"Apology accepted." She paused a moment and got back to work. "So tell me about your daughter."

"It's your turn to tell me something. I know you were in foster care. Do you have any biological family at all?"

"Some."

"Are you in contact with them?"

She had one aunt who sent her Christmas cards. She used to never even open them. But a few years back she started to. They never said much and she wasn't sure if she was relieved or not.

"Not really, no."

"Ah."

Ah? Like he knew? She was touchy when it came to this subject, which is why she so frequently steered far in the other direction from it.

"How did you meet your ex-wife?"

"We're still talking about you. Why did you leave Arkansas?"

"Have you ever been to Happy Bend?"

He chuckled.

"But there are a lot of states between Arkansas and California."

"Sure, and that was part of the appeal." Not that anyone really would have looked for her by that point anyway. "Los Angeles had lots of opportunity. Or I thought it did anyway."

"It didn't?"

"It was harder than I thought it would be. I was homeless for a while when I first arrived. That sucked." Not as much as the place she lived back in Happy Bend though. "But in a few months I had enough saved for a shitty little apartment. I had a few jobs. It got better."

"You were how old?"

"Seventeen."

"Christ. That's young."

"I was never young." She kept working, working to keep herself detached from the details. It was her life; she wasn't ashamed. She didn't necessarily hide it. But she didn't go into it with much depth with many people. With most people, she supposed.

"Yeah?"

"Yeah."

"Tell me about it."

"Not much to tell really. Shitty childhood. It's not a unique story. My adulthood is better. I overcame it and I prefer to keep it that way. My past doesn't hinder me, it serves as a reminder that there's better out there for me and it wasn't in Arkansas."

"I'm sorry. Abuse?"

"Here and there."

"While in foster care?"

"Not always."

He sucked in a breath. "I'm sorry."

"Don't be. It's long done. Be glad your daughter has a bright future and a wonderful past to look back on."

"I am. Her mother, my ex, well, Carrie will probably have stuff to deal with, but she seems to be handling it fine."

"She's got a parent who loves her. She's got a great future. If she can't make something of herself with that, she's not the kid you talk about."

"She and I went to counseling for a while. Did you ever go?"

She laughed but then cringed because there was nothing but loathing in the sound.

"No."

"Don't believe in it?"

"Look, there was no money for that stuff. There wasn't anything. I made it through. That's what counts."

It was easier to talk about it to his back.

She outlined, wiped the ink away, outlined, wiped the blood away. It was what she did. She created new things and didn't think about the old. Looking back slowed you down.

He sighed. "I don't know what to say."

"There's nothing to say. Not really. It was a shitty childhood. It made me into who I am today. I survived it. Lots of people didn't. So, let's talk about you again."

"No, I want to keep talking about you."

"For fuck's sake, why? I'm not a project like a hygiene center."

"I don't think that. I'm trying to know you."

This is why she kept things light. "Don't. I'm sure you've heard. I know you asked about me. I'm not worth knowing. Just fuck me and enjoy it and then move on."

"That's not who I am. And that's not who you are."

She snorted. "That's totally who I am, Jonah. I'm a bitch. I'm a whore. I like to fuck. Lots of people."

He turned then, grabbing her wrist, his eyes ablaze. She didn't even have a moment to be angry at how he could have just made her ink a line across his back if she'd had the needle down.

"You're *not* a whore. I've touched you. I've seen you. Stop."

"Don't make me into something I'm not. I'll break your heart if you expect more."

"I expect all of you. You should know that going in."

Her heart pounded so hard and fast she was a little light-headed.

He tore her defenses down. She barely knew him and he had this much power to affect her. What would it be like if they continued?

"Then we should be friends. I can do that much better."

"Oh, we *are* friends. And we'll continue that. But we've moved past the 'just friends' stage."

"You barely know me. I don't do relationships."

"Oh yes, you do. You're doing it right now. Neither of us is naive. Neither of us is so young we don't know what this is between us. I'm too old to pretend away what this is."

"I told you, I don't do relationships. I'm not a monogamous person."

"When you're in my bed you are."

"Then I can't be in your bed."

He smiled and it sent a shiver through her.

"Oh. Yes. Yes, you can. You are."

"Then you need to accept you may have to share me."

He shook his head slowly. "Gorgeous, I don't even share pizza. I'd never share something as delicious as you. I don't share."

He scared her. Not physically. He held her wrist but if she really wanted to get away, he'd let go. And that scared her too.

It shouldn't scare her. She barely knew him! But this was different on so many levels. The way he spoke to her, the way she found herself speaking back to him. He wasn't shocked by her. He wasn't scared off.

"Don't be a coward, Raven. Give yourself to me and me only. I promise to make it worth your while."

It was a struggle to keep her breath even. A struggle not to run for the door. She *should* run for the door. She was not cut out for this stuff. If she couldn't make it work with a stand-up guy like Brody, she truly was a failure at it.

But Jonah wasn't like Brody. They shared things in common, yes. Both men were both strong and intelligent. But this thing . . . the way her entire system reacted when Jonah touched her or even just spoke to her, well, that was something else entirely.

She understood without a doubt that should she refuse to keep things monogamous, things would be over.

And while she'd been able to accept that and move on every other time this came up . . . she was couldn't just then. She didn't want to walk away.

"It's not marriage. It's monogamy. You can do it. You're the girl who came out to L.A. at seventeen and made herself a life. You sure as hell can fuck me and only me. Unless . . . well, I'd say something like unless you're not really into this thing between us. But that would be a lie. Because I know you are. I can see it in your features. I can feel it around my cock when I'm inside you. You're not a liar, Raven, and neither am I. I won't let you be."

Fascinated, he watched the emotion play across her face. Panic. A whole lot of it. He wondered, not for the first time, what she'd endured to make her this way.

Fear. Oh yes. Not of him. At least not that he'd physically harm her. He hoped his own didn't show. His fear that she'd reject this and back off. Because though he'd made the threat that it was all or nothing, he wanted her too much and he wasn't entirely sure if he could resist her.

Desire. Which he knew mirrored his own.

Hope. Which nearly broke his heart. And reminded him that she was not a thing to be played with, but a complicated woman with flaws and no small amount of baggage. But he wanted something with her. There was no denying it. No denying this woman brought so many things to the surface. More than need, which he nearly drowned in. More than lust and sexual hunger for her.

He wanted to dominate her in all the best ways. Her pupils flared when he'd grabbed her wrist. Her lips had parted, skin flushed. She got off on it as much as he got off doing it. And that only made him want it more. He'd given himself a little; the delight of that crack on her bare ass as he'd fucked her had only whetted his appetite for more.

He wanted to show her the power of what they could have together. Wanted her to trust him enough to give it to him willingly. Wanted to cosset and shower her with delights. If any woman he'd ever met needed spoiling, it was this one.

He wasn't stupid. He knew she was headstrong and it would take a strong hand to set a tone. To keep the balance right. He had to deserve her submission, and once given, he needed to keep deserving it.

Against his fingertips, the rapid beat of her pulse told him she was freaked out. But the way she hadn't just told him to fuck off also told him she was considering it.

He needed to push.

"What do you say, gorgeous? Be mine and only mine. If you want out, you only have to say it."

She licked her lips, her pupils still so huge they nearly swallowed all the color in her irises.

With his free hand he reached up to slide his knuckles down the column of her throat. "You're the most beautiful woman I've ever seen. Vivid. Headstrong. I know you want me."

She still held the needle machine but had turned it off. His back was cool and slightly sticky where she'd been working.

"Take a leap, Raven. I'll catch you."

She sucked in a breath. "I'm not good at this."

"At what?"

"At monogamy." Her voice trembled and this uncharacteristic outward vulnerability tore at him. He wanted to gather her up and hold her close. But he needed to break this stubborn refusal to let him in first. Once he'd done that, he'd show her the gentleness she deserved.

"You've never tried it." Because no other man had ever demanded it of her before. But he wasn't any other man. He'd have all of her and prove she was right to make that decision.

"You're a very nice man. I really don't want to ruin this."

"Have you so little faith in yourself? Hm? If you come across a sudden, unquenchable desire to get laid, call me. I'm ten minutes away. I'll come to you and quench it."

But it wasn't that. He knew it. She hadn't committed before because she needed to be fucked and had no self-control to stop herself from getting it from whomever she could.

"It's not that."

He smiled. "I know. But still, the offer is open."

She smiled back. Victory hovered just out of reach. He forced himself to wait, outwardly patient.

"I don't want to hurt you."

"Is this about Brody? Are you still in love with him?"

She laughed then and the worry he'd pretended he never had faded altogether.

"I love Brody. He's very special to me. But not like that. Even when we were together it wasn't . . . Anyway. But I hurt him. He's a good man and he expected things from me that I couldn't give him. I told him. But he . . ."

He took her chin. Gentle, but firmly enough that she couldn't look away. "You weren't meant for him."

Raven sighed. "All right. I'll agree. You and only you while we're together."

Oh, she thought she could do that little disclaimer and give herself an out. Delightful.

It would be such a pleasure to gentle this woman to his touch.

"All right then." He kissed the hand he'd been holding. "Get back to work." He turned, knowing she probably needed some time to get herself together. God knew he needed that too.

7

She couldn't avoid it any longer. She didn't want to work on him any more that night. She'd gotten a lot done, but she'd worked on his back for nearly three hours and though he hadn't complained, she knew he was going to be sore and tired, and she sure was.

Their conversation had left her sort of off balance, but he'd given her his back and had left her alone with her thoughts for a long while before starting in on small talk again. She'd agreed to monogamy. She hoped like hell she wouldn't fuck it up because she really liked him.

She cleaned off his back. "I think that's enough for tonight. Want to look before I cover it up?"

"Yeah." He stood stretching, his arms above his head as his back cracked a few times.

He checked her work in the mirror, nodding his head. "I like it so far."

"Thanks. Come back so I can get it covered up. You've done the tattoo thing before so you know it's going to itch and you need to keep out of the sun, that sort of thing. I brought a tube of stuff for you to put on it. But then it's on your back."

She covered the tat and he turned slowly, a smile on his lips. "Then it looks like you'll be the one to help. It comes with the service, right?"

He was so . . . much.

"Hm. You promised me food and a martini."

"I'm ordering in. Once that's done I'll get us some drinks." He pulled her in, surprising her. "First I need a kiss."

She held on, careful to avoid his back, as he lowered his mouth to hers, taking it, owning it, and she gave over, opening up on a soft sigh. He tasted so good.

His tongue, sure, as sure as he was, swept into her mouth and a memory of his mouth on her pussy flashed through her brain. She squeezed her thighs together to ease the ache, but it only made things worse.

He nipped her bottom lip and then took a fistful of her hair, yanking her head back to expose her throat. Something warm washed through her as her muscles loosened. His lips cruised down her throat as he nibbled at the hollow, on her thundering pulse.

His skin was hot and hard as he held her tight, one hand in her hair, the other sliding down to take a handful of her ass.

She moaned and he made a sound, nearly a growl.

"Food. Drink. Then I'm going to fuck you."

He stepped back, licking his lips as she struggled to gain her composure. And failed.

Jonah flustered her. She wanted him. That he wanted her with such avarice thrilled her. Her body didn't give one tiny fuck that she was supposed to be annoyed with his caveman-type ways. Her clit and nipples thought it was pretty fantastic actually.

She watched as he swayed to the phone. Broad shoulders led to a narrow waist and a spectacular ass. It was just as hot with his jeans on as it was when he was naked. And that was pretty fucking spectacular.

Raven busied herself by putting her gear away. She put aside the tools she'd need to run through the autoclave before using them again.

Secured the inks. She cleaned off the chair where they'd been working and put the stool she'd been sitting on back.

When she'd finished she'd found some measure of peace, but when she turned back to see him in his kitchen, pulling martini glasses out, she couldn't stop a wistful sigh.

"I like that you wore a red shirt." He pushed a glass to her. "Olive or onion?"

"Olive." And he'd shown a preference for red after all. And she had a million T-shirts, many of them red, so it wasn't like it was a big deal.

He dropped in an olive and clinked his glass to hers. "To beginnings."

She tipped her chin and sipped. He had not exaggerated his skill.

"This is a very fine martini." Nice and dry.

"Food will be here in about half an hour. Come sit in the living room."

She followed him. He sat, putting his feet up and patting the couch next to him.

Raven drank slowly, not quite trusting herself to say much.

"I did ask about you to your friends. Does that bother you?"

She thought about it and he didn't press.

"Maybe. A little." She shrugged.

"I wasn't trying to dig up dirt. I like you. I'm interested in you and I wanted to know more. Daisy likes you. She's a little in awe, I think, which is interesting given how fierce my brother's girlfriend is."

"Well, at least one of you has good taste."

He smirked. "What do you mean by that?"

"Do you think I haven't heard about your sister-in-law? The one who thinks Daisy is a dirty gold digger out for your family fortune?"

He sighed heavily, draping an arm over her shoulder, hugging her close, and to her surprise, she liked it.

"Gwen. Goddamn, she must give head like nobody's business. It's really the only thing I can think of that would blind Mal to her many faults."

"Is that the key then? Cocksucking?"

"You do well with the cock and the rest is sort of easier."

"Hm."

"What's this mysterious *hm* you do? What does it mean?"

"Any and all manner of things at any given time."

"Should you be harboring any ideas that I'm only here with you because of your cocksucking skill, though you've got it, you're not easy."

He was . . . blunt. Surprising. She didn't quite know how to take the things he said.

"Is that what you like then? Easy?"

He took her drink, placing it on the table next to his. He held her chin so she couldn't look away. "If I wanted easy, I wouldn't be here with you now. Easy is overrated anyway. I like prickly. Defensive. Blunt. I want you."

She swallowed, thrown by the heat of a blush working up her neck.

"Easy is boring and you're anything but boring."

Before she could reply, the doorbell rang. "The food. I'll be back."

She stood along with him. "I'll get plates and stuff."

Raven didn't know why she was like this with him. Off balance. She liked to tease her romantic partners, to play. But this was different.

He made her blush. She couldn't recall the last time she'd actually blushed over anything.

He brought the food into the kitchen, humming as he poked into the containers and saw what was inside.

"Here, let me make your plate." She'd paid attention, knew what he liked.

He stepped to her, pulling her close. "I like that you pay attention. I like that you serve me."

She swallowed hard. "I like it too." What else was there to say? She could have lied, but she tried not to. And the look on his face when she told him that pleased her to her toes.

When they sat, he pulled her chair close by hooking a foot in the rung at the bottom. He brushed the hair back from her face and then picked up a spring roll, feeding it to her.

Everything in her stilled.

"I like taking care of you."

His voice was soft. But intense. In command.

"I wager it doesn't happen often."

She licked her lips. "I'm a grown woman. I can feed myself."

"Of course you can." He fed her a bite from his plate.

He took a bite or two and then fed her again. Forkfuls here and there. Nothing overwhelming. He wasn't forcing her to eat.

"Have you ever been to Paris?"

"Twice. I like to travel." She shrugged. "I doubt it's the Paris you visit though."

He raised a brow her way. "Oh? And how so?"

"I've never stayed in a four-star place before. I like pensions and cheap, off-the-beaten-path places. Not because I'm so edgy." She laughed. "But because when I first started traveling I had no money and it was all I could afford."

He snorted. "I do like four-star hotels, I can't lie. Luxury isn't overrated. You said you love travel. Where else do you go?"

"I love Hawaii. There's something about just walking out the door and it being perfect outside. The air always smells good. The water is always gorgeous and warm so you can play in it all day long. The food is plentiful and cheap."

He laughed. "Cheap? It's as expensive to eat in Hawaii as it is in Paris."

"There are so many roadside stands, barbecue grills and hole-in-the-wall places to eat in Hawaii. If you go to the tourist places, it's expensive. If you buy a lot of milk, yes, it's expensive. But when I'm there I eat a lot of fruit and local stuff."

"I think I need to take you to Paris, four-star style. And you need to take me to Hawaii, roadside-stand style. I have a house in Maui."

"You do? A friend has a condo there and he lends it to me a few times a year in exchange for my working at his shop. I used to go more often. But since Alexander I find myself spending a lot more time here."

He fed her another bite and sat back, eating as he listened to her speak awhile.

"You're close with him."

"He's precious to me. Erin is like my sister. She's the person on earth I'm closest to. And Alexander, well, he's impossible not to love. He likes me around so I'm around."

"It's important to children to be surrounded by people they love and can trust. It's a gift you're giving him."

"It's the other way around really. I never thought much about kids one way or the other. Until him. When she got pregnant it was an odd time in my life. I didn't know how it would change our friendship. I was selfish."

"Worried you'd lose your friend, that's not selfish. That's human."

"It was selfish. I can own my flaws. I don't need anyone to make excuses for me."

He loved how her chin jutted out. Defiant.

He fed her another piece of bread. Her eyes closed just a bit as she enjoyed the taste.

"Anyway, she had a rough time. Her pregnancy was hard. There were things going on with Ben's family and it upset her. I stayed to run some interference when I could. Though she's surrounded by people who love her so it would have happened anyway, I suppose."

He knew Erin's brothers adored her and were protective. But he was sure this woman did all she could to help her friend get through her rough time.

"Anyway, when he was born I was there. In the room. It was . . . it was amazing. And she was a fucking queen to have done it. And then Alexander was in the world. I traveled like I usually did, but I found myself coming back more often and for longer stints of time. It worked out for Brody so he could take more time off to be with Elise because then they got pregnant and had Martine."

She downplayed how important she was to people.

"By the time Alexander had his first birthday I figured it would be best if I bought a place up here. He's my little dude. Then Poppy came. Lucky for the kid, she's more like her mom than her dad. But I like kids. Other people's kids even better because after a few overnights with Alexander, I don't know how Erin manages it on four hours' sleep."

"You have a marshmallow center." He poked her belly and she smirked.

"I am a hard-ass bitch, Jonah. I am mean. I am selfish and not to be trusted."

He shook his head. "You moved to Seattle for Alexander."

Her face softened again. "He's my reason to put down roots." Then she found her mask again. "But that doesn't mean I'm still not bad news."

"You are not bad news. No matter how often you tell yourself that. And I will say the sleep stuff is a killer. When Carrie was a baby she was pretty easy. She slept well. But when she started walking she just hated to sit still. She was up at five. Gave up naps before she was two. My ex hated that."

"You were at work all day while she was home with the kid?"

"One of us had to pay the mortgage. We talked about it before she got pregnant. That she'd be home. I didn't expect her to because she was the woman. We had a deal. She . . ."

"I'm not accusing you of being a sexist jerk. It was a question, that's all. Erin is really good at it. The stay-at-home-mom gig. She's got this endless patience with him. It helps that he's a really happy kid. But still, she just goes and goes. Did you have a nanny or a night nurse or whatever?"

He relaxed a little. "She wanted a night nurse but I was really opposed. But she did have a nanny a few days a week. My mother came and helped a lot too. Looking back, the first cracks in our relationship were then. She wasn't cut out for it. Parenting, I mean."

"Yes, well. Carrie has you. Sounds like she's better off without your ex. Who, by the way, sounds like a total moron. Did her tits blind you or something?"

He choked as he laughed. "We were young. She was gorgeous in her way. Her family knows my family. It seemed like the right choice at the time. I did love her. Then." Even as they'd started to get into trouble he'd loved her, wanted to fix things. But once she'd started neglecting Carrie, that had killed it.

"You Warner boys sure do like to marry dumbasses. From what I hear, your mother isn't stupid in any way."

"I thought you liked Daisy?"

"I do. But he isn't married to her. Yet. I'm talking the first one. And your ex. And the dumb, racist one your other brother is married to."

"I'm going to hear your voice calling her the dumb racist one every time I see her from now on. Thanks for that."

She shrugged.

"I think we did what we were expected to do."

"I insulted you."

"No. Not really." He paused, teasing her with another bite. "You say things people don't say. It's . . . I'm not used to it."

"Honesty?"

"*Candor* perhaps is a better term."

"I don't know which fork to use either."

She was so fearless in many ways, but also vulnerable. He saw it all through her words and body language. It got to him. He wanted to gather her up and protect her.

So he did.

She didn't resist, though she was surprised as she wrapped her arms around his neck to keep from falling from his lap.

"I've got you."

The words were simple. Easily understood in the context.

But they were more. It tore at her. Made her lose her grip on her defenses.

He put his head on her chest and she relaxed a little.

"Forks are overrated. Also, you talk a good game, but your table manners are pretty impeccable."

He had a house in Maui. Good lord.

"I'm full, but you hardly ate."

He sat straighter and pulled her plate over. She moved to take the fork, but he grabbed her wrists with one of his hands, holding them fast at the small of her back.

A pulse of warmth flowed through her. Narcotic.

He fed her, pausing to kiss her here and there as he did.

She couldn't explain to herself why she tolerated it. That he restrained her and fed her and she made no effort to stop him.

But it did something to her. Filled a crack that had been forming since he'd come into her life.

"Candor is important. Most people aren't honest on that level."

"Erin says I'm sort of feral." She shrugged. It was true really. It's not like she was ever in any one place long enough growing up for a responsible adult to teach her how she was supposed to act.

He smiled. "Not feral. You're just not affected like so many people are."

"I'm really not trying to offend people. Well, most of the time." She smirked. "I can be a total bitch when I put my mind to it."

He laughed. "I bet you can. And I bet you're aces at it."

"Not worth doing if you don't do your best." He kept feeding her, holding her hands, keeping her on his lap until she was nearly catlike in her laziness. She leaned into his body, warm and lethargic. "I'm full. I promise."

He put the plate aside.

"Do you trust me?"

She managed to tip her head back enough to look at his face. She didn't trust a lot of people. But there she sat, on his lap after he'd held her hands captive and fed her. After she'd told him about growing up in the system.

Ludicrous. But no less true.

"Yes."

"Good."

He stood, keeping her in his arms, though he did let go of her wrists to keep from dropping her.

"I can walk."

"I know. And I can carry you. What's the point of going to the gym if I can't carry a hot woman to my bedroom where I'm going to strip her naked and fuck her?"

"Put that way."

She had to admit she was impressed by the easy way he carried her. As if she weighed nothing, and heaven knew that wasn't true.

He nudged the doors to his room open with his foot and put her on the edge of the bed. "You need to be naked."

She quickly complied, pulling her shirt off.

He sucked in a breath. "Mmm, I know you love purple, but red really looks gorgeous next to your skin."

She was glad she'd worn the red bra.

She bent to help him get his jeans off and then his shirt, which luckily was a button-down so he wouldn't have to pull a shirt on over his head with his back sore.

She pressed a kiss to his shoulder. "You have a fantastic body. Really."

"Thank you." He tipped her back to the bed and pulled her jeans off. Pausing to look at the tiny red panties she wore.

"I'm not sure I'd have pegged you for matching lingerie. But I like it. A lot."

"I have a slight problem. I love lingerie. So much that it's one of my favorite things about finally having a regular place to live so I can store it all instead of carrying it around."

"Clearly I need to come to your place so I can check it all out."

"Maybe. If you're extra good."

He grinned, looking rather like a pirate.

He crawled up the bed toward her body, nibbling up her thigh until he got her panties off, tossing them behind him. He paused as he held her gaze and a change came over his features.

"Hold on to the headboard. Don't let go unless I say."

She obeyed as if he'd pressed a button.

The cool of the wood was real against her palms. An anchor as he nibbled up her belly and then bit the underside of her breast until she hissed. Then he licked over the spot and warmth flowed as he hummed against her skin.

"Gonna leave a mark."

That appealed to her. Knowing she'd be able to see it the next day. A tangible reminder of the time they'd shared.

"I like knowing it'll be there. Knowing my mark will be on your skin. Like a secret."

He left her breathless with the stuff he said. Good gracious.

The edge of his teeth found her nipple. First the right and then the left. Over and over until she was writhing. Grabbing the headboard so hard she wouldn't have been surprised if she'd broken it.

"What shall I do next? Hmm?"

She'd been about to answer when he sat up.

"Don't move."

She didn't as he disappeared into the next room. She heard him rustling around for a few minutes and then returned looking rather triumphant.

"I'm not sure if that look bodes well for me."

"It bodes well for *me*, anyway."

He pulled out a blindfold. "I use it while sleeping on long plane rides, but it'll work just fine for you too."

The material was cool against her face as he slid it on. It smelled faintly of lavender and of him.

Her skin came alive at the loss of her sight. Gooseflesh rose as he drew a fingertip down her collarbone and then over her nipple.

"On your belly. Hands out to the side."

He took one of her wrists and she felt the clasp of a leather cuff as he tightened it on one side and then the other. Then he moved her wrist up and attached it to the poster of the bed somehow. He followed with her ankles.

Now, she wasn't a stranger to sex. She'd been tied up for shits and giggles a few times. But *this* was different. This wasn't a game. He was far too good at it to have been a game.

Part of it was—a big part of it—how hot it seemed to make him. She heard his breathing change as he moved. The brush of his cock as he worked let her know he was more than a little turned on by what he was doing.

His hands on her were sure and strong. And though what he was doing was binding her, those hands did not harm or misuse. This was out of her normal repertoire, but she knew that she liked it and wanted more. And that was enough.

"You're so beautiful this way. Your back, your gorgeous ass and those long legs. Goddamn."

She couldn't quite put her words together so she didn't say anything, though she managed a grunt of assent.

She wanted to know what he was going to do next. Wanted to experience it.

He'd never seen anything better in his bed. Ever.

Her dark hair a river over her shoulders and her back. Her muscles corded with her arms up, bound to the bed with the cuffs he'd actually never used before today. Though he'd taken them out and thought about using them more than a few times. He'd never been alone in the house with a woman he'd trusted enough to use them with.

Charlotte had barely tolerated his taste for rough sex. But she'd never submitted this beautifully. There had been others since the divorce. A woman he used to visit at her apartment. He'd learned a lot. His likes and dislikes. How to wield the tools that appealed. But it had been more like training than a relationship. He'd never been invested in her beyond her bedroom door.

This though . . . Raven was something far more. It had been a very long time since anyone had called to him the way this woman did.

So much to do with her. He let it take over, that part of himself he kept leashed deep inside. It settled in easily. As if it had been waiting for Raven.

Provocative. Her eyes covered. Naked on his bed. Her skin a riot of color from her ink, the roses curling up her inner arms. Her ass jutted out because she'd arched her back.

His. No one else around. Hours and hours.

He leaned down and bit one juicy cheek and she shuddered on a moan.

This strong, bossy woman had given over to him with such ease it had startled him. And, he realized, it startled her too.

He picked up the slapper, testing it on his palm, liking the sound. She stilled.

He drew the edge of it over the curve of her ass. "Still with me?"

She managed a moan of assent.

And then he brought the leather down against her skin, the sound loud, more startling then the actual slap, he'd wager.

He dipped to lick up the line of her spine before he slapped her ass several more times. Slowly. Building heat. Building pleasure to beat back the pain.

"Your skin turns the most beautiful shade when it's being paddled." He blew over her ass cheeks and smiled to himself when gooseflesh rose in response.

Her legs were spread wide, leaving her pussy open to his touch. When his fingertips brushed against her labia he found her wet and hot.

She moaned low and ragged when he parted her, swirling a finger around her clit, tugging lightly on the hoop.

His pulse pounded in his temples. His cock was so hard it nearly hurt. He wanted to slide into that hot, wet cunt and fuck her. Right then.

Instead he drew it out.

Her muscles trembled as he slowly built her orgasm.

Her skin, so much of it, soft, taut over curves that stretched forever, called to him. He kissed the dimples at each side of her spine. Licked the small of her back. He kissed the blades of her shoulders and across her back.

Every once in a while, he returned to her cunt and she strained back to get more.

"Do you want it?" He surged up to nip her ass again.

She made a frustrated growl, her muscles tightening.

"I need you to tell me."

"Yes!"

"Yes what?" He blew against her pussy and she groaned as he tickled her clit.

"Yes, I want you to make me come."

"There you go. That wasn't hard, was it?"

She growled again and he resisted laughing. Only barely.

He went back to her cunt, one hand there, the other he slid between her body and the bed to play with a nipple. Her body gleamed with sweat and a flush as her climax began to build in earnest.

She smelled so good he couldn't resist leaning in to lick over her ribs. She whimpered and he nipped her skin. The whimper smoothed into a moan.

She rained honey on his hand as her nipple hardened against his palm and fingers.

With a strangled gasp as he pressed his palm against her cunt, still stroking her clit with his fingertips, she came hard and fast, her muscles tightening as she strained against the cuffs. He was thankful for the sturdiness of his furniture; her upper-body strength was nothing to sneeze at.

And when she finally went boneless on a satiated sigh, he kissed her skin.

"Mmm, you're so fucking delicious when you climax."

She mumbled into the mattress.

"It's my turn, Raven."

He sat up enough to undo her cuffs from the bed, though he left them on her wrists.

She was still boneless and lazy. He wondered how often she was this way and figured it probably wasn't very often.

He pulled the blindfold off and she blinked at him. "Hello there, beautiful. You need to climb up and fuck me."

She managed to get to her knees on the bed, and then he hooked the cuffs on her wrists together, binding them behind her back.

"My balance . . ."

He put a finger over her lips to silence her and he nearly came when she sucked it into her mouth.

"Goddamn."

She smiled, catlike.

"I'll handle your balance. You said you trusted me. Prove it."

She licked her lips and then relaxed as he kept hold of the chain between the cuffs to help her remain upright.

"Your back . . ." Her words were slightly slurred. "Either sit or put a bunch of pillows under your head and neck or you're going to hurt."

He hadn't thought of that but she was right. He moved to a nearby chair and brought her along, helping her off the bed first, sliding a condom on before she straddled him, her knees to either side of his body.

Looking up at her this way brought pause. This wasn't play. This was more. He was breaking her in a sense. Battering all her defenses until she submitted to him totally. There was a lot of responsibility he was about to take on. If he wanted her to submit to him, he had to deserve it. To continue to deserve it every day.

This woman was strong. Vibrant. She was wild and willful. But beneath? She was fragile and he needed to tread carefully so as not to harm that. He wanted her total trust. He had to earn it.

One-handed, he angled his cock, brushing it against her pussy a few times before he lined up and pressed in. Her lips parted on a sigh and she pushed down, taking him into her body completely.

He held her wrists, letting her know he wasn't ready for her to move again just yet.

His gaze danced over her body. Lingering as he took in the curve of her hips. The weight of her breasts. The glint of the silver bars piercing her nipples. Her face, those gorgeous, lush features, her full mouth, the slumberous, slightly wary eyes.

And then there was the sight of his cock as she drew up on her knees, nearly leaving her body, and then slowly disappearing as she fell slowly down on him again.

Dark, slick with her honey, the sight of his cock disappearing into her cunt seemed to hypnotize him. Seduce his senses.

She arched, jutting her hips as she slid herself back and forth on his cock. All while he held her to keep her from falling. Watching her face as she closed her eyes. He wanted her to look at him, to know it was Jonah who gave her this experience. But he sensed she wasn't ready for that kind of exposure. Not yet.

He'd demand her gaze when it was time.

For then, her body surrounded his in a hot, wet embrace. The weight of her body against his kept him aware of her curves.

"You make my mouth water. So lush and sexy. Goddamn."

Her smile was a little shy. She was touched. The hesitance there only served to dig in under his skin even more.

"Slow. I want this to last a while."

She pouted then and he laughed.

"Someone doesn't like to wait."

"I have instant-gratification issues."

He tugged on the cuffs a little and she swallowed hard, her head falling back.

He'd thought he was being smart, but all he'd done was render her even more attractive. The long line of her neck offered up along with her tits. The window behind the chair let in moonlight and it caressed her skin.

He growled, unable not to. He leashed his impulse to thrust up hard and fast just to see her tits jiggle. Though he would the next time.

He wanted to savor this. So he did. On and on as he drew closer and closer. His orgasm built, filling him bit by bit, more and more, until there was nothing else to do but let it take over.

But before he did, he wanted her with him.

He moved his free hand to her clit where he squeezed it between his fingers. Fingers he'd gotten wet in her mouth. Hot, hot, hot.

"I want you to come all around my cock."

She shifted to look down her body at where his fingers played against her clit. He watched her watch him. Orgasm bore down on him. His balls crawled up close to his body and he came on a snarled curse. But he kept his fingers squeezing over and over until, just a few seconds after he'd begun to come, she did as well.

It drew his climax out longer, the tight grip of her inner walls around his cock. Wave after wave until it felt like there was nothing left in his body.

He unclipped her wrists and gently helped her stand, leading her to his bed before darting to the bathroom to get rid of the condom and returning to her.

She watched him as she stretched. "Wow."

He grinned. "Why, thank you. Back atcha." He watched her carefully, so carefully that she cocked her head.

"What? Did I do something wrong? I'm not . . . well, this was new for me." She blushed so prettily he couldn't help but lean down to kiss her.

"You did everything right. I just want to be sure you're with me all the way. What we did was good. Really good. I want you to be good with it too."

She smiled, sliding her fingers through his hair. "Yeah? I don't know what to say to you sometimes."

"That's got to be novel for you."

Her laugh relaxed him.

"That's pretty true, as it happens. I get the feeling this is normal for you. No, not normal, that's a judgment word as Erin would say. Regular? I guess I figured you just said what needed to happen and that was that. Your lifestyle? I don't know, I'm saying it wrong."

He understood right at that moment that Raven Smith hated to be uncertain about things. Liked to be in charge.

That she was willing to be off balance with him—for him—meant quite a lot. More than he wanted it to, but it was too late to feel anything else for her but the way he did. That he hadn't known her very long was pretty irrelevant at that moment.

"I resist terms like *lifestyle* because playing golf is a lifestyle, gardening. Whatever. To me, this isn't a lifestyle. This is how I like to have sex. Other people may say differently and that's how the world works. Regardless, I'd be a prick to do things with you, especially when you were bound, that you didn't like as much as I liked doing them."

"Oh. Yes, I liked them. You should do them more."

He laughed, pulling her close. "Gimme a few minutes to recover. You're hell on my cock, gorgeous."

"That's probably one of the best compliments I've ever received."

8

"I can't believe I let you talk me into this."

Erin laughed as she hooked her arm with Raven's and steered her toward the front door of Tart, the home of Mary's supper club, Delicious.

It was, of course, already full of the people who made up the whole extended group of friends and relatives Erin was part of.

Mary had to stop doing the public one after it had become so well known she was involved with Damien Hurley, uber big rock star. But she still did them for her friends on occasion.

"And I can't believe you didn't tell me Jonah Warner was a kinky motherfucker. Jesus, you totally hold out on me all while telling me you love me?"

Erin said it in an undertone so no one else could hear, but Raven felt the heat of a blush anyway. Damn it, she did not blush!

"I told you yesterday. I'm sorry. I figured it would scar Alexander for life to hear his mother and Auntie talk about how Auntie's man loved to whip her with a slapper while she was blindfolded and tied up."

"I love it when they blindfold me. Makes all my other senses come alive."

They'd actually not been able to get into the whole Jonah discussion too deeply the day before either, as they'd run into Elise and Rennie while they were out shopping and had ended up spending the afternoon together.

"He's so hot. My god." Erin's grin made it impossible not to grin back.

Like this was news? The man messed with her head. Made her break all her rules. He was a tornado in her life.

"I agreed to be monogamous while we were together."

Erin turned, her brows flying up. "Get out! Really? Damn, he must make you come so hard."

"Well yes. Didn't I already say that? He demanded it. And I like him and it seemed silly to argue. I'm too busy to fuck anyone else right now anyway, and this will burn out in time and I'll move on when we're done. I'm a big girl, I can do it." She chewed her lip. "I think."

Erin cocked her head.

"God, what if I mess it up?"

Erin put an arm around her shoulders and squeezed. "You're not going to mess it up." She took a drink from the table and handed it to Raven, clinking her glass to it. "It had to happen sometime. My baby is growing up."

Raven snorted before she took a sip.

And then she heard him.

"Well now, I'm extra glad I came tonight." Jonah walked straight to her as if no one else was even in the room. He took her free hand and kissed her fingertips. "Hello."

She knew she did one of those cartoon gulps but she really couldn't help herself. "Hi. Fancy seeing you here."

"I called your place, actually. To ask you to dinner. But you weren't there and Levi bugged me to come here and I was hungry. But this makes everything so much better."

He made her skin tingle. His voice did things to her nipples. Flashes of how he felt deep inside her as he fucked her kept running through her memory.

"Hey, Raven."

She tore her gaze away from Jonah to catch sight of Daisy approaching wearing a big smile.

"Hello, Daisy."

"We saved you a seat. Next to Jonah, I mean." She fluttered her lashes at Raven, who managed to wrestle her left eyebrow into staying put.

Jonah did some fancy thing with her hand. He turned as he put her hand on his arm, his own hand firmly over it, keeping her at his side as he walked her over to their table.

Erin simply moved their things down to that end of the table. "That was pretty nifty there."

Jonah gave Erin a look, but she wasn't the type to be scared off by a big alpha male face, as she had two of her very own anyway.

"That little spin as you directed her, I mean. So how have you been?"

Todd sat on one side of Erin and Ben the other. He kissed Erin quickly. "Smooth. You totally could have been a CIA agent with your sneaky skills."

"I'm not sneaky. He's smooth. I'm not waterboarding him or anything."

Jonah leaned in closer to Erin, clearly amused. "Would you?"

"I don't know. I might. Have you done anything worthy of being waterboarded?"

"Not yet. I don't think."

Raven cleared her throat. "Just ask him whatever you're going to ask him already." She turned to Jonah. "You need to give in now. She won't give up. She's like one of those little dogs. She'll bark and nip at your ankles until you submit. It's her way."

Erin laughed, clearly delighted. "I'm just getting a feel for him. If he wants to take my daughter out, I should know his intentions."

Raven couldn't help but laugh. "I'm a big girl, Mom."

"She's concerned." He put a hand over hers briefly. "I promise not to despoil her. And to have her back by ten."

"What if I like being despoiled?"

"I tell you, you walk away from a table filled with these people and you return to talk of despoiling."

Mary shooed her fiancé, Damien, to the table. "Sit. Don't get any ideas."

"I can help you in the kitchen." He mooned over her, which Raven— though she'd never admit it out loud—thought was sort of sweet.

"You are not my helper tonight."

"I am. So back off, buster." Daisy sent him a lovely smile that sort of ruined her gruff words. "You get her all the time. It's not enough that you stole her away to Oregon? You get to be in her kitchen every day. You need to learn to share."

"That sounded sort of dirty. Can we watch?" Adrian leaned back in his seat, his arm around Gillian's back.

"Only if you want me to poke your eyes out." Levi sipped his drink. "If anyone gets to watch, it's me. And Damien I guess, if he's nice."

Raven breathed a sigh of relief when the conversation moved past the grilling of Jonah. Oh, she knew people thought she loved being the center of attention and none of them mattered enough for her to correct their misperception. But she didn't like it.

Erin leaned closer. "So we need to continue our discussion later."

Jonah slid his hand up her spine, stopping to cup the back of her neck. She shivered and Erin's eyebrow slowly rose as she took in Raven's response.

"Yes. Later."

"Oh, is it a secret? What'll I need to give you to let me join in?" Jonah's words were playful, but his grip on her neck made Raven tingly.

Todd laughed.

Erin sniffed but wore a grin. "This is what I'm trying to get her to tell me. What you give her, I mean."

Raven knew this was her payment for being so provocative with all her friends. Now Erin was going to be merciless.

"So what's on the menu tonight?" She grabbed the card on her plate to look it over.

Jonah turned to her, amusement in his gaze. He tipped her chin up with his fingers. "Are you trying to change the subject?"

She leaned in close. May as well get him as worked up as she was. "I'll tell her all the details later. When we're not surrounded by fifty people. Don't worry, I'll be sure to tell her how hard you make me come."

He laughed, kissing her quickly. "Good to know. I have a reputation to uphold."

Levi looked sideways at his brother and Jonah sent him a raised brow. Levi shrugged, but Jonah knew he'd have to have a long talk with him about Raven.

But for that night, he wanted to be with her. It was clear by the way the others seemed to react that Raven hadn't brought dates around. Then again, he never had either.

He stroked the smooth skin at the back of her neck.

"So I hear most of the outlining is done on your back piece." Brody spoke this time.

"Yes. It's looking good. He's a champ. I worked on him for several hours and he never complained."

Jonah snorted inwardly. He had a high pain tolerance and really, she was so good and he was so distracted by everything else that had been going on between them that he'd barely noticed.

"Itchy today though."

"Means it's healing. That's a good thing."

"My mother says he has superhuman healing powers," Levi added.

"Levi and I used to beat the fuck out of each other. I always healed first."

Daisy sighed. "You're supposed to unite and beat *other* people up, not your brother!"

"He's the one who hauled me out of bed and made me finally see reason and grovel to you." Levi smiled at Daisy, who softened immediately and sent a look to Jonah.

"Yeah? Well, I guess it's okay that you may have punched him over that."

Jonah laughed. "Well, to be fair, we always united against anyone who tried to hurt our family and friends."

"That's what family does." Daisy shrugged and flounced off to help Mary in the kitchen.

Raven looked down at her hands.

He kept stroking her skin.

Erin glanced his way and then back to Raven. The storm had passed and Raven pulled her gaze from her hands and back up to Erin.

Brody spoke again. "Make sure to take photographs of the back. Step by step. For the book."

Raven nodded at Brody. "I did."

"The book?"

"Raven is being featured in a piece about tattooing. There's a short film with it too. Anyway, they're using some of her bigger pieces. From her design for you, I think it would be a good one."

"You saw it?"

"Of course I did." Brody gave him a look that told him he was dumb for thinking otherwise.

Jonah didn't quite know what to make of the closeness between Brody and Raven. It was totally and utterly clear Brody Brown adored his wife. They had a connection so strong, so tangible, it was nearly a physical thing. Brody was protective of Raven. Like he was of Erin in many ways.

But it rankled that she had this history with another man.

Stupid. He had an ex-wife he had a kid with. It seemed hypocritical when Raven didn't seem overly bothered by his ex. But there it was. Jonah figured he wasn't entirely reasonable when it came to Raven.

"I show all my work to Brody. He's a great sounding board. He tossed out a few of my sketches so you should be thankful."

"I'm sure they were just as amazing as the others."

Brody raised one brow and Elise blinked, hiding a smirk behind her hands.

"She's a pretty amazing artist. I'm sure all the designs were good. I'm sorry I didn't see them all."

Brody sipped his drink, clearly taking Jonah's measure. All around them pockets of laughter and conversation rose and fell, ebbed and flowed. These people, all of them, had a deep connection to one another. He liked it. Wanted a place in it. But he had to deal with this man sitting a few seats down, who clearly saw himself as Raven's protector. Jonah wanted that job.

"She is. I agree. But it's a process. Design, I mean. Some ideas don't make the cut."

Raven put her hand on Jonah's arm. "Some of the designs he tossed out, as an example, would have been too large on your back, or too small. Because you're doing black and gray, the balance is really important. You're too . . . elegant . . . No, that's a feminine term, I think . . . Anyway, all that ink wouldn't have fit you. Not your personality or your body type. It's why I bounce ideas off him. He's been doing this longer than I have. He's better at it."

On one hand, he liked that she explained. On the other, he hated that she was defending another person to him. That she'd feel she had to, that he was being a pissy fool, that she'd said anyone was better than her.

"You're the best." He kissed her again and she sighed.

"You're going to ruin my reputation as a hard-assed bitch," she murmured against his mouth as he pulled away.

"You're not a hard-assed bitch."

She laughed. "I am. Thank you for the compliment. I am good at what I do. But it's okay to admit he's better. He's like . . . he's amazing. Gifted. You're born with that potential. I'm good, I'm not gonna lie. But he's in another league."

"I don't want you to put yourself down."

She paused, looking at him for long, quiet moments. "I'm not. This is real life, Jonah. There will always be people who are better than you at things. Richer people. People with nicer houses. Skinnier people. Whatever. That's life."

He softened, smiling at her. "All right. You have a point."

The first course came out and he leaned back as he ate, watching her interact with the others. She was open with Erin and Brody. Open with Gillian. But with the others less so. She was friendly, yes. Asked questions here and there, but it was clear she was uncomfortable on some level.

That bugged him.

His phone rang and he saw it was work related.

"I need to take this. I'll be back shortly." He paused to kiss her temple and then moved outside to answer.

"He was not happy with me." Brody grinned at her like a total loon.

"He didn't like it that she said you were better than she was. I thought it was sweet." Elise patted her husband's arm.

She'd never had anyone like him. He touched her. A lot and not in a creepy, hey-let's-fuck-all-the-time way. He touched her like he couldn't not touch her. Like he wanted people to know they were together. Which was odd. He was possessive but in the best sense.

And then he was mad when he thought she'd been putting herself down. That made her nervous. She knew how to deal with people who liked her well enough to have sex and hang out. But this was more. *He* was more.

"I noticed that."

"You *are* better than I am at tattooing."

"Ah, but he reacted like a man protecting his woman reacts."

"I'm no one's anything."

Brody shook his head. "You're wrong about that. This guy is going to show you just how wrong."

"If you'll let him," Erin interjected. "And you should. He's gorgeous. And he digs you."

Raven scrubbed her hands over her face.

To her surprise it was Ben who spoke next. "Leave the poor woman be." He smiled Raven's way and she shoved back her impulse to snarl. He was being nice and she really should learn how to accept kindnesses from people. Plus he was Alexander's dad and she never wanted to give them any cause to get in the way of her seeing that boy.

"Creeps me out when everyone is nice to me. Like I'm sick or something," Raven mumbled, getting up and heading to the ladies' room.

Erin watched her friend go. "Be back."

Brody nodded her way and Elise leaned into him, understanding as well.

Erin knew Raven was nervous. She hadn't wanted to come to Delicious at all, but Erin had pushed it. Knowing. No, wanting her to understand these people could be better friends if she just let them in. Wanting *them* to know Raven was so much more than what she appeared on the surface.

Erin caught up to her just inside the bathroom. "You all right?"

Raven broadcasted her annoyance in her stance and the look on her face. But Erin had known her a very long time and it didn't put her off. Raven could be fierce, of course, but she was all façade when it came to Erin and Brody and those she let inside.

"Just had to pee. Been a long time since I needed an escort for that."

"Don't be a bitch. I know this is a little much. I admire your restraint. You haven't snarled at a single person. The sex must be really good to keep you so calm."

Raven groaned as she turned to wash her hands. "I'm fine. I'm not going to punch anyone. Yet anyway. Stop provoking me."

"I live to provoke you. God, stop being a joykiller. Let me have my fun." She softened. "He's nice."

"Sometimes." Raven looked confused by that. "Other times he's bossy and he likes to tie me up and use a slapper on my ass." She blurted it and looked quite vexed that she had.

Erin tried not to smile but it was impossible. "I like the slapper." She shrugged. "I like being tied up too."

"Don't you think it's weird that I do? Am I that fucked up that the first guy who does this to me gets me all hot?"

Erin wanted to hug her, but she also knew it would have made Raven really uncomfortable and on the verge of losing her shit, which she clearly worked so hard to keep together. So she kept her distance.

"You think it makes you fucked up to like being tied up? I guess I'm in big trouble then. Does he do it against your will?"

"No! Do you think I'd stay with someone who did something I didn't want done?"

"Nope. Which is why I don't think you're fucked up. Or, well, I do, but in the way that everyone is fucked up somehow. So why do you think that? Because adults who should have protected you when you were a kid didn't means you shouldn't like a little rough-and-ready fucking? Puh-leeze. That's bullshit. That was *abuse*. Is he abusing you?"

"No. You said it yourself, he's a nice man. Mainly. He's also bossy

and annoying. He's nosy and in my business and doesn't like being told
no. He's very stubborn."

"Thank God or he'd have dumped your grumpy ass by now. No
matter how cute it is."

"This is a mistake. You know that."

"Why? Because he likes you on a deeper level than how you look?
Because he demands your monogamy? Because he touches you like he
thinks you're precious? You don't think it's obvious to anyone with
eyes? I'm checking him out, wanting to see how he is with you and
he's . . . enchanted by you. He listens to you when you talk. He's got
that super alpha male thing where he touches you to be sure everyone
in the room knows you're with him. But not in a douchey way like he
owns you. Tell me please, how that is a mistake? Unless being with
someone who wants you for longer than five minutes and a few orgasms
is a mistake? God, do you have so little value in yourself that you'd
think those jerkwads you banged in the past were better than this?"

"Fuck off."

"Whatever. I know you. No one else but a guy like him would
work out. Because he won't let you put him off with that attitude of
yours." Erin allowed herself a touch of Raven's hand then. "He values
you. Like you should let someone value you. It's about time you let
someone in who isn't me or a kid." She went into the stall.

"This is all bullshit. He's a dude I'm fucking. That's it. We're not
getting married or anything. It's just a few weeks."

Erin sighed, annoyed. Once she finished up she came out and
sneered at Raven before she started washing up. "You be quiet. I'm not
one of those people who can't see past your crap. This is already different. You're not eighteen. This isn't the first man, or woman, who made
you come. Some stuff just is. You can walk around it and say it's new,
and it clearly is. But that doesn't change what it is. Sometimes you just
know from the start." She turned to Raven as she started to leave. "And
you're not a coward, so stop running away from it."

9

Jonah hit the button to have the car answer his ringing phone. He was on his way over to Raven's to pick her up. He'd tried to coax her into sleeping over and she'd refused.

He didn't get to where he was by taking no for an answer, but he knew strategy well enough to understand Raven had deeper reasons for not wanting to sleep over than how much she liked her own bed. And he was beginning to know her enough to detect the edge of something he'd have to be careful about getting her to reveal to him.

It was Levi, his voice coming through the car speakers. "You have the day off? It's a Monday. Are you sick?"

"Nope. Taking a vacation day. Is there a problem?"

"I was going to see if you were free for lunch. I have to be at the courthouse downtown in a few hours."

"Raven and I are heading up to look at leaves and have lunch."

Levi got quiet and Jonah wished his brother could see how hard he'd just rolled his eyes.

"Okay, well, I guess I'll see you this weekend at dinner. You going to bring her?"

"Are you suggesting she's not good enough?" Considering how much Levi had gone through with Daisy he'd be surprised if his brother could have the balls to take any other tack with Raven than acceptance.

"No. I'm suggesting she's not . . . bring-home-to-Mom material."

"I don't plan to bring her around until we've got some more time under our belt. Not because she's not bring-home-to-Mom material, as you say. But because she's going to need some preparation before I expose her to the Warner household."

"So this is serious?"

Jonah sighed again. "Yes. I didn't think it would be when I first met her. I thought she was beautiful. I wanted to bed her and get a new tattoo. But it's more. I can't explain it all. I'm still processing it really."

"Why so suddenly now? Why her?"

Agitation rode him. "I can't do this while I'm driving and I'm coming up to her block anyway. But she's different. There's so much more to her than you see at first glance."

"I'm not attacking you. I'm on your side so don't take that tone with me. I'm trying to understand."

"So am I." He didn't bother trying to find a parking spot. It was nearly impossible in that part of town and he had no intention of calling her and meeting her at the curb as she'd suggested.

"Let's have drinks on Wednesday. After the board meeting."

"Sounds good."

He found a pay lot and then headed across the street and down the block to her building.

Fifth floor, corner. The place wasn't bad at all. The building was safe enough, though he'd have preferred a doorman.

He tapped on her door and moments later she opened it up with one brow hiked.

"Ready?" He breezed past her into her place and she closed the door behind him. At least she wasn't going to push him out and slam it in his face. He knew he was being pushy. Knew it was out of her comfort range too.

"I don't know that I would have pegged you as this tidy."

Tidy was an understatement. The place was organized. Everything in its place. Her shelves . . . "Are these organized by color?"

"I told you I'd meet you outside." She took a book from his hand and put it back and he grinned before hauling her close for a kiss.

"I wanted to come in to get you. I am not the man who will honk at the curb."

"Mm."

"Not just color, but alphabetically and by color. I'm impressed by this level of obsessive detail."

"I like things in order." She grabbed her jacket and a bag. "I have snacks. Shall we go?"

"Wait. Give me a tour."

She gave him a very fine side-eye as she sighed. "It's a studio. This is pretty much it."

He moved around, peering at her shelves. "What are these?"

"Sketchbooks. Books. Photo albums. The usual."

He pulled one out and she shifted, clearly uncomfortable. "May I look?"

She licked her lips, chewing on her bottom one a moment. "Sure. They're just sketches, nothing special."

But they were special. Page after page of drawings. Sometimes they were of people or landscapes. Sometimes they were clearly ideas for tattoos. But they were all amazing.

"You've got a great deal of talent."

"I'm okay."

"Prolific too." He indicated the multiple shelves.

"This is all of them. You know, since I was twelve or so. Some of the earlier ones . . . they didn't . . . I didn't keep those."

"How long have you been drawing?" He led her to the sliders and then out onto the deck. The traffic in the distance was a hum, but not annoyingly so.

"Since I was six or so. We should go."

"Your only appointment is me. And I'm right here. You're my only appointment. No rush. Why weren't you able to keep the ones from before you were twelve?"

"They didn't let you bring a lot. When you moved to a new place. Later I started keeping them at school, or in my great-grandmother's shed. But I didn't know much the earlier years."

He touched her then, sliding a hand through her hair, which she'd left loose around her face. "Awfully young to have to learn stuff like that. Did you lose her then? Your great-grandmother?"

"She lived until she was a hundred and one. But she"—her voice thinned but didn't quite break—"she couldn't care for me after I turned three. She had several strokes and she couldn't get around well."

"I'm sorry. Your mother?"

"Couldn't be bothered. We should go."

"You keep saying that. I want to know more."

"Fuck off!" She wrenched herself back, eyes flashing. "I'm not a reality television show. I'm not your dancing monkey."

"I never said you were. People share, that's how they build relationships. I don't want to hurt you. I just want to know you."

She hated how he stood there so fucking calm after he'd rooted through her memories that way. Hated too that the way he'd touched her had calmed her, how hard she'd had to fight the desire to lean in and take comfort.

"So let's get to know you then."

"Go on. Ask. I've answered all the questions you've asked."

She blew out a breath and tried to go back into her place but he stood there looking so reasonable she wanted to kick him in the balls.

"Look, I said I wouldn't fuck anyone else while I was with you. But that doesn't mean you get a full pass into my life. Into my memories. It sucked. Growing up the way I did sucked. It was horrible and I don't want to talk about it for a reason. You didn't grow up like that so I get how it's a story to you, but it *happened* to me. It happened to me and I'm not giving it to you on demand."

He moved to her slowly, but he kept moving until he'd gathered her up against his chest, holding her tight.

"I'm sorry."

She hated how he got to her. Hated how easy it was for him to waltz in and get past all the walls she'd built to defend herself.

"We should end this. You're looking for something I can't give you."

He snorted. "Be quiet. Let's go look at leaves. Bring your sketchbook. I'll buy you a glass of wine and lunch and make you come a few times before we go to dinner."

He turned and did that thing with her hand on his arm, leading her inside.

Of course he had a car that looked like a panther. Sleek. Powerful. Tinted windows. He escorted her to it and opened her door. When he closed it to go around to his side, all sound from outside was gone.

The seats were soft leather and it smelled a lot like he did. It wasn't necessary but she put her sunglasses on anyway, trying to find some way to filter him out.

"I like the sunglasses."

Of course he managed to sound suggestive. He drove calmly, but in charge. Easing into traffic like no one better get in his way. And really they didn't.

"Are you warm enough?"

Despite it being late October, it felt a lot more like November. But she'd worn a sweater and brought her jacket and gloves.

Soon enough though, her seat got warm.

"Jeez, are these heated seats?" She tried not to sound like she'd just eaten an entire bowl of ice cream, but it made her languid. Spoiled like a cat.

"I like luxuries. We established that. So when can I get the next piece done on my back?"

"I like to wait at least two weeks between sessions. I'll look at it the next time we're naked to see how it's coming along. But I want it healed before I do the next part."

"I like how you made that fun."

She rolled her eyes, relaxing a little when she realized he wasn't going to push about her past.

"That's me. More fun than a barrel of monkeys. Though, to be honest the idea of a barrel of monkeys doesn't sound fun to me. It sounds like there'd be fleas and bites and shit involved."

"I do think Raven fun is better than that, yes."

"Who even thinks that stuff up? Monkeys in a barrel?"

She noted that his mouth quivered as he tried not to smile. It was a seriously sexy mouth.

"Who knows, darlin'. Maybe someone without any idea of what fun is?"

"Probably. Anyway, two weeks. Maybe three, depending on how you heal. Though I doubt your immune system would have the audacity to take more than two weeks."

He chuckled. "And what exactly do you mean by that?"

"You know what I mean by that. I'm sure your immune system is just as stubborn as the rest of you is."

"I come by it honestly, I'm told. My mother is just as bad."

She snorted. She'd heard.

"I figured we'd head up around Snoqualmie. I saw a lot last year when Carrie and I went up. Work for you?"

"I'm just along for the ride. I wore shoes I could hike in, just in case."

"Hm, a hike. After I wake up in a warm cabin and have hot sex with a willing woman covered in ink. But just as a general rule? Not gonna make you hike without telling you up front."

"Good to know. I don't camp much. I like hot showers too much to really get into it. Erin did con me into going to the Sleeping Lady a few years back. We've gone several more times. If it comes with a spa and gourmet food as well as some pretty swank accommodations, I can swing that."

"I lived in the dorms my first year of college. I hated the communal showers. I hated wearing flip-flops."

Imagining him in cheap flip-flops did a good job eroding her annoyance. "You lived in the dorms?"

"Don't mock. My parents thought it would be a good experience. I met a shitload of girls. Lots of furtive, very quick fuck sessions before roommates came home. That was the good part. I got an apartment my second year when I worked at the firm part time."

"I bet you met a lot of girls. I can't even imagine the Jonah in his early twenties. Though, I do admit to the fairly overwhelming appeal of the Jonah in his forties. I like a man who knows what he's about."

"Good to know. I was more reckless then."

"Who isn't when they're twenty?"

"I bet you weren't."

"I'm reckless now, Jonah. As for when I was twenty? I was in my own way. I was trying to figure out everything. Trying to raise myself, I suppose."

"Trying to survive?"

"By the time I was twenty or so I knew I'd be all right. I had some skills that I could pay the rent with. I realized how much I loved to travel around that time, too."

"Do you ever go back? To Happy Bend, I mean."

"I went back once. For my great-grandmother's funeral."

"How old were you then?"

She licked her lips, trying to ignore the pain in her chest. "Twenty-three."

"Do you still have family there?"

"I imagine so. I don't have much contact with any of them. I hear from an aunt from time to time."

"They never took you in?"

Erin had urged her to share more with people and she was usually right. So she'd give it a shot.

"Sometimes. They were dirt poor, most of them. The aunt I have contact with sometimes, she and my mother are sisters. Were sisters. Whatever. Anyway, she's been plagued with health problems and a variety of addictions." Like the rest. Alcoholics and crazy people. She came from such fine stock.

"I lived with her on and off until I was six. She went to jail a few times. Had to move from one run-down, piece-of-shit place to another."

She shrugged but he took her hand, saying nothing.

"Don't." She pulled her hand back.

"Don't what?"

"Pity me. I don't need your pity." It's why she hated talking about any of it.

"I don't pity you. I care about you. I can hear the pain in your voice. I offered comfort. It doesn't make you weak to take it."

"This is all easy for you to say. Academic even."

"Is that what it is? Only people who've suffered like you can understand what it means?"

"Don't be an asshole."

"You already told me I was one. Don't be a bitch."

"I already told you I was one as well."

"That must be why we work."

She crossed her arms over her chest, staring out the window.

"Are you going to close off?"

"Back. Off."

"No."

She whipped her head to get a good look at this man she'd been so silly to think she could be with. Pushy!

"Just take me home."

"You agreed to come spend the day with me."

"That's before you started being all pushy and nosy."

"I was born pushy and nosy. Ask anyone. You knew that when you got in the car with me. You knew that when you opened your door to me this morning."

"Look, this is . . . We're just having some fun. You're making it more than it is."

It was his turn to snort. "Bullshit. Evasion is one thing. Lying is a whole different thing and, frankly, beneath you. This is far more than just some fun and you know it. If it was just fun you'd have told me to fuck off when I demanded your monogamy."

"I should have."

"But you didn't. Because you know it's more than just fun. It's more and you can't deny it. I won't let you."

"Why?"

"Because I like you. You're nothing like anyone I've ever known before and that appeals to me a great deal."

"Oh, so I'm your walk on the wild side then?"

"Fuck you. Fuck you, Raven, for thinking you can use that to keep me out."

The slice of anger in his tone didn't scare her. Well, it did, but not for her physical safety. Just her everything. It should have made her feel better, but instead, she knew it had been a tactical error. He wasn't going to be scared off. He was too damned stubborn for that.

And maybe that's why she'd done it. To test him. But he wasn't a boy to play with. He was a man. A man who knew what he wanted.

"I have a life. Everything is in order. I like my schedule and how I live. And you come in and in less than a month you're turning shit upside down and demanding I . . ."

"Share? Tell me about your life? How dare I? Is it that you think I'd judge you? That you don't think you can trust me to keep your confidences?"

"Look, sometimes you say things and you can't unsay them. You can't unknow them."

"But you already know them. They happened to you." The anger was gone and his calm was back, laced with a kind of gentleness that tore at her.

"Living them was enough. I've spent most of my life trying to forget!" She slammed her fist into her thigh so hard she knew she'd have a bruise.

"Baby, maybe you shouldn't. Maybe you should get it all out and slay those demons."

The endearment nearly pushed her to frustrated tears.

"Which is so easy for you to say! You grew up with a family. You grew up knowing exactly where you'd sleep every single night. I bet your parents tucked you in. I didn't even know that was a reality until I was fifteen years old."

"It *is* easy for me to say. Certainly easier than for you. And yes, sometimes we got tucked in. Enough that I knew how important it was to tuck my own child in every night. What happened? When you were fifteen, I mean?"

"No. That's not open for discussion."

He froze. "Someone hurt you."

"Lots of someones hurt me, Jonah. Don't try to avenge me now. I'm past it."

"No, you aren't. Or you could talk about it."

"Have you ever stopped to think, just once, that people don't like to discuss unpleasant things?"

"Sure. But this is more than that. What happened to your mother?"

She blew out a breath. "She was a drug addict. She had me, dumped me on my grandmother, who was just as much of a mess as my mother was. So I got dumped on *her* mother."

"So you never saw her? In your childhood?"

"A few times. She'd come to town, promise me she was better. She stayed with my great-grandmother too. Once she even rented us a house and had a job."

Tears threatened and she clamped her lips tight, willing them back. Pushing the humiliation, the shame and disappointment as far away as she could.

He must have sensed it because he backed off. For a few minutes anyway.

"What's your favorite food?"

"Pot roast."

"Really?"

"Yes, really. Why do you sound so surprised? Am I not allowed to like pot roast?"

"No." He laughed. "God, you're so fucking defensive about everything."

"And yet you can't get enough."

He took her hand, pulling when she tried to snatch it back. He kissed her knuckles. "This is so goddamned true you have no idea. For what it's worth, I like pot roast too. With roasted potatoes."

"Hm."

"That sound manages to be dismissive, annoyed, sexy and funny all at once. I even hear it when I'm not with you."

"Part of my many charms."

"They're legion. My favorite food is tacos."

"Really?"

"Now it's my turn to ask why you sound so surprised."

"You seem like a well-aged-steak-and-scotch sort of dude."

"No denying the appeal of a good steak and some scotch. But tacos are something I can make. They're portable. Most places manage to do them well if they're on the menu."

"The next time you go to L.A. I can tell you a few places I love."

"You seem pretty fond of Los Angeles. Why did you come up here then?"

"Brody."

"Really?"

"Yes, really. At first anyway. I met him in L.A. through a mutual friend who does tattoos. I liked him immediately. I mean, what's not to like? Anyway, then I met Erin and she and I hit it off. She lived in L.A. too. But I came up here a lot to see Brody. He took me under his wing, taught me a whole lot. I started working at his shop. Filling in here and there. He never tried to make me into something I wasn't. He let me come and go.

"Plus, its cool here. And green and clean. Far, far from Happy Bend. I still go to Los Angeles at least once a year. But I suppose I've ended up calling Seattle my home. As much as I have a home anyway."

"What went wrong with Brody?"

"He's a good man. In the end he wanted something I couldn't give. I told him that but he . . . I guess he expected better of me and I disappointed him. Hurt him. And then we were on and off. Truly, better as friends than we were as lovers. Elise came into the picture. God, I hated her at first. Well, that's not entirely accurate. I didn't really mind her at first. But once I saw he was really into her, that the thing between them was way more than just a flirtation, *then* I hated her."

"Why?"

Raven laughed. "Have you seen Elise? She's gorgeous. She's perfect. A wonderful mother. She was—is—good to Brody. She's what he needed in a way that I never had been." She paused and then just said it. "Erin adores her. Adrian thought she was perfect. And my place there, I was—"

"Worried you'd lose them."

It had taken a few weeks of some hard-core, unflinching introspection to get there. But she'd always credit Elise for it. "Yes. I was a bitch to Brody, tested his loyalty. She put me in my place one day. But it was that she was also kind to me even as she told me she would fight for him. She knew why. It . . . Anyway, I left town a while. Got my shit together, and when I came back, it was with my head on straight. I didn't want Brody that way. He's my friend and I wanted him happy. It took a while for me to get on the right track with Elise, but we're good now."

"You're probably one of the most well-adjusted adults I've ever known."

She burst out laughing. "Well, you're a lawyer, so that explains a lot."

"It takes guts to be truly introspective. To look at your actions and take responsibility for them. You own what you are, though you see yourself as more of a villain than you are. There's an emotional maturity there." He shrugged.

"I grew up around people who never took responsibility for anything. Ever. I vowed to not be like that. Sometimes I succeed."

⁓

"I think you should take a shower with me." He waggled his brows at her. They'd come back to his place after their day trip so he could shower and change for dinner.

"Hm."

"There you go with that sound again."

"I'm beginning to think you want to agitate me. It's like foreplay."

"Everything about you is foreplay, Raven. Have you looked at yourself in the mirror lately?"

"Hm."

"So? Your clothes are here." He'd convinced her to stop off at her

place first to grab a change of clothes so they could leave directly from
his place. But really it was that he wanted to watch her get ready.

"Let me look at your bathroom first."

He pushed open the doors, gesturing her inside. When they'd been
here before she'd used the one downstairs. Still a nice bathroom, but
this one. Well, he was proud of this bathroom.

"Holy cow." She turned in a slow circle once she'd gone inside.

"I like a long shower."

"I should say so."

His shower stall was quite large with benches on both sides and six
showerheads. The bathtub was a modernized version of a clawfoot,
only far larger and deeper.

"This is awesome. You can shower with me but only if you let me
have some alone time with this place."

"Should I be jealous of my bathroom?"

She turned to him. "Yes. You really should."

She undressed and he leaned back against the counter to watch her
fold each piece of clothing carefully. He was emotionally raw after
their discussion on the way up. She'd revealed a side of herself that had
brought all his protective instincts to the fore.

She'd been routinely neglected by the very people who should have
protected her. That made him insanely angry. And he only knew a
small bit of it. He understood that she had revealed a lot to him, but
it was just the tip of the story. Just the outline.

He wanted to gather her up and hold her until he'd made it better.
But he couldn't. He couldn't slay her dragons. Not for what she'd survived.

He'd gone and fallen in love with her. He hadn't meant to. God
knew she was complicated and it hadn't been that long that they'd
been together. But he knew what he knew. She'd come into his life for
a reason and this was it. She was meant to be his.

She got into his shower and bent to fiddle with the settings. He quickly disrobed to join her, sliding his body against hers.

"Back off. I'm not done yet."

He should have known she was a superhot-shower type. He'd thought himself a lover of hot showers until her settings had nearly scalded his top two layers of skin off.

"Jesus!"

"There are three shower heads right there. All for you."

"I thought you weren't supposed to use really hot water on a tattoo."

"You aren't. But I'm a rebel." She leaned back, groaning as the water rushed over her and he simply watched as the water cascaded over her curves.

"I'll get your hair."

He looked at her shampoo. "I thought I scented coconut."

"I get it in Hawaii. I love the way it smells."

Clearly she didn't skimp on her cosmetics.

He poured it into his palm and then braved the water to slowly lather her up. She stretched against him like a cat. He massaged her scalp and she rewarded him with a soft sigh that shot straight to his cock.

He started to soap her body up but she smirked, stealing her washcloth back. "I'll never get out of here if I let you wash my body."

"Who says I want you out of here?"

She rolled her eyes but kept her distance. "Let me do this and I'll get your hair. I can stand on the bench thing to reach."

"Fine. But I'm fucking you when we get back tonight."

"You can drop me at my place before you come back here. Not that I'm ruling out fucking."

"Why won't you spend the night?"

"I don't spend the night. We already had this discussion." She soaped up and he watched, his mouth watering as she ran her slick hands and the washcloth all over her skin. It was then he noted the scars.

He took her hand, turning her wrist to see her inner arm more clearly. "You did this?"

She looked up into his face with no shame. "It's been a long time. But the roses and thorns remind me that once upon a time I hurt myself to feel anything at all."

He sighed, pulling her close as the water came down all around them.

"Baby, you wreck me. You turn me inside out. I want to help but I don't know how."

"It's long past. I don't cut myself anymore. I don't hurt myself, though I let hot older men tie me up and slap my ass because it makes me wet. But I don't need to punish myself for other people's sins. You don't need to fix me."

She held his heart in those soapy hands and she had no idea. She was like those roses climbing up her inner arms. Beautiful and strong. Slightly dangerous.

She was the most amazing thing he'd ever seen.

10

She unlocked her door and he came in with her, wearing a hungry expression.

Five seconds after she'd locked the door behind them she'd found herself picked up as he walked them over to her bed. The rain had started, the sheets of water pelting her windows, soothing.

But there was nothing soothing about this man who unbuttoned the bodice of her dress so nimbly. He uncovered her skin like he'd found treasure. It . . . touched her. As much as she tried to keep it to just sex in her head, it was more. She knew it and couldn't hide from it anymore.

He kissed her chest, above her heart and she cradled his head to her body. Tenderness rushed through her system, making the way for the desire that barreled through right after.

He licked up her neck, suckling on her earlobe.

"I want you."

She shivered at this declaration he'd whispered.

"Take me, then."

"I plan on it."

He hauled her upright. "I don't want to rip this dress you look so damned delicious in, and I will if I try to get you out of it. Take it off."

She got to her knees and pulled it over her head, tossing it to a nearby chair.

On her knees, she watched him, waiting for whatever he wanted next. Something about that had settled into her system. Letting go of the control eased her, unknotted her muscles.

"You're amazing."

He pulled his shirt off before stepping from his shoes, shorts and socks. Naked he was breathtaking. The ambient light from the street outside only highlighted the masculine power of his muscles. His cock, so hard, tapped his belly.

"I want that." She indicated his cock.

He laughed and she shivered. He had a way of laughing when he meant to tease her. So much promise there.

"You'll get it. Hands behind your back. Clasped. That's how I want you every time we're like this. Unless I tell you otherwise."

She swallowed past a very dry mouth, complying with his request. Ha, request. His order.

Her back was arched and she knew she got to him. Knew her beauty appealed. It filled her with power, the allure she held. Just the way he looked at her made her feel beautiful. Incomparable.

He moved to her like a predator. Her nipples hardened impossibly.

She watched as he took each one between thumb and forefinger. Pinching. Tugging.

Her breath gusted from her lips as pleasure ripped through her belly.

He stepped away and she couldn't stop the sound of disappointment that bubbled up from her belly.

"I'm coming back." He rustled through the bag he'd brought up from the car, turning as he held a small box. "I have something for you."

She kept still long enough that he understood. "You can move to take the box and open it."

Inside lay two new hoops for her nipples and a long silver chain.

"I saw these in a movie once. I'd like you to wear the chain. Between your nipples and then to your clit when I'm not with you."

This was more than not fucking other people. This was a stamp on her in a way she'd never allowed. The appeal of it set her heart thundering.

She nodded slowly.

"Put the new hoops in."

She pulled the bars from her nipples and replaced them with the pretty silver hoops he'd presented her with.

Then he wove the chain through the hoops, tugging and bringing a gasp from her. Sensation, quicksilver, flitted through her like lightning.

He petted down her belly and thighs, easing them wider. His fingertips brushed her clit and she moaned at how good it felt.

"I think I'm doing this right."

She agreed when the cool of the chain slid against her cunt and then through the ring he'd exchanged for her old one.

"They told me the chain goes best with the rings I gave you. I like you like this, but I don't want to harm you. Does it feel all right?"

He stood, straightening as his gaze slid over her skin like a caress. "Y-yes."

More than all right.

"You're so ridiculously beautiful."

She smiled past the lump in her throat, luxuriating in the feel of the chain against her flesh.

"I have little weights too. We'll deal with those next time. For now you look like the best present I ever received and I'm going to fuck the hell out of you."

"All right." She put her hands back into position and watched his pupils swallow a bit more of his irises.

He blew out a breath and stepped closer again.

He fisted his cock over and over as he watched her. She couldn't tear her eyes from the way he touched himself. So sure and unashamed.

But *she* wanted to be touching him. So much that she ached from it. "Please."

He paused. "Please what, darlin'?"

"Please let me do that. Please touch me. Please fuck me. Whatever. Just please." She'd never in her entire life begged a man or a woman to give her something sexual.

He moved to her, reaching out to caress a hand over her hair, stopping to tip her chin up so he could brush his lips over her mouth. "So pretty. How can I turn down a request from such a beautiful woman?"

He straightened, sliding the head of his cock against her mouth. The salt of him awakened her senses and she had to clasp her hands tighter to keep from reaching out. He hadn't told her she could.

She swirled her tongue around the head, smearing that pre-come as she did. He grunted when she took him into her mouth totally, sucking him back as far as she could without losing her balance or doing something undignified like gagging.

He fucked into her mouth slow and easy for some time. Long enough that the rhythm of it lulled her senses.

Jonah watched her as he clenched his jaw to keep control. He wanted to spin her around and thrust his cock into that sweet, juicy pussy. But this was too good to stop. Her compliance, the way she was with her hands clasped, wearing the hoops he'd given her in her nipples and clitoral hood, the chain against the pale cream of her skin, he wasn't ready to let that go just yet.

"Yes, yes, like that."

She'd had her hair up for their dinner out but when they'd danced it had come loose a little, sending tendrils around her face and at the back of her neck. He pulled the pins out, letting it all free, so cool and soft against his hands and wrists. Thick and dark.

He held her head, cradled it between his palms as he began to fuck her face. To press his cock deep and pull back, watching the slick, dark stalk of his cock, the swell of her lips. The sound was enough, wet around her moans and hums of pleasure.

She got off on this as much as he did. Thank God.

Finally he couldn't hold it back any longer so he pulled out, letting go. "That's enough for now. I want you on your back. Hands above your head. Spread your thighs."

She complied, moving slow. Her expression was dreamy, in direct contrast with the swollen, dark nipples.

Her scent hung in the air, beating at him.

"You smell good enough to eat."

He grabbed her ankles, pushing her feet back and her knees up, keeping her open to his gaze and his mouth. She was dark and wet, swollen.

There was no more waiting. He had to take her.

He took a long lick, tugging on the ring with his teeth. She shivered and then moaned.

"You're so juicy. Do you like this, hmm?"

"God, yes!"

He smiled before he went back to work. Licking, sucking, loving every dip and fold. Her pussy was as delicious as it was sensitive. He knew she wasn't far from climax. Felt the tremble in the muscles of her thighs as he sucked her clit slowly and slid two fingers up into her cunt.

He picked up his pace, flicking his tongue against her clit relentlessly, keeping the pressure even until she breathed out his name and came against his lips, her hips rocking to take what she wanted from him.

After she'd stopped trembling, he pressed a kiss to her inner thigh.

"Hands and knees. I want to fuck you from behind."

He'd put a condom near when he'd brought the nipple jewelry

over, so he got it on quickly as she moved into position. Her back was gorgeous this way, her hair over her face. He'd let her hide for the time being so they could both keep their bearings.

He wanted to roll around in her scent. His hands smelled like her skin. Like coconut and sex and whatever it was that made up Raven.

He aligned his cock and slid deep in one hard thrust and she groaned so deep in her gut he felt the vibrations of it to his balls.

He grabbed her hips and began. Slowly but surely, stroking into her deeply. Over and over as he drove himself up, back toward the climax she'd nearly toppled him into just minutes before.

The muscles and curve of her hips played against his palms as he held on.

Being with her was totally natural and yet utterly unreal all at the same time. She was so much more than he'd bargained for. Everything.

He pressed in one last time with a snarl as he let himself fall into climax before toppling to the bed, holding her close as he came.

He slid onto a barstool next to his brother.

"I ordered you a scotch."

Jonah tipped his chin. "I knew there was a reason I kept you around. I haven't eaten yet; you have time for a bite?" He really wanted to bounce some stuff off Levi, who in addition to being his brother, happened to also be his best friend. He knew anything he said would be kept in confidence.

"Daisy's got some shindig with Delicious so I would just be eating leftovers of some sort anyway. They have a decent bar menu here."

They did, and he and his brother ordered food and headed to a booth when one opened up.

"The server was giving you the eye." Levi lifted his glass. "Still got it, even for an old guy."

"I fucked her once. Right after the divorce."

Levi snorted. "Damn."

"It was all right. She made a lot of noise, but I don't think she really meant it."

"Maybe you need me to show you where everything is?"

Jonah snorted. "I know where everything is. I never felt compelled to call her again. Because as Raven points out, I'm an asshole." He laughed.

"She said that?"

"As it happens, she was making a very good point." He explained it to Levi, who shrugged and nodded.

"She's pretty smart. But sort of . . . wild. You having a midlife crisis or something?"

"Fuck off. You're shacked up with a girl nearly half your age."

"Dude, there's a lot to be said for midlife crises. Mine came with a hot artist with tits that defy gravity. What's not to like? I have all my hair and I'm in love."

"A crisis implies there's something wrong you need to make up for. This isn't a crisis. It's the opposite. I feel totally clear for the first time since Carrie was born. I'm head over my ass in love."

"*Love?* Jonah, you've been seeing her what? A month?"

"Not quite. But I'm not a teenager. I've been to the rodeo, so to speak. I know what infatuation is. I know what lust is. Lust was me fucking the server over there. This woman gets to me. Not because she's gorgeous, though certainly that's a bonus. Not because she's insightful and intelligent, talented, artistic. Not just because she makes me feel like no one ever has in bed. There's a connection with her that I've never, ever had before. I click with her. She . . . I don't know how to put it into words that do it justice, Levi. But she makes me *feel.* She makes me work harder than I ever have with a woman. Goddamn, she's defensive. Bitchy. Sharp and prickly. But so vulnerable. Fragile. The sum of her is irresistible."

"So you're going to save her? Is that it? Be the guy who's done what no one else has?"

"First of all, Dr. Phil, I already have done what no one else has. I listen to her. I accept her. But I don't take her shit. And I don't let her push me away. I'm not with her because I'm some fuck-drunk frat boy who has a hard-on for ink and piercings. *She's something else.* More than I ever thought I'd find in a partner. She's a grown-up. She listens to me. She sees things in a way most never will. I don't need to save her. She's a woman who's done plenty of her own saving. She's endured a lot." He sipped his drink.

"I'm just saying it seems sudden. You're not a sudden type of guy."

"Isn't love really about someone being something no one else has been? Isn't that what you have with Daisy? What you didn't with Kelsey? What I never did with Charlotte? Isn't it about that connection that clicks and settles down all that noise in your head? She excites me. She challenges me. I'm on fire when I'm with her. Not just the sex, though, wow. She's that part inside I never knew I'd been missing. But now that I've found her, I don't know what I'd do without her."

Levi dug into the sandwich he'd ordered. "Wow. Well, congratulations then. For what it's worth, I like her. Though she's prickly, no doubt about it."

"Now I just have to convince her I'm in it for the long haul. A lot of people have failed her in her life." Jonah paused, wiping his mouth. "This is going to make us both uncomfortable, but here goes. You're into the D/s stuff right? I mean, we've skirted around it . . ."

Levi nodded. "It wasn't something I was really able to get into with Kelsey. I dabbled before Daisy. But she, Daisy, I mean, she just—it works with her. You and Raven?" Levi ate a while as he thought. "I'd be careful around any possible stuff that might bring up her abuse. I'm assuming she's got some in her background and that's what you were referring to."

"I don't want to say too much about that. She's given me her confidence and I can't betray it. But it hasn't been an issue. Her sexuality is strong. She's vibrant. She knows what she wants and I have zero doubt that if she didn't want it, she'd let me know. This isn't therapy for her. Or me for that matter. She needs . . . a strong hand. She needs to let go of all her control."

"So you're going to take her in hand?"

"Not in a paternalistic sense. Like I said, she's a grown-ass woman. But all her bullshit notions about what a relationship is, what it means to be with someone, they need to be broken apart. She submits, holy shit, she gives over and it's like everything just feels perfect. I need to break down her defenses, so she knows she can count on me."

"That makes sense. Bind her perhaps?"

"I can't believe we're having this discussion." Jonah snorted, taking a few hearty gulps of his scotch.

"Ha. You started it."

"I'm going to collar her."

Levi sat back. "Really? I can't imagine she'd go for that."

"Not to own her. But I think she needs that underline on my commitment. It's a declaration from me, a tangible one. I think she needs to be peeled open, layer after layer, and since we really click sexually, I think that's our key."

Levi nodded. "I can see that. But I'd be sure my first-aid kit was stocked. Just in case she sees it differently."

Jonah snorted. "She's dangerous enough to kick my ass if I push too hard."

"Hot though. Daisy undoes me when she's like that. So, when are you seeing her again?"

"She's coming over next week to do some more on my back. But I'm trying to get her to agree to be my date for the museum benefit this weekend. You and Daisy will be there, right?"

"Yes." Levi gave him a look. "You sure about that?"

"Why?"

"Don't give me that face. Mother is going to be there. Have you told her about Raven yet?"

"I'm a forty-two-year-old man. I don't run my romantic life past my mother. Anyway, she and I are having lunch before the board meeting on Thursday so I was planning on it then." He shrugged. "I mean to make Raven part of my life. I'm telling Carrie about her this week. I wanted to do it face-to-face, but she's getting ready to go to Paris with her friends and I wanted her to know before I took her around anywhere she'd come into contact with Mother."

"How do you think Carrie is going to react?"

"If she isn't happy for me, I raised her wrong."

"True. It's not like you've been bringing all manner of random chick around since you and Charlotte split. Mother, on the other hand . . ."

"Whatever."

"You know I've got your back. You kicked my ass when I messed things up with Daisy. We want you to be happy like we are. And in case you're wondering, those are her words. I'm more prone to bad words and threats to keep you in line."

Jonah grinned at his brother. "Hopefully it'll be all right."

Raven lay on her belly, dancing a plastic horse around as Alexander made growling sounds with his.

"Dude, horses don't growl." Ben grinned at his son.

"Mine do." Alexander nodded once and went back to growling and prancing.

Raven tried not to laugh.

"Good thing you came over. Brody and Elise will be here in a few minutes with Marti and Rennie."

Alexander clapped. "Yay! Pizza!"

"I was thinking tacos."

Alexander got serious for a moment and then nodded. "'Kay."

"Want some help?"

"You're not going to try to beg off?"

"You'd only guilt me into staying. I haven't seen the girls in a few weeks, anyway."

Erin liked the change in her friend. It had been a very long time coming. But Raven seemed comfortable with Elise at long last. And maybe even herself.

"Ben, you need to take over horse duty." Raven handed the plastic horse to him and he settled in with Alexander.

They went into the kitchen and washed up. "So?" Erin began to pull ingredients from the fridge.

"Things are good."

"I didn't even have to poke at you for ten minutes to get you to tell me. Must be good."

Raven looked up from where she'd started cleaning the produce. "It is. They are. Whatever."

"You two have spent a lot of time together lately."

"We have. We spent pretty much the entire day together on Monday. Went up to Snoqualmie to look at the leaves. Walked a lot. He's a hand holder. Opens doors. Pulls my chair out. He glowers at people if they don't move out of my way when we're on the sidewalk."

Erin loved that about her men. Loved the way they always made her feel protected. Cherished.

"It's not that I can't do it for myself. But he likes to and I let him. He sort of gets that I'm letting him. He's nice to me. Though, he's so pushy. Always wants to know about my childhood and stuff."

Erin stilled a moment and then kept moving. "And?"

"I told him some. He saw the scars. I told him about that. He knows I was in foster care. Not all of it," Raven added quickly. "I don't want his pity. I don't know if I could stand it. If he pitied me, I mean."

"Sometimes, just saying it out loud lifts the weight." Erin knew about this personally. Knew what it felt like to hold all that pain inside until she'd finally shared it with Todd and then Ben. Knew that it had brought them all closer to have shared her grief.

Knew too that Jonah Warner would keep pushing Raven to share and that hopefully, if Raven didn't balk and run off, she might have found a person worthy of her confidences.

Raven lifted a shoulder. "It's hard to say it out loud sometimes."

"I know. But it's not you. You did nothing wrong."

"Academic."

Erin knew about guilt over things that weren't her fault too.

"Sometimes you should listen to your head as well as your gut."

"I'm trying. He wants to stay over. God."

Erin snorted as she began to shred cheese. "I imagine he's not one to take no for an answer."

"No."

"Why don't you just tell him?"

"Tell him what? I don't need therapy, Erin, so don't start on me with your freaking psychological mumbo jumbo about why I like to sleep alone."

"Alexander has slept over."

Raven smiled, softening. For her baby. Love swamped Erin just then. Raven would take a bullet for Alexander. She loved that boy and he loved his auntie right back.

"He's my best guy. Clearly the rules can be broken for him."

"I'm just saying, rules were meant to be broken. Especially when they exist to bandage some long-ago trauma that may need a little sunlight and fresh air."

Raven grunted and went back to work.

Brody came over before Erin could do much more nosing around. Marti, Brody and Elise's toddler, came into the kitchen at a full run, her arms open. When she saw Raven as well as Erin her face lit even more. She squealed with total joy as Raven stepped to her and swung her up into a hug.

"Martine, my love. I think you're a foot taller now."

Marti threw chubby arms around Raven's neck.

Rennie came into the room and it struck Erin that her niece was nearly a teenager. In just a few months she'd be thirteen. But she had her mother's beauty. Pale hair, big blue eyes. A dancer's long, lean body.

"Why hello, Rennie." Erin hugged her.

"Hey, Aunt Erin." She grinned. "Thanks for the awesome paints. I'm working on something now. You know, to thank you."

Elise came in, smiling at the sight of her daughters with Raven and Erin.

"I want to see too." Raven handed Marti to Erin and then tipped her chin to Rennie, who still looked at her like she was the most awesome fireworks show ever.

"My art?"

"Yeah. Your dad showed me some the last time I saw him. He's got like forty pictures of it on his phone. But that's not the same as in real life."

Rennie blushed and then bent when Alexander came in, patting her thigh. "Yo, Nee!"

"Hey, Alexander." She knelt to hug him and he handed her a horse. "Come play."

Rennie waved at them and followed Alexander out.

"She's a great kid," Erin said before turning her attention back to Marti, kissing those chubby toddler cheeks. "Where's Brody?"

"Jeez." Raven went back to work. "Hello, Elise. How are you? Sorry about Erin's manners. You know how she gets when she's got a baby in her arms."

Elise laughed and Marti did too. "Down, please."

Erin kissed her one last time and put her down. With one wave over her shoulder, she headed toward where Alexander and Rennie were playing with Ben.

"He's on his way up. He's bringing the pies and some other stuff. He and Todd met in the lobby and there was secret stuff happening."

"Halloween stuff most likely. You're coming, right?" Erin turned to Raven.

"Uh."

"Miles and his band are playing. There's going to be a little Halloween parade thing."

Raven groaned. "Miles doesn't need me there."

"Pfft. Alexander does. And Marti. And Rennie. And of course, me. Plus, Gillian and Elise and Brody."

"You already used that one for Thanksgiving."

"It's all-purpose."

"You're coming to Thanksgiving?" Elise's bright smile was genuine and Raven relaxed.

"Yes."

"That's wonderful. I'm glad you'll be in town this year."

"I'm planning on bugging her relentlessly until she agrees to make cinnamon rolls." Erin flashed a grin and Raven groaned.

One of the only happy memories Raven had from her childhood was of her great-grandmother teaching her to make cinnamon rolls. She was too old to do much more than sit in the kitchen and tell Raven what to do. But on those rare visits once she'd gotten a little older, Eula Mae's kitchen would be filled with scents that still made Raven smile to that day.

"Maybe. If you ask nicely."

"I should ask Jonah too." Erin fluttered her lashes.

"His daughter is coming home for it. She's in Europe on some study-abroad deal. I'm guessing there'll be some big dinner at the manse with Ma and Pa Kettle."

Elise laughed. "The stories I've heard about his mother scare me. But she seems to like Daisy so she can't be all bad."

"In any case, he'll be otherwise engaged."

"You can go over there. I'll give you a day pass for that."

"I am still vexed I allowed you to guilt me into Thanksgiving day with you. I'm sure as hell not going over there. Plus, we're not at the meet-the-parents stage. We're just dating. Or whatever."

He'd want to spend time with Carrie and there was no way Raven would get between them. The girl needed her dad and she had no doubts how much Jonah adored his daughter.

Elise sent Erin a look and Raven kept her head down, biting her tongue. See? She was learning.

11

Raven looked at her phone and saw Jonah's number. Smiling, she answered. "Yes?"

"That's what I like to hear. Just yes. All the time. No matter what I ask."

"It does me no good to encourage you in any way."

"Oh, but it does." His voice went all low and silky and she shivered. "I remember you encouraging me just fine the other night."

"To what do I owe the pleasure of this call?"

She sat on her small deck, the rain falling, though she was dry beneath the overhang.

"What are you doing right now?"

"I'm sitting on my deck, drinking a beer, wrapped in a blanket, listening to music."

"Damn, that sounds pretty nice. Wish I was there with you but instead I'm going into yet another meeting shortly. What are you doing Saturday night?"

"Nothing yet." She'd been invited to dinner with some friends visiting from out of town, but anything he'd be offering would be better.

She was officially at the stage where she turned down things with friends to be with a guy.

Man.

"Good. Come out with me. Be my date to a benefit. We'll dress up, drink champagne, eat appetizers, and afterward I'll take you to sushi."

"Um."

"Too late. You already agreed."

"*Um* is not agreement. What benefit is this?"

"It's a museum benefit. Daisy will be there. Levi too."

"I'm not really benefit date material, Jonah."

"Bullshit. You're beautiful. I know you can dress up. Don't forget I saw you all fancified Monday night. You don't pick your nose or spit on the floor. You are indeed benefit date material."

Against her better judgment she accepted it in her head. But that didn't mean she wasn't going to drill him for more information and make him work for it. "Is it like formal?"

"I sent you something. I'd bring it myself but I have a meeting in a few minutes and then tomorrow I'll be slammed all day and into the evening. It'll arrive at the shop since I didn't want it sitting around on your doorstep all day."

"What did you do?"

"Has anyone ever told you you're a very suspicious woman? It's a dress. I saw it and I wanted to see you in it. Wear it for me and I'll show you why doing what I tell you to is always in your best interests."

"I don't know, Jonah. I'm not much for society stuff."

"I know you like art. I know you like me. I know you like doing some good. I already bought the tickets. I already have a driver. I already bought the dress. Oh, and some shoes. It'll be fun."

"You have a strange idea of fun."

"I want you there with me. This is important to me."

She sighed. "All right."

She knew he was grinning, though she couldn't see his face. "I'll pick you up at seven. We'll get drinks first with Levi and Daisy."

"Okay."

"See how easy that was?"

"Hm."

"You know what that sound does to me." He paused a moment. "You doing okay? I miss you."

"You just saw me on Monday."

"But that was three days ago."

She smiled, flattered. "Yes, well. I'm good. Busy. Worked ten hours today so my back is killing me and my wrist is messed up. You all right?"

"Better now. I'm talking to Carrie later on tonight. I like to catch her first thing in the morning, before her classes start. She's actually off to Paris in a few days so I want to check in."

"Have a good talk with her." She knew he missed his daughter.

"I will. Sweet dreams. I'll see you in a few days."

He hung up and she was still smiling to herself when she went inside nearly an hour later.

Jonah stood when his mother approached their table. He pulled her chair out and then settled, ordering her a glass of wine.

"You look handsome today."

Of the brothers, Jonah was closest with his mother. Mainly because she'd tried to break him multiple times as he was growing up and she'd never succeeded. She liked to make a joke that he was the most stubborn being she'd ever known, but really, all she had to do was look in the mirror. He came by it honestly.

Still, she could be a stone-cold bitch and a pain in the ass, especially when it came to how people might perceive what her sons did and how that might reflect on the family and their position.

"Thank you. Carrie gave me the tie for Father's Day last year."

"She's got good taste. Thank heaven she takes after you and not her stupid twit of a mother."

"So." He moved on, not wanting to get into a bash-Charlotte conversation. It wasn't that he still cared, but that he didn't. He didn't want to spend any time on her. "I'm seeing someone." He figured it was best to just get it out there. Not present it like it was an issue, but a done deal. He was mainly telling her because he wanted to answer in the affirmative if Raven asked if he'd told his family about them.

His mother gave him a look as the wine was delivered to the table. "Do I know her?"

"No."

She narrowed her gaze. "Well, stop evading. Did you get some girl pregnant or something?"

He laughed and they held off discussing it further until after they'd ordered.

"I know how to use birth control and I wasn't evading. I'd only gotten a few sentences in. No you don't know her. Her name is Raven. She's an artist."

"An artist? Well, with a name like Raven I guess that's appropriate. Who does this girl come from? Where did you meet her? She's not twenty or anything, is she?"

Jonah laughed. Everything was going to be just fine.

She gave herself one last look in the mirror on her way to the door. The dress he'd sent, she had to admit, was perfection. Black. Simple but elegant.

She'd worried her ink would show too much, but the sleeves, though sheer, gave her enough cover to feel comfortable and yet not that he'd wanted her to hide.

The bodice had pretty beading to add some shimmer, but not so much it looked tacky or shouted "hey, look at my boobs." Though the cut was generous, she also wasn't concerned she'd be having a wardrobe malfunction. It was figure hugging without being tight.

The material was gorgeous. The dress was really well made. It was clear he'd paid a pretty penny for it. But at the same time, also clear he'd really given thought to what her personal style was.

In short, instead of feeling bought and paid for, she felt treasured. Spoiled even.

She'd done her hair in a chignon at the base of her skull. One of the first hairstyles she'd learned when she came out to Los Angeles and one she had used time and again.

He'd also sent along shoes. Shoes she'd actually drooled over a few months before so she knew how much they'd cost because she'd said to Erin that she couldn't, in good conscience, pay that kind of money for a pair of shoes.

She smiled, looking at herself one last time. She was still Raven. Only fancified, as he'd said. And the shoes were a dream and made her legs look a million miles long.

Partial payment for the hell she was sure to endure at this thing.

He knocked again. Impatient.

She opened the door and he sucked in a breath. "You look magnificent."

She blushed but got a load of him while she did. "Says the gorgeous man in the tux standing in my doorway."

He handed her roses. "Just because. I saw them and knew you needed them."

She took them, burying her face, inhaling. "Thank you. Come in while I get them in water."

She grabbed a vase and got the roses settled, taking one, trimming it and adding it to her hair.

"Oh, I like that." He took her hand, kissing it. "Do you have a wrap?"

"Yes. Thank you for the dress and shoes, by the way."

He looked her up and down. "I really have to take credit here because you look so good. I had to guess on the sizes."

"You know women's bodies well. Though that's not really a surprise."

He took the wrap she'd picked up after she'd unwrapped the dress and put it on her shoulders.

Outside, at the curb, a sleek black car waited with Daisy and Levi already inside.

"Hey, Raven. Wow, you look fabulous." Daisy smiled and Raven couldn't help but smile back.

"Thanks. You too."

"I think it's necessary to say just what good taste the Warner men have." Levi tipped his chin at his brother. "Evening, Raven."

They drove to the hotel where the benefit was being held. "We can get a drink here. The bar at the top is quite lovely." Jonah helped her out and then kept his hand at the small of her back as they went up.

"I'm really glad you're here tonight." Daisy sipped her martini. "These things were fun before I got together with Levi. But usually I was working at them." She laughed and Raven relaxed a little. "Being here as Levi's fiancée is different. It makes me nervous because they're always sizing me up."

Jonah and Levi had excused themselves to hit the men's room so it was just the two of them at the table.

"Who sizes you up?"

"All the women who figured they'd be making a play for Levi."

"So there you are all vibrant and young and really hot. My god, they must flip out."

"You're really good for my ego." Daisy grinned. "The artist thing helps. I know many of these people in my own right. But the whole society thing? That's Levi's neck of the woods."

"Which makes you . . . What do they call it? A power couple. I mean, he's the money and you're the talent. Both of you are easy on the eyes. You're all charming in that way only a very few people are."

"I am?"

"Um, yes. Unlike me. I'm just going to try really hard not to say anything at all tonight."

Daisy's eyebrows flew up. "For god's sake, why?"

"Look, I like Jonah. He's a lovely man and he's good to me. I know I'm . . . an acquired taste. I don't want to embarrass him."

Daisy's expression softened as she reached out to pat Raven's hand. "You're who you are. More than anyone else I've ever met. And that's a good thing, believe it or not. I'm just saying, sure, sure, don't blurt out that such and such has clearly had her lips done no matter how much she tells you she's just got that youthful glow or whatever, but you're not going to embarrass Jonah. He wouldn't have invited you if he'd had any worries at all."

The ballroom was glittery and lit with what seemed like a zillion candles. The awesome thing was that candlelight hid a multitude of sins and made everyone look lovely.

Jonah handed off her wrap and his overcoat to the person at coat check and they waited for Daisy and Levi to do the same. She'd never admit it out loud, but having Daisy there made it better. Oh, not by comparison, because Daisy wore a bright smile and waved at people who seemed delighted to see her.

That wasn't Raven's wheelhouse. At all. But she knew Daisy, and Daisy had been very nice to her. Raven didn't feel so totally alone.

People did look though. In fact many of them did a double take when they noted she was on Jonah's arm. Inside she told herself, "You are Raven Smith. You are beautiful and amazing and these people can fuck off sideways." As affirmations went, it was useful and one she used more than once. It helped her keep her back straight and her eyes up off the floor. She'd vowed a long time ago that she'd never let any-one make her avert her gaze again.

Daisy seemed to float through the crowd and Levi followed, nod-ding and saying hello.

"Usually Carrie is my date for these things. It's nice because I can use it being a school night or something like that to leave early. But there are definite plusses to you being my date instead."

She paused as he grabbed a glass of champagne for each of them. "Yes? And those would be?"

"Well, when I get bored and start to daydream I can imagine all the things I'm going to do to you later. Also, I can laugh inside and be smug every time one of these men looks at you and has to stop them-selves from drooling. Oh, and I like to imagine your mental dialogue. I'm guessing it's priceless."

Off balance, she laughed. "You're trouble."

"I am. I didn't get kicked out of as many schools as Levi did but I had my share of trouble."

"And yet you went to college and law school and now you drive a sleek black car with heated leather seats."

It was his turn to laugh. "I know. It's pretty awesome."

He nodded at a passerby. "That's my brother Mal's mother-in-law. Want to meet her?"

"Do I?"

He shook his head. "You really don't."

She clinked her glass to his. "All right then. No."

"That's her, by the way. Gwen, Mal's wife."

She was beautiful on her husband's arm. Mal was certainly Jonah and Levi's brother. A younger version, yes, but he had the same mas-culine features. Handsome. He wore his tuxedo perfectly. As perfect as the champagne-toned cocktail number his wife wore. Gwen clearly knew how to look pretty. Her hair was done well and her makeup job—most likely a professional had done it—was exactly right for the evening and her outfit.

Her ring was so huge Raven could see it from where they stood.

And then she noted Gwen's expression when she caught sight of Daisy. Her eyes narrowed and her lip curled. She really, really didn't like Gwen Warner. Not one tiny bit.

They moved through the crowd, Jonah introducing her here and there.

And then there was Liesl.

"Ah, Jonah, there you are." The Warner matriarch paused to kiss her son's cheek and then turned to Raven. "You're Raven." She held a hand out and Raven took it, shaking, hoping she wasn't too soft or too rough or wrong in any way. She wanted to be perfect for Jonah.

"I am."

"I'm Liesl Warner, Jonah's mother." The older woman gave her the once-over. Jonah moved closer to Raven, putting an arm around her waist.

"Raven Smith."

"I know Smith is a common name, but I can't tell you the last time I actually met someone with that name."

"I took it on when I emancipated myself from the state. I was seventeen and had been bounced around from home to home for so long I didn't really belong to anyone or anything and had no affinity with the people whose biological stock I carried. I figured Smith was generic enough so I took it on. I belong to myself."

Liesl drew herself back, narrowing her gaze for a moment.

"I apologize. I meant no offense." And it was genuine; though she had when she said it, she was sorry at that moment and that was what counted. God knew Raven said things all the time that offended people.

Raven nodded. "I'm probably the one who should apologize."

Jonah squeezed her to his side. "No, you aren't. It's fine now. We're moving on and changing the topic."

Liesl actually smiled at Raven and then her son. "Indeed. Jonah tells me you're an artist."

Raven laughed. "Well, I'm not like Daisy. I do tattoos."

She'd half expected Liesl to frown, but she didn't. Instead she nodded. "Daisy is one of a kind, I agree. As for art in general? One of the pieces on sale this evening is made of spit and gum. Art comes in many forms. Jonah says you're doing one on his whole back and that it takes several sessions, each taking many hours. He wouldn't show me what you've done so far, but he assures me you're quite talented."

"I wasn't going to remove my shirt in the middle of the restaurant, no. But yes, she's very good."

"He says you have a wait list."

Raven looked toward him quickly, so surprised by this entire exchange. "I do, yes. My boss is the draw, but I have a decent client base. People like my work. It's good because I like doing it and it pays my mortgage."

"Making a living with your art is a good thing." Liesl turned to her son. "You should figure out how we can put Raven to work for the next auction. If Levi can convince Daisy to donate her art, I'm sure you can be equally persuasive."

"Mother—"

"What auction is this for?"

"Created Families. We raise money and awareness for adoption and foster care support."

Jonah made a cute, frustrated sound.

"Quit that, Jonah. The woman has a history in the system. Why shouldn't she want to help?"

"Have you ever stopped to . . ." He clamped his lips closed. "We'll talk about this later."

"If you'll both excuse me. I need the ladies' room. Then you can talk about me while I'm gone. I'll give you about ten minutes."

She stepped out of his grasp and he started to speak. She placed her finger over those talented lips. "Shh. I'll be back."

Jonah turned to his mother. "Did you ever stop to think her experiences in the system might have been terrible?"

"I assume it was, given the way she spoke about how she changed her name. And my, the girl has some spunk. Put me right in my place." His mother was impressed, Jonah could see it, and frankly, he was too.

"She did, and don't think we won't talk about how rude you were later on. For now, why push for this auction stuff?"

"Just because the woman had a rough time doesn't mean she wouldn't want to make it better for others. I'm sure she's not an idiot and understands it wasn't the system who harmed her, but some of those in it."

"You should have discussed it with me privately. I don't want her hurt. You need to understand that. She means something to me. Being with me doesn't mean you have carte blanche to play with her like a cat with a bug."

His mother reached out to squeeze his arm. "Darling, she's no bug. Your Raven can handle herself quite ably."

"This isn't a game. She shouldn't have to *handle herself.*"

"You really do have feelings for her. I can't recall if you were ever this protective of Charlotte."

"Probably one of the many mistakes I made that led to the end of my marriage. But I'm trying not to make mistakes with her. I'm in love with her. She deserves respect and kindness. I won't have anything else."

His mother raised a brow his way. "You're introducing her to a world she's a novice in. She'll have to earn that respect. And I suggest you let her. She'll draw blood a few times and that will be that."

"I'm not interested in this social engineering discussion. If anyone fucks with her, I will end them."

His mother's delighted laughter surprised him into silence for several long moments.

"What?"

"All I can say is that it's about time. You were a late bloomer for other things so I suppose it's only right you were to love as well. Love is exactly what you're feeling. Do you know, once when I was twenty, one of your father's ex-girlfriends—well no, her mother—spoke to me rather harshly. And your father took her aside and whatever he said worked because no one ever messed with me again. But I had to stay hard. And she will too. Being with a Warner comes with responsibilities. That's reality. She'll have to scorch her own earth and again, I think you need to let her to a certain extent."

"Every time I think I have you figured out, you surprise me."

"It's one of the mysteries of motherhood, darling. Now, you can make yourself useful and get me a glass of champagne."

Still amused by the interchange between Jonah and his mother, Raven made her way across the room toward the ladies' room.

Daisy joined her. "Well, you're not bleeding."

Raven must have looked confused because Daisy explained. "I take it this was your first time meeting Liesl?"

"Ah. Yes. She's all right. She and Jonah are having a discussion. Just imagine air quotes around it. But really, she's fine. She pushed, I pushed back."

"Everyone is afraid of her. And for good reason, she's pretty scary. But she respects other strong people. As long as they're not a threat to her family anyway. I bet she thinks you're fabulous."

"She's got a lot to lose." Raven shrugged. "I get it."

"If she thought you were a threat to it, you'd be bleeding. Trust me."

Raven paused to reapply her lipstick and check her hair, and that's when she made Gwen Warner's acquaintance.

Raven turned to find the other woman standing there, a sneer on her lips, hands at her waist.

"Didn't your mother ever tell you your face would freeze if you did that?"

Surprise skittered over the other woman's features.

"I see Jonah has picked up on Levi's bad habits. You're nearly as bad as that whore Levi is shacked up with."

"I take it you're Gwen. Who I am is of no concern to you."

"Not really, no."

She turned back to the mirror and Gwen stomped up and grabbed her arm.

Daisy came out of the stall. "Whoa! Get your hands off her."

"You're about to make a very bad mistake." Raven leaned in, her nose nearly touching Gwen's. "You can let go, or I can make you."

Daisy pushed Gwen back and Gwen sputtered some incoherent rage. "You listen here, you're trash!"

Raven stalked to her again. "You need to get the fuck out of my face. I'm beginning to wonder just why you're so concerned about the love lives of your husband's brothers. Are you pissy because you wanted a different Warner?"

"I ask myself that same question all the time." Daisy's voice was laced with a hostility Raven had never heard her use.

"Look at yourself. Then tell me you're worthy of the Warner name."

Raven turned and looked at herself in the mirrors, pausing to blot her lipstick and touch her hair up. "I'm pretty fabulous. Daisy over there looks like a magazine ad."

"You have tattoos!"

Raven laughed, her anger sliding away. "I totally do. I give them to other people too. Now you want to tell me what your real issue is? Because I'm really bored with this."

"You two are not right for this family."

"First of all, I don't really care what you think I'm right or not right for. I don't give a shit about you one way or the other, so your opinions on anything really are totally meaningless. Secondly, this seems like a plot from a movie. Jonah isn't next in line to be king. If he wants to date a tattoo artist, what's it to you? You got your Warner and your ring. Be satisfied with that."

"Jonah is the oldest. He's going to take over when his father dies. He needs a suitable wife. As the only wife in this generation—"

Raven looked to Daisy and tipped her chin toward the door. "Does she always yap like this? I'm hungry and Jonah promised sushi after the benefit."

Daisy grinned as she washed her hands. "Sadly, she does."

Raven went to the door and opened it before looking back over her shoulder at Gwen. "Bored now. Let's just leave it at this—if you touch me again, I'm going to punch you so hard you lose a tooth or two. Trash like me doesn't take kindly to being manhandled by dried-up bitter bitches who wished they'd been able to fuck their way higher up the societal food chain."

"Holy shit." Daisy breathed it out as they headed back to where Jonah was now standing with Levi. "If you made semen, I'd totally have your babies."

Raven snorted. "Um. Thanks, I guess. Has she done this before?"

"She went off on me once in the middle of a restaurant. And she's made comments under her breath. But she's never touched me. I thought for sure she was going to end up with a black eye."

"It's been a very long time since I've had to solve a problem with a fist. She nearly broke that fast. I imagine Liesl's probationary like of me is going to dissolve away now. That was pretty tacky of me."

"Of *you*? Are you kidding me? You did nothing but defend yourself."

Levi sidled up to Daisy. "What's got you bouncing around like a bee in a jar?"

"Nothing." Raven tried to stop it, not wanting the scene, but both men were far too smart for that.

"It was Gwen," Daisy finally said, throwing an apologetic look Raven's way. "She flipped out in the bathroom. She grabbed Raven's arm and yelled in her face."

Jonah's features darkened and a slice of emotion nearly cut her in half. That was defense, protection.

"Do I need to call an ambulance?" Levi tried to make light, but he wore a similarly dark look.

"It's fine. She made her point. I made mine."

"It is most assuredly not fine, Raven. This bitch has done enough damage as it is. What did she say?"

Daisy told it and Raven made a mental note to go over a little thing called discretion with her friend.

"This is going to make a scene." Raven linked her arm with Jonah's. "You promised sushi. I had to deal with your mother and your sister-in-law. I deserve ice cream as well."

Across the room Gwen burst from the women's room and Raven blew out a breath. From the look on her face, things were only going to get worse.

Jonah stalked over, his arm around Raven's waist. Levi did much of the same with Daisy.

She dug her heels in. "I said no."

He paused. "Why? Damn it, Raven, I can't allow this sort of behavior. It's bad enough that she's said what she has in the past to Daisy. But she grabbed you. She had no fucking right to touch you. It is not acceptable."

She leaned in close. "I appreciate that more than I can even say. But I'm begging you not to make a scene. Please."

He stopped, emotion filling his eyes. He turned to face her fully, kissing her right there in front of God and everyone. "I don't want you to feel like this is how it's going to be. Being with me, I mean. She can't get away with this."

"Can you please just deal with it any time and any place not here? People are looking. I don't like it."

Levi had turned a few feet away, watching. Daisy was talking to him, brushing a hand down the front of his lapel.

But on the other side of the room Gwen was giving Mal an earful.

"If we stay, I'm going to have to deal with it. She's over there with Mal right now."

He wanted to go punch his brother in the face for having such bad taste. He wanted to slap Gwen hard enough to leave a mark. But he saw the misery on Raven's face and it cut him deep. The pain in her whispered plea had wrapped around his heart.

"Come on, I have some sushi and ice cream to procure. Levi, why don't you and Daisy come along?"

"Because you know this needs dealing with."

"I do. But not here. We can go see him tomorrow."

Levi looked to Raven and then back to Daisy. "This shit has gone on long enough."

"It has. I agree."

"This is a benefit. It's not about your family." Jonah heard the anxiety in Raven's voice.

Levi huffed a sigh and turned Daisy toward the doors. "I need a drink with that sushi."

They'd made it to the drive of the hotel, waiting for their car when Mal came out, Gwen at his heels. Raven gathered herself up to her full height and Jonah held her close. "I'm going to handle this, all right?"

"Is that your way of telling me not to punch your sister-in-law?"

He grinned a moment and then turned back to Mal. "Be careful now. There's not a full ballroom here to protect you and your wife."

"Your fucking date attacked my wife."

Raven snorted. "Is that what she told you?" She looked at Gwen, who had the good grace to keep her gaze averted.

"Why should I believe the likes of you?"

Jonah stepped forward, bumping his brother with his chest. "You best watch what you say, Mal. Think real carefully about what comes out of that mouth of yours next. And think about what a lying bitch you're married to before you go tossing accusations around."

Daisy spoke, breaking the tension. "We were in the ladies' room when Gwen came in. Before Raven said a single thing she started in. She called me a whore. She insulted Raven, repeatedly. It was Raven who tried to end it by leaving. It was Gwen who grabbed Raven. It was Gwen. It's always Gwen, Mal. I wish that wasn't true, but you know it is."

"You're lying. You just want me out of the way." Gwen's voice carried a mean edge.

"For what? Out of whose way? You speak like you're important in any sense." Levi stood next to Jonah, both men keeping Raven and Daisy behind them.

"This is really stupid." Raven touched Jonah's arm. "Are you really going to get into a fistfight with your brother over some stupid shit his wife said and did?"

"If my brother doesn't apologize for the *likes of her* comment right now, he's going to find out the answer to that."

"My god, Gwen, are you really going to let your husband get punched for your lies? Do you care so little about this family you profess to respect so much? What if the papers get wind of this?"

Gwen sighed at Raven's words, touching Mal's arm. "It's not worth it."

He turned to her. "Did it happen like you said or not?"

"Why would I lie?"

"That's a good question. This is my family. My brothers and the women they're with. I need to know the truth."

"She was out of line in the bathroom."

Mal scrubbed hands over his face. "Jesus, Gwen. What do you think you're doing?" He turned back to Jonah. "I apologize for what I said. It was ugly."

"If your wife comes near Raven ever again, or speaks to her in that manner, there's going to be a reckoning. Do you understand, Malachi?"

"Same goes with Daisy. Gwen has done enough damage."

"I understand." Mal turned and walked away, Gwen hurrying in his wake.

12

They'd gone out to sushi and it actually hadn't been bad. Levi was growing on her and it was impossible not to like Daisy.

She knew Jonah had been holding back all he wanted to say for hours, so it wasn't a surprise that when the car pulled up in front of her building he paused, his hand on her arm. "Can I come in?"

"I don't know. It's late."

"I don't have to be up early. Do you?"

"I . . . I really don't want to talk about it anymore. I just want to go to sleep."

He tipped her chin to look into her face. "Baby, I want to talk. Alone. Lots of stuff happened tonight. Please?"

She blew out a breath and nodded. The driver opened the door and Jonah got out first to give her a hand.

She was so tired. Emotionally and physically. She just wanted to pull the covers up over her head and sleep for twelve hours.

He put an arm around her, taking her keys and opening her door when they got to her floor.

"I need to change."

"No, you don't. You're perfect just the way you are."

She found the energy to roll her eyes as she slid her shoes off and put them into the box before putting the box on a shelf.

"You're very organized."

She sighed heavily.

"About tonight . . ."

She unzipped the dress at the side and took it off, careful not to rip it before she got it on the hanger.

"Damn, it's hard to talk when you look so good."

She pulled on her pajamas and he followed her into the bathroom where she undid her hair and took her makeup off.

"I love to watch you do this stuff. Get made up, take your makeup off, put lotion on. I don't know what about it appeals so much, but it's like a secret woman code. It's so beautiful."

Raven had *rules*. She had rules and she kept people back. But he disarmed all her defenses. He made her break her own rules, and there she was after an evening where she just spilled her fucking truth all over the place.

Worse? It felt . . . all right. She'd probably be sick in the morning. Probably have bad dreams all night. But at the same time her burden was lighter. He hadn't walked away. God, he'd defended her, all bared teeth and furrowed brow. No one ever had. Not like that.

He stepped up and brushed her hair aside enough to drop a kiss on her shoulder, and tenderness filled her to the point where her eyes swam with unshed tears and she had to close her eyes against them, and against the way he looked standing there.

"I'm sorry. First my mother and then Gwen and my brother. Christ. I'm so embarrassed."

She shook her head, pulling herself back together. "Your mother was fine. As for Gwen, I had it handled."

"I want to say something and I don't want you to take this the wrong way."

She met his gaze in the mirror, trying to stave off disappointment and panic. But she didn't see the hey-it-was-nice-but-it's-over face.

Still, she braced herself as she moved back into the main room to settle on her bed.

"It's not okay with me for anyone to grab you the way Gwen did. The way she spoke to you was bad enough. But to physically get into your business? No. I'm not having it."

Oh, well, that was better than breaking up with her. She relaxed a little.

"I didn't either. I. Handled. It."

"You wouldn't have had to if not for me."

"Which is why I told you I wasn't benefit material."

"Fuck that!" He pulled his tux jacket off, having long ago gotten rid of the bow tie. She'd have been lying to herself to deny how much she enjoyed how worked up he was getting. As it happened, he was pretty hot when he got agitated. And it was in defense of her.

"Look, you're with me. This stuff, dinners and benefits and that jazz, comes with the territory. There is no way I'm going to tolerate any sort of disrespect toward you. Period. Gwen is out of her fucking mind. Jesus. First of all, she's lucky you showed restraint. You're a good four inches taller and I'd put money on you ten times out of ten."

She smiled at him. "You really do give good flattery. Anyway, she's probably the type to cry at the sight of a bug. She doesn't matter. She touched me and that was when we had the problem."

"I'm never sure how you're going to react to anything I say." He took his shirt off and she sent him a raised brow. "What? Don't you want me to be comfortable?"

"I told you I was feral when we first met. You're the one who keeps poking around."

She kept replaying the part about how she was with him and how he wasn't going to tolerate any disrespect of her. Over and over, like a shiny treasure.

But she wasn't some society babe. She nearly got into a fistfight in the ladies' room.

"I can see the look on your face. You stop with this feral crap. *You're* not the one who caused a scene in a bathroom at a charity benefit."

"Well, let's be real here, Jonah. It's not like I tried to heal her with the love from my heart when she came in and started getting crazy. I poked her. Plus, I said that stuff to your mother."

He took her face in his hands. "She needed it. And I did too. When you reveal stuff like that it breaks my heart. Even as I am so amazed by you and your strength."

"Don't build me up into something I am not. I shouldn't have popped off. She's your mother."

He snorted. "She was being rude and you slapped her with it. It's good. She respects that. I know that's sort of psycho. I can't make excuses for her. She's very protective and sometimes it turns her into a total bitch. But you held your own."

"Look, I'm no stranger to how women relate to each other. It was just a lot in one night."

"I'm worried about Mal. I have been for some time. This situation between Gwen and Daisy has been simmering for nearly two years. She had avoided Levi because she knew he'd skin her alive if she did another thing. I don't know what finally pushed her into action. But thank you for defending Daisy. You didn't have to."

"Of course I did. Also, she insulted me too. I hate to point out the really totally obvious but how has it escaped your notice that she's unnaturally obsessed with who Levi is fucking? And you now? Did you? Or did Levi, you know?"

The horrified disgust on his face answered before he said a word. "*No.* Good god. She's been with Mal for several years. I was with Charlotte when they first got together. Levi with Kelsey. Neither of us would have done that to our wives or to Mal for that matter."

"All I'm saying is that she's really interested in something that's really just not her biz. And so why? It is my belief, given the little I've seen, that she's got a hard-on for Levi. And because you and Levi are close, now that I'm around, she just sees it all as one bad thing."

"I'm thoroughly creeped out now."

She laughed, pushing him to his back. "You don't find her the least bit attractive?"

"Fuck no. She's not my type. Is she yours?"

"No. I never went for dainty women. Or helpless women. Or helpless men either. She's got a barely leashed sanity thing, not cute. But she's married to your brother."

"I saw his face tonight. He looked really sad. I don't know how this will shake out for him, or for them. Back to my mother for a second."

"God, why? It's like you keep throwing cold water on me."

"The whole auction thing. I'm sorry."

"It's fine. It's what people do when they get involved with a charity." She shrugged. "It's a good thing. I don't mind helping out."

"But you don't seem to have a lot of positive memories of your experience in foster care."

She sucked in a breath. "Look, I really don't do vulnerable well. I've said a lot today, more than I have in a really, really long time. I'm *raw*." Horrified, she heard the tears in her voice and tried to turn away, but he was there.

"Shh." He gathered her close, even when she tried to push him back. "Let me. If not for you, for me then."

She let herself believe the lie that it was for him instead of her. Let herself go still, burying her face in his neck, breathing him in, holding on tight.

"Will you let me sleep over? So I can hold you?"

She tried to get free and once he knew she really wanted it, he let her go and she got some distance.

"I'm not . . . comfortable with it."

"Why? You've shown me the most intimate parts of yourself. Do you think I'd care about morning breath?"

She rolled her eyes. "Don't."

"Do you think I'd hurt you?"

If he'd asked in a different tone, one absent a thread of hurt, that curiosity that was really about her and wanting to know her, she might have resisted. But she was too tired to hold the words back.

He saw it break over her. The moment she decided to tell him. And he braced himself.

"I don't sleep over. I don't couch surf. I don't let anyone sleep with me. I don't sleep with anyone in the room with me. Not ever. There are times I might sleep at someone's house, but I barricade the door from the inside. I have these mini alarms that go off if someone opens the door when I'm asleep."

He sat up, needing to be near her, but he could see in her body language that he needed to give her some space.

"When you're asleep you're vulnerable. People can do stuff. And you don't know until it's happening."

Sick, he clenched his hands into fists.

"So I had enough of that. When I left . . . when I came out to L.A., I made myself many promises. That was one. I don't think you'd hurt me." She started to cry and it seemed to startle her as much as it did him. "I don't. But I don't know if I can do it. I don't know. I'm not normal, Jonah. I'm jagged and fucked up and I don't know if this is going to work between us because you have a normal life and you have people who love you and you can sleep in the same room with someone and not have nightmares about being raped."

He was up, moving to her before he knew it. He pulled her into his arms and they both went to the floor. He rocked her, her tears on his skin, her entire body trembling as he stroked a hand over her hair and made wordless sounds to comfort what couldn't ever be comforted.

He held his own emotion back. Just barely. But he knew she needed to get it out. The way she sobbed he bet she hadn't given in to tears in years. This needed to be about her, and if he let go of the rage simmering in his belly, she'd hold back. And God knew she'd held back more than enough for far too long.

She finally quieted down and after a time he pulled back enough to look into her face. Her gaze was down and he kissed her forehead. "Hey."

"I'm so sorry." She tried to move but he held her in place.

"I don't accept your apology. You don't get to apologize for having emotions. Now. How about some tea?" He stood, bringing her to her feet along with him. He kept an arm around her waist as he moved to the kitchen area.

She said nothing as he deposited her on a stool at the kitchen island and rustled through her cabinets. "Christ, who knew you'd be the type to have ninety types of tea?"

She sighed and he looked back over his shoulder. "You're going to have to help me. Which?" He waved a hand at the array of tea she had in her cabinet.

"The one with the sleepy bear on it."

"Ah. Makes sense I guess."

He put water in her teakettle and teabags in the mugs.

"I don't know what to say. Other than I'm honored you shared so much with me. And that you're amazing."

"I'm not amazing. I'm someone who had some bad shit happen to her. It's not unique. It doesn't make me special or amazing. I told you this before."

"And you were full of shit then too."

She sighed again, so much emotion in such a simple thing. He knew he had to back off, to let all the stuff she'd said—and the fact that she'd said it—percolate. She needed it, that space. But he wanted so badly to gather her up and take care of her.

"So I have a proposal."

"Does it involve your cock and any part of my anatomy?"

He grinned at her. "You know me so well. But actually, not this time. Maybe later though. I have several guest rooms. How about you come back to my house. You can use my bathroom to your heart's content. You can sleep over in one of the spare rooms."

Wariness warred with exhaustion in her features.

"There are locks. On the doors, I mean. My house has a great security system too. No one can get in without my knowing it. I'll leave you be. Until the morning anyway. We haven't had morning sex yet and so, well, when you wake up you can come to me."

She wanted to say yes. Really badly. Not least of which because she really loved his bathroom and that claw-foot tub looked like heaven on earth.

"I promise to leave you alone." The kettle whistled and he turned to take care of it and pour the water to steep. "I'll be there if you want me. But I'll let you make the choices. Don't be alone tonight. I'm going to worry about you if you're not with me. And I know that's selfish."

"And manipulative."

He handed the mug her way. "That too. I want you there. For both of us. But you're so fucking stubborn you'll say no, thinking you don't need it. But you do. And it's been a hard day and I want you to have it. I want you to sleep tonight knowing I'm just down the hall if you want me. I want you to be in my house when I wake up. I want you to sit at my table and drink coffee with me in the morning. Let me take care of you. Let yourself be taken care of."

"Why does it matter to you?" She needed to know, though she wasn't sure how she'd feel when he answered.

"It matters because you matter. I can't remove your past. I can't kill anyone to avenge you. I can't make it better that way. But the thought of you here alone after all the stuff you've revealed tonight? After the shit with Gwen and my mother, after what you've told me about sleeping alone? It tears me up. Because I care about you and I want you to know you mean something to me. I want you to understand I'd do anything for you, including going back to my house alone if that's what you need. But I don't think it is. I think you've been alone for so long you think it's normal. But it's not. Let someone care about you. Let me fucking help in some way."

She took the bag out of her mug and sipped. Chamomile would soothe her nerves and her stomach too.

"All right," she said at last.

He sighed, his shoulders relaxing. "Good. Drink your tea and we can get a bag together for you."

13

He tried to ignore the sound of her in his bathroom. She moved slow, like she'd been in a car accident or something. And he supposed in a sense she had.

He'd brought her to his place. She even let him drive her car. He'd put her bag in the guest room just a few doors down from his. She'd run her fingers over the lock on the back of the door as she'd left the room and his heart broke anew.

He'd urged her to his bathroom, telling her he'd return with a glass of wine in a few minutes, and she'd nodded without saying anything.

For then though, he stood in his hallway, leaning against the wall where pictures of his daughter, of his friends and family hung and felt, in no small amount, like that car had hit him too.

She was damaged and jagged. It was true. No one who lived a life like the one she had could have escaped it without a healthy bit of baggage.

That she was so bold and blunt and brutally honest, even with herself, didn't make her weak. It made her strong. He wished he knew how to make her see it. But he desperately didn't want to fuck it up. Didn't want to make her regret sharing.

She seemed confused—befuddled even—that he hadn't rejected her. That he wanted to take care of her and hadn't walked away. The helpless rage of it battered his heart.

Because he loved her.

God help him, he loved her so fucking much it hurt to breathe as he thought about her just on the other side of the door. Holding it together because that's all she had.

He sucked in a breath and stood taller. He'd be what she never had. He'd love her with the same surety he did everything else. There was nothing but that to be done. He knew he had to be careful not to feel sorry for her, though goddamn, he did in so many ways. But she didn't want or need pity. His pity would only drive her away, or worse, make her think the reason he wanted her was to fix her.

He tapped on the door. "Ready for wine?" He didn't go in, though he wanted to. There would be time, later, to dominate her and help her let go of the control she clung to so hard right then. But she needed it for the next little while.

"Sure."

Her voice was small, but a little better than it had been earlier. He'd take that as a win.

She was in his bathtub, her hair wet, slicked back from her face, leaving her young and vulnerable. "You're beautiful even without makeup." He shook his head as he brought the wine to her. "Enjoy it. I'll be back in a while to see if you want another glass. Just call out if you need me. For anything. I'll be in my room."

She let out a shaky sigh as she sipped. "Do you have music?"

"I do. What would you like to hear?"

"Surprise me."

He bent to kiss the top of her head. "All right."

"And then . . . you can come back. If you want."

He tried to remain nonchalant but inside he was celebrating the bit of ground she'd just given up to him.

"Give me a few. I'll be back." Always.

She sipped a rather fine glass of red and sighed when Beth Orton began to fill the air.

He wasn't irresistible enough? He had to like Beth Orton too? How much was a girl supposed to take anyway?

He gave her space. She needed it and he'd known that. For a man like him—so infuriatingly pushy and bossy—to have backed off and let her process had been important.

He came in a few minutes later with a bottle and another glass.

"This okay?"

"I love Beth Orton. Also, this is a very good wine. I should probably get out. The water will be getting cold." But she made no move to do so.

"I have a pretty big water heater tank. Want me to freshen the water with hot?"

She cracked open an eye. He stood here, his hair tousled, wearing a T-shirt and low-slung sleep pants. He was a thousand kinds of hot. Protective. Dominant.

"You scare me sometimes," he muttered, though he smiled and ruined the effect. Or rather, made it a million times hotter.

"What have I done to be scary? I mean right now."

"You look at me and I know you're thinking stuff. Sometimes it's stuff that makes me really lucky. Other times I worry for my safety."

"Keeps you on your toes." She stood and felt better at the way he took her in. It wasn't the gaze of a man who felt pity, or that she was damaged goods. His eyes were hungry, lit with appreciation and desire.

He put the wine down and wrapped her in the towel when she stepped out.

"Let me."

She struggled, taking the towel and stepping back. She'd only just managed to get her control into place. The lure of letting him take over was a lot to get past. But she needed to or she'd fall apart.

"I need to do it myself."

"Fair enough." He leaned against the counter, sipping his wine as she dried off. He handed her the lotion and she slathered it on, filling the room with the scent of coconut.

The rhythm of it soothed her, the scent, the warmth of the room and the slight buzz from the wine. And him. She should not get used to him, get used to drawing comfort from him, but it was past that.

"I forgot a brush." She squeezed the water from her hair with the towel.

He opened a drawer and moved things around before holding one up. "Will this do?"

She nodded.

"Can I?"

She nodded, turning to face the mirror. He moved up behind her and began to slowly brush her hair. She closed her eyes and held on to the counter in front of her to keep from melting into a puddle.

"How about you get dressed and then we can go into the guest room and you can settle on the bed while I finish brushing? It's been a long day and you'll be more comfortable. Plus, you're all glisteny and you smell good and you're naked. A guy can only take so much." He smiled at her reflection and she leaned back against him before nodding.

She pulled panties and her pajamas on and then socks. He smiled at her the whole time. "What?"

"What's not to smile at? There's a sleepy, gorgeous woman in my house. Also, it's sort of cute how you wear socks."

"There is nothing cute about me. Anyway, my feet get cold. It's fall." She frowned, but it didn't last long as he settled on the bed and she joined him. He was so gentle with her she sort of melted into him, totally relaxed.

After what felt like a very long time, he leaned down and kissed her. "Go to sleep. I'll take you to breakfast tomorrow if you like. Wake me when you're ready."

He went out, locking the door before he closed it, and she realized she was in way too deep with Jonah.

She pulled the blankets up and snuggled down. The room smelled like him, which calmed her jangled nerves.

She figured dreams would keep her awake, or nervousness would mess with her sleep, but it didn't happen. She was asleep before she'd been able to obsess over it too much.

14

He woke up early, as he usually did, even on weekends. Decades of being up for 8 a.m. meetings had pretty much ruined his ability to really sleep late.

But she was there too. That's what woke him. She stood in his doorway, hugging the doorjamb, looking hesitant.

He pulled his blankets back and she came to him. "Best wake-up I've had in ages," he said as he snuggled her up against his body.

"Yeah?" She climbed atop, grinding her cunt against him.

"Well, I do like to say there's *always* room for improvement. You've got a good start." She was glorious in the morning. Her hair tousled and soft around her face. No makeup. She was warm and soft and goddamn, he wanted more.

The shadows from the night before were gone. He knew those memories took up a permanent place inside her, but he was glad she looked better.

"How'd you sleep?"

"Bed is very comfortable. It's quiet. You have a great house. Thank you for . . . you know, everything."

He cupped her neck. "Anytime."

"Yeah?"

He tried to focus on the words, but hello, nearly naked woman grinding herself against his cock. "Careful there, missy, you're playing with fire."

She pulled her shirt up and over her head. "I am? Gosh, I sure wouldn't want that."

He rolled and she landed on his bed on her back. One quick movement and her pants and underwear were gone and she was gloriously naked on his sheets. Where she should be.

"Now then. Are you being deliberately provocative?" He tugged a nipple between his teeth and she moaned.

"What gave me away?"

He laughed, really liking this side of her.

"Don't move." He got out of bed and she watched him, a smile on her lips.

He went to his drawer, the one he'd begun to think of as Raven's drawer. He kept his toys in it. Things he'd bought with her in mind. The chain he'd bought for her was there and he thought of a good use for it. Just not right then.

He saw what he was looking for and pulled it out, turning.

Her gaze went to the collar in his hand, one of those imperious brows of hers rising.

"Kneeling please."

She did it immediately and he liked that more than he could put into words. Her hands went behind her back.

After he'd gotten her in bed the night before he'd stayed up very late thinking about the entire situation. Whether or not it was a good idea to continue with the D/s nature of their relationship. The last thing he wanted to do was harm her. Or push any of her buttons related to what he knew was a pretty fucked-up childhood.

But then he'd realized that if he had pushed buttons that way she would have told him. Probably not directly, but Raven Smith did not do things she didn't want to do. And she got off on their relationship just as much as he did. It wasn't therapy. It wasn't a balm to her wounds. She liked it when he dominated her and he liked to do it. All the other stuff wasn't a part of it. And if it ever became part of it, she'd call a halt to it.

"You see, I was thinking about you. As I often do. And I realized how much it would please me if you wore a collar. My collar. But you're not a leather-collar type of woman. I wanted something that would be unique. Like you are. He held up the platinum choker.

"You want to collar me? Like a slave?"

He laughed. "No. I don't want a slave, and if I did, you and I wouldn't be together. I want you to be reminded of me; of the way you're mine. All day. Every day. I don't need the whole world to know it. Just you and me."

Her eyes glittered. Not with anger. Not with fear.

"I'm not one to make a commitment."

"Because none of the people before were right for you. I am. You know it or you'd have stormed out of here two minutes ago when I first held up the choker. You like it. When you get these fool ideas about how flighty you are, or how you don't do monogamy, you can think about what you're wearing around your neck and know you're lying to yourself. You're mine, Raven. Try to deny that. I dare you."

She sucked in a breath, her mouth opening to speak. He waited.

"No one owns me," she said at long last.

"No one but you. I said, I don't want to own you. When I say you're mine, you know exactly what I mean. And you're scared. Scared I'll fuck you over, or run away or whatever. I'm telling you right now that you're here with me. Like I want. Like I've wanted since the first conversation we ever had. I get what I want and I want you. Not to own. Not to harm. But to cherish."

He held the choker closer to her and she examined it. But her hands were still clasped at her back.

"And if I wear it, what does that mean?"

"I told you what it means to me. What would it mean to you? Hm? That's not something I want or even am prepared to tell you. You own your own feelings, your own reactions. When I put it on and you're wearing a declaration of your connection and commitment to me, what would it mean to you?"

She took a slightly shaky breath.

"I don't know."

He smiled at her. She was scared and he didn't blame her. "Yes, you do."

He stroked a hand down her neck with the backs of his fingers. "Cosseted? Hm? Protected? Safe in the knowledge there's someone out there who adores you, flaws and all? Confined, but in the best way? All these others who tolerated your refusal to commit, they were one thing. I'm another. We're another and you know it. Will you wear it?"

She swallowed hard and then nodded.

He slid it on and it felt totally right as he secured the two clasps to hold it. It glittered against her skin, fitting perfectly. It was a lovely piece of jewelry. Something she could wear and no one would think twice over. But she'd know. And he would too.

"Beautiful."

Her gaze dropped and he tipped her chin up. "Mmmm. Can't deny it, gorgeous. Beautiful. And mine. Like I'm yours, and that's good too. Makes me hard."

"Would you like me to do something about that?"

She knew that he found her attractive, yes, but there was this way she had, she got right to him. It wasn't coy, it wasn't practiced, and though she certainly wasn't innocent, the way she got to him was.

He shoved his pants down and off, kicking them to the side. "Now you can. Suck my cock."

She gave him one last look. "Can I move my hands? This angle will make it hard to keep from falling off the bed."

"Yes."

She bent forward, kissing his belly and over to his hip bone before doing the same on the other side. He watched her back, the shock of how alluring she was ricocheting through him.

With one hand braced on the bed, she grabbed his cock at the root with the other and held him out so she could take him into her mouth. First she sucked slow, keeping him really wet. She licked around the crown, sucking hard and then soft, enough to bring a grunt and a flex of his hips, demanding more.

She slid her fist down, holding the skin taut as she followed, taking him deep. She stretched her fingers out to stroke his balls. Up and down. Over and over. It was so good he let it go longer than he should have. He was right up against climax when he put a restraining hand on her shoulder and stepped back.

He struggled for breath as he looked down at her.

She licked her lips and he grinned. "Goddamn. I'm going to fuck you."

The choker was cool against the skin of her neck. It was wide enough that she knew it was there. It wasn't a piece of jewelry she'd forget about, which she guessed was the point after all. It made her feel . . . it anchored her, the solid weight of it, the way it seemed to caress her throat the way he held her throat in his palm at times.

It made her pussy slick, hardened her nipples and her clit. She wanted him to fuck her so badly it had taken all her control not to beg him, to keep sucking his cock the way she knew he liked. Knowing he'd take care of her.

It was a big step and one that had scared her spitless. Trusting anyone else to put her needs first and foremost wasn't something she did often. The number of people she trusted like that, she could count on one hand.

But this man, this reason she broke her rules, well, there seemed to be nothing else she could do. She was still scared enough to shake a little. But she was so sick of being scared and alone.

"I want you facedown on the bed. One leg bent, knee up. I want you open."

She did it quickly. Placing her hands high, like she knew he'd tell her to.

He hummed his satisfaction and she knew she'd made the right choice.

One cuff slid over her hand and to her wrist where he tightened it. He hooked it to the strap on his bed. A few ticks later and she was stretched. Not painfully so, but certainly very aware she was giving over to him.

The other wrist, same movements, and she had to close her eyes against it. Nothing in her life had ever felt like this. She wasn't even sure what *this* was. Only that it kept her from floating. His hands on her, his attention and focus made her feel beautiful and desired. Not as a thing. Not as some white-trash whore as she'd been regarded for many years. But as this man's woman.

A shiver ran through her as he ran covetous hands from her fingertips, down her arms and back. He stopped at her hips and held on, his fingers digging in.

"You're so fucking beautiful. It drives me out of my mind to see you this way in my bed."

She heard the condom wrapper tear and knew he'd be in her soon. Even so, she couldn't help but arch as much as she could to take him deeper when he finally nudged her open with the head of his cock.

He swore under his breath and she loved it. His fingers tightened on her hips and she loved it. She did it again, taking him deep, and he let go, slapping one ass cheek so hard she could picture the red mark he would have left. It burned against the coolness of the room, burned against his skin when he adjusted, fucking her in earnest now.

His weight pressed her into the bed, limited her range of movement. And she loved that too.

"More," she managed to gasp out.

He let go of her hip and she waited for the slap on her ass. But he slid a hand between her body and the bed and found her clit. He managed to squeeze her clit with the tips of his fingers as he continued to fuck her deep.

"You can't come until I say so."

She wanted to argue. It was ridiculous after all to order such a thing. She'd come when she wanted to, damn it. It wasn't as if she was a yogi with that sort of mind/body control.

But she knew it would be a lie. Knew she'd do her damndest to make it happen however he wanted it to.

He kept thrusting and she sort of floated awhile, the pleasure flooding her system, lulling her even as it excited. She wanted to come. Wanted him to come. Wanted to please him.

She squeezed her inner muscles over and over and he hummed. "Well now, that's quite lovely." And then he growled as she kept it up. His fingers on her clit sped up a little, squeezed just a little harder. "I'm ready. Come around my cock."

Like he hit a switch, orgasm burst through her with alarming speed. Brilliant. Sharp shards of pleasure seemed to slice through her as she heard him say her name, knew he was coming too.

It went on and on for some time until he pressed a kiss to her shoulder and pulled out gently. The bed moved as he got up, but she was content to keep lying there, her arms up above her head, wrists bound. On display.

All the noise quieted when he touched her. What all it meant she didn't really know, only that it made things better.

"What's your plan for the rest of the day?" He asked her this as they sat at a diner, their breakfasts piping hot on the table in front of them.

"I promised Erin I'd go out to Bainbridge to a Halloween party thing. They're doing a costume parade and Miles—Gillian and Adrian's son—his band is playing. I tried very hard to get out of it, but she guilted me."

He smiled at her. "Why try to get out of it?"

"It's exhausting trying to behave all the time." She poured syrup on her stack of pancakes.

He laughed then. "Oh, gorgeous, you're something else."

"Hm."

"Behave how?"

"They're all so nice. Perky. Everyone loves everyone else and they're close and blah. I go because Alexander will look adorable in his little costume and I'm sure Martine and Poppy will too. Rennie tells me she's too old for that stuff, but she's old enough to get a little giggly around Miles's friends who, thankfully, are old enough to think she's an annoying-little-sister type instead of make-out material."

"I notice you're talking about the kids and not the adults."

"I like children better." She chewed for a while, sipping her coffee, before she spoke again. "Though *some* adults do all right."

"I never really pegged you for an earth-mother type."

She laughed. "Stop, you're going to make me choke. I'm not. Not in a million years. But I'm a decent aunt. And Alexander, Martine and Poppy are too young to judge me for anything but the quality of snacks in my cabinets and how many of those tiny board books I'm willing to read."

"Just when I think I'm getting you figured out, you go and prove me wrong. Do you ever, you know, think about having a child of your own someday?"

"I'm getting older. I come from some fucked-up stock. My family was enough. What kind of person would I be to do that to a kid?"

"I had a child and my mother . . . well, you've met her."

"Your mother loves you. She's a hard-case bitch with her nose a little too high in the air, don't get me wrong. But I can guarantee she never left you alone for ten minutes, much less dropped you off at the corner convenience store and didn't come back for nearly two years."

He blinked at her.

"I'm sorry. I . . . It's like telling you stuff has loosened my tongue."

He took her hand, his fingers tangling with hers. "Don't apologize. I'm glad you're sharing with me. I can't get past that initial moment of rage when I hear how you were treated when you were at your most vulnerable."

"So I come from a bunch of assholes. There are already a lot of assholes who had kids and fucked them up. I'm not sure I can overcome my DNA to not do the same. I mean, can you imagine me at a PTA meeting?"

He grinned. "I totally can." He shrugged. "I've seen you when you talk about Alexander. I know you love him, and from what I understand, he loves you right back. Seems to me what your situation was had a lot more to do with how they acted, not their biology. Hell, Charlotte, my ex-wife, her parents were really involved when she and her siblings grew up. And she's a terrible mother. It's not always biology, Raven. Some people are just, as you so eloquently put it, assholes."

"Anyway, I don't know. I have a studio apartment and I like to travel. Having a baby isn't in the cards for me."

But he could see her holding a baby. Their baby. He didn't say that out loud, not wanting to scare her away and also needing to process, yet again, how fast this was all moving. He wasn't impulsive. He was the type of man who took forever just to decide what to order off a menu. But the way he felt for Raven was apparently outside all the rules in his life. The way he felt for her simply was. He *knew* it as sure as he knew gravity existed and that he had to pay his taxes.

"Do you . . ." She shook her head and went back to eating.

"What?"

"Never mind."

"No way, you don't get to do that. Do I what?"

"Do you want to go with me? To this Halloween thing tonight?"

It was the first time she'd done the asking, and he liked it.

"Yeah. I'd like that. I want to get to know your friends better. I'm sure Daisy and Levi will be there. I know Daisy and Gillian are close. She's got pictures of Poppy and Miles all over her and Levi's house."

"Okay then. I need to go home for a while. I really need to exercise. I've done nothing but eat too much and drink a lot of beer since you came along. My clothes are going to get tight."

"Want to go kayaking with me and my brother Eli?"

Warily she considered that. "I don't know."

"He'll like you. I told him about you earlier this week. He's sort of feral himself."

"Don't you want to do the brother thing? If you spend a lot of time with me, you're going to figure out I'm sort of a bitch."

He laughed, having to put down his cup of coffee before he started to choke.

"Gorgeous, I figured that out weeks ago. I'm still here."

She pulled her phone out to check her calendar and noted she had several bookings starting in just a few hours and lasting until about an hour before the party. She frowned. She'd told Maggie, the woman who ran the shop, that it was all right to give her appointments, so it wasn't like anyone had done anything wrong. The business was good. She liked having money in savings. But, she had to admit she liked the idea of spending time with Jonah and meeting his brother.

She looked up from the phone and shrugged. "Apparently I'm going to be inking people for many hours today. I'm sorry. I love to kayak though, so if you want to in the future and feel up to having me along, I'd go."

"That's a deal."

15

"Nope. Wait." He gave an imperious look her way before he got out and walked around to her side to open her door and give her a hand out.

Then he kept her hand and she didn't quite know what to do, so she let him.

The place was awash in kids and it made her smile.

Erin was out on the large lawn with them and she looked up, waving. Alexander looked to see what his mother was doing and caught sight of Raven, his little face lighting up.

She let go of Jonah's hand and bent to grab Alexander up into a hug when he came running her way.

"You're here, Auntie!"

"Of course I am." She kissed his cheeks, hugging him again.

"I missed you. We have candy."

"Dude, candy? I'm really glad I came now. Would you like to meet a new friend?"

"Sure!"

She turned to face Jonah. "Alexander, this is my friend Jonah. He's Levi's big brother."

"Yo, Jonah!"

Jonah grinned; all that imperious masterful Dom stuff had melted away in the face of this little boy. "Yo, Alexander. Raven told me all about you. I have to admit I ate some of your Goldfish. I promise to replace them before you come over again, though."

Alexander, in a very fine Brown imitation, narrowed his eyes for a moment before he stuck his hand out. "Okay."

Erin approached, holding Poppy, who clapped when she saw Raven. "Hello, there, Jonah."

Poppy leaned out, toward Raven.

"Hang on a minute, baby girl. Alexander is with Raven, then it's your turn, all right?"

Poppy frowned but seemed satisfied for the time being.

"Dang, you're like the Pied Piper." Jonah winked and Alexander laughed.

"I'm glad you brought Jonah. Levi is around here somewhere. Mary and Damien got here a few minutes ago so Gillian is out back with them."

Alexander was done being held so Raven put him down and he tore off. "Pop!" Ben and Todd came around the corner. "Daddy!"

"Yeah, poor kid, no one loves him." Erin turned back to Raven before she pulled her into a hug, Poppy still in her arms. "Hello you. I called you twice yesterday."

"I was really busy. Loooong day, and not now, I'll tell you later. Now give me that baby before she jumps from your arms."

Poppy squealed, tipping her head back, utterly confident that Raven wouldn't drop her. That meant everything to Raven.

Erin took up next to Raven. "Let's go around to the back. Martine has her tricycle and is riding all over the place so watch your toes."

Jonah put an arm around her shoulders as they walked and Erin shot her a look, waggling her brows at the choker Poppy was eagerly trying to grab.

"Not for you. That's my pretty. Don't break it." Poppy frowned. "I know, it's super hard to be you."

Then she grinned, clapping her chubby little hands.

"The jig is up, sweet girl. Auntie Raven knows your game." She kissed Poppy's nose. "It'll be our secret."

Out back, the vista overlooked the water in a sweeping and rather breathtaking view. Adrian had designed the house for Gillian as a wedding present. It made it more difficult to think he was an uptight asshole when he was so good to his wife and children.

Gillian turned, a huge smile on her face when she caught sight of Raven.

"I have no idea why she likes me so much," she said in an undertone to Jonah, who snorted.

"Because people can see past your crusty exterior and know there's a big heart in there."

Emotion swept through her like wildfire as she tried to hold it together.

Erin squeezed her arm, leaning close to speak quietly. "You and I totally need to catch up. Don't even try to get away without it. I'm glad you're here and I'm glad you brought him. Also? Nice necklace."

Poppy loved Raven, but she adored her mother and at the sight of her, she reached out to Gillian, who caught her up with a smile. "Hello, darling. Have you brought Raven to us? Nicely done." She gave Raven a quick hug and looked to Jonah. "Hello you. Your brother is just over there. There's cider of the mulled and child-friendly variety."

Jonah kissed her so quickly she didn't have the time to be stern. Instead she smooched him back, blushing.

"Would you like a glass?" He was so gentlemanly. She never knew how to deal with it, but it made her belly all fluttery.

She nodded.

"Be back in a few then. Good to see you, Gillian."

The three women watched him amble over to the group of men Levi was part of.

"Well now." Gillian clucked her tongue, amusement on her face.

Raven rolled her eyes.

"So things are serious now. I knew you'd been seeing him, but you brought a date to a family party. That's special. I quite like that. Come over this week. Adrian is off to Los Angeles and he's taking Miles. It's just me and Poppy and we'd love to have you for dinner and some gossip. Mary brought enough food to feed me for months."

"Let me see what my week looks like. Brody is down a few people at the shop. I'm helping out there and then I have an evening appointment on Thursday. I'll call you. I promise."

Levi looked him up and down as Jonah eased into a chair near the cider.

"Wasn't expecting to see you."

"My lady brought me along. I figured you'd be here with yours."

"Indeed. Couldn't stop her if I wanted to. She's helping Miles with something or other. I just bring her and she squeals and giggles and runs off. Like I'm going to complain?"

Jonah snorted. Raven wasn't giggle-and-squeal material. But he sure did like that she'd invited him along.

"I've got three messages from Mother. I went kayaking with Eli earlier and she'd called there looking for me too." He'd wanted Raven along but she'd had to work.

"She called me a few times too. I'm going to guess she got wind of what happened with Raven, Daisy, Mal and Gwen last night."

Brody, who'd been sitting across from them with Adrian, leaned in. "What happened?"

If Jonah meant to make a relationship with Raven, he knew he had to deal with Brody as well.

He gave them a brief overview.

Brody sat back, shaking his head. "She's lucky Raven didn't pop her one. You know she does kickboxing, right? Four days a week. She's really strong."

He didn't actually. He knew she worked out, but not more than that.

"She tried very hard not to make a scene. But she defended Daisy. Daisy would take a bullet for her for that." Levi shrugged. "So of course I would too."

Adrian didn't say much as Jonah had spoken. "So what are you going to do? Seems to me Raven probably told you she wasn't the society type. Gillian loves her; I don't want to see her hurt."

Jonah took Adrian in. "It's been handled. My mother and Raven had a"—he paused, trying to remember how Raven put it—"a come-to-Jesus. My mother was rude. Raven put her in her place. I think this situation is going to be more about my brother and his wife and their marriage than Raven."

"There were cracks before, but I think this might really be a point of no return for them. I don't know." Levi nodded. "Anyway, we're on Raven's side here. I promise you. Even if I wasn't on my own, Daisy would never let me touch her boobs again if I didn't back her up."

Both Brown brothers nodded, easing back.

He wouldn't tell her about this conversation. She'd be uncomfortable and that's not what she needed. He grabbed two mugs and stood. "If you'll excuse me, I promised Raven some cider."

Levi stood as well. "I'll come along with you."

She smiled as she saw him approach and give her the cider. "That hits the spot, thanks. I'm just about to go in and help Alexander get his costume on. I'll be out in a few."

"What's he going to be?"

"That's a surprise, Jonah. Sheesh." She turned to Levi. "Hey, Levi."

Levi tipped his chin at her. "Hey, Raven, nice to see you."

She went into the house after a quick kiss from Jonah and his brother gave him the eye. "So you're not limping. Is that necklace the collar you mentioned?"

Jonah nodded. "Yesterday . . . last night . . . all of it. A lot of emotions. We talked for hours. It felt right this morning and it was."

"Okay then. She's okay then? I could tell how tense she was, though she was pretty good at dinner. I guess I just misjudged her, thinking she was sort of bitchy. But she protected Daisy and I owe her. You love her too, so I can admit I was wrong."

"Oh, she can be bitchy. But people take one look and make up their minds. She's a lot more than you see at first glance. She had a hard time, but she's resilient. I'm ass over teakettle with that prickly woman." He shrugged. He usually shared most everything with his brother, but he knew how difficult it had been for her to trust him and he didn't ever want her to regret it.

"I get it. If you need to talk about it more, you know I won't tell tales out of school."

"Appreciate that."

"Do you want me to do a background check on her? I mean, you're getting serious about this woman and you don't know much about her. It might be better to be safe than sorry. You've got a trust fund and a big bank account. Attractive to some women. We know she hasn't been very constant in the past."

Of course it was then that Erin Brown came at them from the left. She must have been walking around the porch. Her eyes were on fire and he flinched at the rage in them.

She pushed him away from the steps and Levi hurried to catch up.

"I can't believe you!" She kept her voice down but the rage radiated off her in waves.

Jonah put his hands up. "I was going to say no."

"You are the first person she's let into her life this way other than me and Brody. She's not some whore you fuck and throw away because you're worried she's going to steal from you. She never, ever took money from me, and I can *guarantee* I've got more than you. You asshole."

He took her hands. "Erin, I don't think that about her. I swear to you. I love Raven. She's independent and strong and the last thing I'd believe about her is that she was using me."

Levi put himself in the line of fire. "Christ, it was all me. I'm so sorry, Erin. I didn't mean it as an insult. I want to protect my brother. But it was my suggestion, not his. I'm protective of him and my family."

Erin rounded on Levi and Jonah felt sorry for him. "Protective? You mean how she was of *your* family last night? You think I haven't heard how your sister-in-law acted? How your mother acted? You think you're so much better than her? She's not constant? Fuck you. She's in there helping my little boy change into his Halloween costume. One she *made* for him. He wanted to be the Doctor from *Doctor Who*. But the one with the scarf, Tom what's-his-name. *She* knows his name and he does too because she watches the show with him. No matter where she's been or what she's doing she will always be back here for his birthday. Don't you fucking talk to me about constant. That woman is my best friend and no one is more constant than she is."

Levi lost the tension in his spine and he shook his head. "I'm sorry. I was wrong. But it's *me*, not Jonah. Don't hang him with something I did. He had nothing to do with it."

"Erin?" Raven called out from the back porch and Erin tossed such a look of malice over her shoulder that Levi flinched.

"On my way." She turned and walked away without another word.

"Holy shit. Do you think she's going to tell Raven? Oh my god, I'm so sorry, Jonah. Jesus. I would never want to hurt her. I swear to you. After Charlotte . . . I'm sorry."

Jonah felt sick, but he understood where Levi was coming from and he also knew his brother got how wrong he'd been.

"All I can do is hope she won't say anything. If for no other reason than to spare Raven's feelings.

"Everything okay?" Raven asked Erin when she came back from the yard.

"Yes. Fine. What's up?" Erin's smile was brittle at the edges.

"I've known you an assload of years, Erin. What's wrong?"

Erin sighed. "Nothing. I was just thinking about stupid stuff that got me wound up. I'm fine."

Raven looked her over carefully but let it go. "If you say so. I'm looking for the hat. Have you seen it?"

"Oh crap. I left it in the car. I'll be right back." She raced out the front and Raven went back to the room where the littlest ones were getting ready.

"Your momma is going to get the hat and then you're ready to rock." Alexander did a little fist pump.

Martine was dressed as a pirate ballerina. She'd wanted both so Elise had just gone with it. She wore an eye patch and a tutu and it worked.

Ben's brother Cope and his wife Ella's daughter Maddie was a princess, complete with one of those pointed hats with the tulle on it. As Cope treated his daughter like the sun rose and set with her, it fit. Ella, who'd always been sort of sweet and shy, had come out of her shell as a mother. Raven had watched confidence take hold as she poured her love and attention into the job. It was a good thing to see.

Poppy was a ladybug. She had a headband with little antennae and a red and black bodysuit.

Rennie had two friends along; one of them, Nina, was Arvin and Maggie's daughter. Both parents worked at the shop with Raven and Brody.

The girls had said they were too old to dress up, but since they were there and all, they'd do it for the little kids. Raven had kept a straight face and nodded, thanking them for being so cool about it.

Miles, of course, was sixteen and totally not interested in anything but his band.

Erin came in with the hat and Raven plopped it on Alexander's head, standing back. She'd spent months putting the costume together after Alexander had said he wanted to be the "scarf Doctor" for Halloween. Finding the right vest, hat and scarf for a nearly four-year-old took time. But she'd done it, though she had to cut the scarf and the blazer down some.

"He's just like Tom Baker. I grew up watching him. To this day I consider him my Doctor, though truth be told, Eleven does do that nerdy bada . . . bad guy thing really well." Gillian smiled.

Alexander examined himself in the mirror quite seriously and then smiled up at Raven, giving her a thumbs-up.

"I think that means you're a success, Auntie."

"All in an auntie's day's work."

Elise patted Erin's arm. "Let me go check on Rennie and the girls and then I'll have Adrian start the music for the parade."

It was pretty much impossible for Adrian to take his child trick-or-treating. A person who was as well known a celebrity as him couldn't really go door to door in a regular neighborhood without causing a ruckus. Gillian didn't want to ruin anyone else's Halloween with surprise visits from the paparazzi either, so they'd decided a fun Halloween fest at their house would be just fine, especially as young as most of the kids were.

Raven bent to adjust Alexander's neck scarf. "Excited?"

"Yes! I'm gonna march." He marched in place and Martine, seeing him, began her own version of a march, which was actually more like the maniac dance from *Flashdance*. Maddie, a relatively new walker, just sort of bent her knees over and over.

"Jeez, I'm going to die of cute." Erin put her head on Raven's shoulder.

"You have a good life. All these kids are going to grow up so loved."

"Yeah. I'm grateful for them. And that you're part of it. I'm so glad you're here more now. That they get to grow up with you as their aunt-ie. His costume is awesome. I'm creative and all, but you two have that *Doctor Who* connection. He's going to remember this."

"Well, I know I will."

She stepped back and started taking pictures again. The shutter speed was set for action shots and she knew there'd be plenty to give to Gillian, Ella, Elise and Erin.

Elise came back in. "They're ready."

The kids filed out and Raven kept taking pictures. The music came up as they went down the stairs, Elise holding Martine's hand and Poppy riding on Gillian's hip.

It was a really good night. The best Halloween Raven had had . . . well, ever.

16

"How are you recovering after the candy coma?" Raven teased Brody as they sat at their stations in the shop.

"Fortunately we left most of it at Adrian's place. Now that Miles has his braces off I'm sure he'll go to town on it. In any case, at least it's not at my house hopping my kids up. Well, more than usual."

"Rennie is a knockout. Just sayin', Dad. She looks a hell of a lot like her mother, all blonde and big blue eyes. And she showed me some of her art on Sunday. Wow."

Brody's clear discomfort at the realization his daughter was growing up was alleviated a little by the mention of her talent.

"Elise and I have decided to send her to the same school Miles is at. Heavy arts concentration."

"I think that's a great idea. Miles seems to have thrived there."

"It's a great school. We took a tour a few months back. Elise may actually do some classes there. One of the dance teachers recognized her when we were there."

Raven smiled. "That's pretty awesome."

"She had to give up a lot. Makes me happy to see her do well. She still loves to dance and her school is doing well, but this is a good opportunity and I can't lie, a huge part of the appeal is that Rennie's tuition would get a hefty discount."

Raven imagined that kind of private arts school would cost a pretty penny. She had no doubt Adrian would have offered to pay, probably even Erin, but Brody wouldn't have taken money from his siblings. And it wasn't like they were paupers, just not gazillionaires like his rock-star siblings.

"Oh, that's a big plus."

"Rennie is sad to leave her school and her friends, of course. But once she took a look at the classes? She got really excited."

"I think that's really cool. I'm glad. She's a great kid and has so much talent. I'm happy she's got this opportunity. The stuff she showed me is like years beyond what anyone her age can do."

Brody looked up from his client. "Yeah, and you're part of that. Always encouraging her. Elise and I appreciate that. Rennie adores you."

She looked down, fighting a blush. "Daisy has more connections of that type than I do."

"Meh. Daisy's a nice lady, but she's not you. You're family."

She blinked back tears. Tears that seemed to come so freaking ably all a sudden. She cleared her throat and kept on working. Brody, who knew her so well, backed off and made small talk with his client while she got herself back together.

When she'd finished and was waiting for her next client, he approached again. "So Jonah Warner."

"Yeah. Unexpected, huh?"

"I dunno. You tell me."

She nodded. "He is. I have rules, Brody. Lots of them. He makes me break them. Left and right."

"The dumb rules like no sleeping over? Or the good rules like you'd never stay with anyone who harmed you?"

She rolled her eyes. As close as she was with Brody, she'd never revealed why she never slept over to anyone but Jonah.

No one else was close enough to hear. "Well, he does like to use a paddle on me. He also ties me up. But that's not really harm. At least not in a bad sense. And the only man who has slept over at my place is a nearly four-year-old who likes frozen pudding cups and pees all over the seat."

Brody laughed. "Rough sex is one thing. Harming is another. He seems protective of you. I like that part. I like that you're letting him in. You seem calmer lately. Must be all that spanking."

She burst out laughing. "Could be. I certainly feel so very mellow when he's done. Who knew? I used to think all that stuff was just role-play. But it's more than that with us. He takes over and . . ."

"And you don't have to be in charge. For once in your life, someone else makes the decisions and choices."

She blew out a breath. "Yeah. I think that's part of it. If you want to get all psychological about it and all. Anyway, he's good. We're good. His family? Well. We'll see about that. But who am I to talk?"

"I heard part of what happened over the weekend with the mother and sister-in-law. Wasn't really happy about it. Did like his reaction though."

"If I mean to do this relationship thing, I'm going to have to find a way to deal with her. The mother anyway. The sister-in-law can eat a bag of dicks. She may never know how close she came to eating my fist."

Brody laughed. "Maybe she needed that."

"Not at a charity event, for fuck's sake. The evening was about raising money for the arts, not for some stupid play for attention by a sister-in-law who wants to bang the brother she couldn't marry, if you know what I mean."

"Ah. You think that's the issue?"

"I don't know for sure. All I can say is she seems unnaturally interested in where Levi puts his dick."

"Some people can't be happy with anything."

"Don't I know it. But I'm good. Jonah is good. What it is more than that I don't know. But for now, I'm happy."

"How much have you shared with him?"

"More than I intended to. He's got . . . I don't know, this way about him. I find myself sharing stuff I haven't talked about in a long time. If ever. But he never looks at me with disgust or pity."

He put a hand on her shoulder. "Sweetheart, there's nothing to be disgusted over. Not with you. Everything you survived was about you overcoming other people's shitty behavior. None of it was your fault."

"I'm no angel, Brody. I was not very nice to Elise when she first came around. I tried to break you up. I broke your heart before that. And you're still my friend. Thank you."

He smiled. "You did break my heart. And that sucked. But if I'm being honest—and since I'm an old family man now and all I guess I have to—my heart got broken because I didn't listen to what you told me. You never made me promises. I just wanted them to be there. And you made your peace with Elise. You went to her and apologized and whatever you said—she won't tell me—was enough to make her not only forgive you, but be fond of you. You have flaws, no lie. But you own your shit and a hell of a lot of people don't. Just let this guy love you. Understand you're worth loving. Because you are. What I have with Elise makes everything different. Better. You deserve that too."

It couldn't be avoided any longer. Jonah had ducked his mother's calls until Wednesday morning when she simply waltzed into his office, dragging his father and his brother Eli.

"As you have deigned to ignore the woman who gave you your very existence, I had to hunt you down. Your father and Eli as well."

"If you want to count a coy call for lunch that she then sprung on us as 'let's all talk about Mal and Gwen,' yes."

"You stop that." Their mother gave Eli a look and he sighed, dropping into a chair at the conference table in the room.

"I've been busy. I called you back."

"You called me back at midnight when your call would go straight to voice mail. Honestly, I don't know why you boys think I'm so stupid."

Levi poked his head in and then froze when he saw what was going on.

"Don't you try to scamper off, Levi. Come and sit." Liesl pointed at a chair and he obeyed.

"You get conned with a lunch date too?"

Levi nodded. "It was a call from Jonah's assistant."

"Mother, leave my staff out of it. She's already petrified every time you come into view." Jonah put his phone on Do Not Disturb and headed to the table.

Their father would never say anything to disagree with their mother, especially not at a time like this.

Toby, another brother and Eli's twin, popped in and then groaned.

"Now, we're all here. Food will arrive shortly. I did not lie. We will be eating. I figured you were all busy enough that you'd need to eat while we discussed this mess."

True to her word, Jonah's assistant brought food in just two minutes later. She gave him a look full of apology and he waved it away. He knew how his mother was; he couldn't blame his assistant for getting caught up in her whirlwind.

"It has come to my attention that some sort of kerfuffle occurred between Gwen, Daisy and Raven on Saturday evening at the benefit. It has also come to my attention that whatever this kerfuffle was, it spilled out to the hotel's drive where Jonah and Levi got into a heated argument with Malachi. Do I have this correct?"

"Mother, I'm not sure this is any of your business."

Oh, Eli; so naive about their mother.

"Elijah, if it is not a mother's business when her children are in trouble, whose business would it be?" She turned a hard eye to Levi, knowing Jonah would hold out longer than anyone else. Levi knew he was the weaker link of the two and he sighed.

"It was resolved. If Mal wanted you to know what it was, he'd have told you. Leave it be. He's got to deal with his wife on his own."

"So it was Gwen, clearly. Stupid woman. What happened in that bathroom? Don't lie to me. This is one of my boards, you know. People came to me who'd seen the aftermath. I need to understand whether or not I should be sure Gwen is never invited to such events in the future."

"Yes, don't invite her to anything in the future." Jonah spoke quietly.

"Boys, your mother is rightfully concerned. We all know Mal has been having trouble. His work is suffering. You have to share with us. We want to help him. He shouldn't have to deal with this on his own. That's what family is for."

Eli blew out a breath and looked to Jonah. "Tell them."

"I think Mal should be here for this. I am not comfortable talking behind his back." Jonah sat back, looking at their mother. "He's an adult. He's married. We can't just talk about him like he's a kid. Any of you would be angry if this was about you and no one bothered to include you."

Liesl smiled like the cat who ate the canary and he knew he'd been outmaneuvered. "As a matter of fact, he'll be here in a minute or two."

"You're good." He nodded her way.

"Where do you think you come by it, boy?" his father asked.

They were eating when Mal came in. He paused in the doorway and then came into the room and sat down with a resigned sigh. Jonah pushed food his way.

"You will be pleased to know Levi and Jonah would not tell me the details of whatever transpired on Saturday evening. Jonah rightfully pointed out that you should be here when we discussed this issue. And of course I completely agree, which is why you're here now. What is going on, Malachi?"

"This is really not your concern."

Jonah kept eating. Mal was the youngest. He'd been spoiled more than any of them had been. But he was weaker against his mother than the rest as well. It was only a matter of time before he broke, and everyone in that room knew it.

"Now you know that's a lie. Of course it's my concern. It's all our concern. Your wife is clearly unbalanced. She's driving a wedge between you and your family and she has been for some time. We love you. We've let you go your own way. But this has to stop. At the very least give me your version of events."

"She hates Daisy." Mal put his fork down and ran a hand through his hair.

"Whatever for? She's delightful."

No one had ever told their parents about the strife that had been between the two women since Gwen had made a rather ugly and pretty blatantly racist scene. Since then Levi hadn't spoken more than the words it took to warn her to keep her distance from his woman or there'd be hell to pay.

"What else have you all been keeping from me?"

Then Toby spilled. The entire story about the first time Gwen met Daisy when Gwen had accused Daisy of being a gold-digging whore, complete with racist overtones, to the situation on Saturday night.

The other brothers stared at him, mouths open.

"What? Fuck this noise. There is no way Gwen should have gotten away with it for so long. She's an ugly bitch. I'm sorry, Mal, but she is."

"Tobias, please limit your use of the word 'fuck.'" Liesl sighed and looked around the table. "Why you didn't tell me this, I do not know. There's no way I would have had her in my home over the last few years if I had known."

"Which is why they didn't tell you." Mal spoke and sounded so tired. "They've been protecting me."

"What is your version of what happened Saturday night?"

"I can tell you Gwen's version. But I believe Daisy and Raven's version. Gwen says she wandered into the bathroom and was beset by both women. She was so upset I believed her. Even though in my heart I knew she was lying. I've moved out."

"Jesus, Mal why didn't you tell one of us? Where are you living? I have extra space. You're welcome to stay as long as you like." Jonah felt sick for his brother.

"Or with me. Daisy would be happy to have you with us, too. She doesn't blame you and neither do I."

"I'm looking for a house. I've got an attorney. We're filing tomorrow or the next day."

Liesl leaned close to him. "Darling, we love you. I'm sorry you felt you had to do this alone. Please tell us what you need."

"Well, that was pretty nice." He smiled at their mother and then around the table. "I needed to do it on my own. I was licking my wounds. I've known for a while that things weren't going to get better."

"How long?"

"About two years."

Jonah snorted. They'd only been married two years as it was.

"I shouldn't have married her. But I thought we could work it through. That once she got to know Daisy she'd lighten up. But it's more than that."

"She's got a thing for Levi."

"Subtle, Eli. Well done." Levi sighed.

"Well, am I lying? I mean come on. The way she is about Daisy is ridiculous. It's more than racism, though clearly that's part of it. It's that she would react that way to anyone with him. It's Levi, not who he's with. It's that Mal isn't Levi."

"Sweet Christ." Levi looked to Mal. "I hope you know I'd never do anything to facilitate this crush, if there is indeed one."

"There is one. It's more than that. She's obsessed with you. She had an affair last year. The guy looked just like you."

There was an uproar around the table and Jonah rapped several times on the tabletop to shut everyone up. "Okay, so we're outraged. Let's not make it worse on Mal. He's doing what is right."

"Indeed. Thank heavens for the prenup."

"Cal Whaley did a great job on it."

"Honestly I just want to be free of her. She can keep the house. I have no desire to turn her out into the street or anything. She's got a good job. We have no kids. It could be worse. So much worse."

"Yes, well." Jonah agreed wholeheartedly.

"What does she say? Have you told her?"

"We had a very big fight on the way home from the benefit. I moved out that night. She thinks I'm working out my mad. My attorney advised me against telling her I was going to file. She'll be served at work and I'll have a moving crew go in and take my stuff at the same time. She can have the furnishings that aren't Warner antiques. I just want what was mine when we got married. The rest is all hers anyway."

"Well, there's some hope for you, darling. Levi and Jonah have done much better on their second choices. Just get this marriage dissolved and move on. We're behind you all the way."

17

The weeks passed as Seattle moved from the delightful color of early fall to the dreary gray of rainy and cold late November.

To Raven it used to be the time she hightailed it out of the Northwest and sought out Los Angeles or Hawaii. But she had roots now. Reasons to stick around. One of them currently looked through a book of birthday cakes Jules Lamprey, a friend of Gillian's and a pretty wonderful baker, had brought over to Erin's.

His fourth birthday was approaching and Erin was planning his party to coincide with Thanksgiving and their annual football grudge match thing that Raven made a point to miss every year. She usually made it a point to fly in after dinner and right before Alexander's birthday. She'd never miss that.

But now she'd be coming over to Gillian and Adrian's place to help with the food prep while they all played their football game outside. Because Erin had asked her to.

But for the time being, Alexander was trying to choose a cake.

"I bet Jules could make a TARDIS cake."

His eyes widened and Jules laughed. "I could. I've never made a TARDIS cake, but it would be lots of fun."

"Can I have a Dalek cake?"

Raven looked it up quickly and turned her iPad to Jules. "Just in case you didn't know."

Jules's smile was one of those brilliant girl-next-door things that seemed to enrapture males of all ages. Birds sang and mice made clothes. Or something. She was pretty okay though, as people went.

"I'm a huge *Doctor Who* fan. I think a Dalek cake would be really awesome. I bet we could put mini doughnuts down the sides."

Raven nodded. "Doughnuts on a cake? Alexander, I definitely think you should have a Dalek cake."

His eyes were so wide there wasn't much to do but lean down to kiss his forehead.

"Yes, please. Doughnuts, Daleks and cake!"

"All right then. I'm sort of excited about this one." Jules closed the book. "I hear you're both coming out with us tomorrow night. I haven't been out dancing in so long."

Jonah had actually craftily conned her into this "group date" thing. His daughter was coming back home for Thanksgiving and he'd be busy with all that stuff so he wanted a fun-filled evening to tide him over. She assured him she wasn't upset that he wanted to spend time with his kid, for heaven's sake. He then told her he wanted Raven and Carrie to meet while she was back in town.

No pressure.

When she opened her door at his knock he took a long, meandering look from the toes of her shoes up to her face. He paused at her nipples, of course.

"You wearing it?"

He meant the chain he'd left in a box on her bed before he'd left to go home several nights before. In it was also the dress she currently wore.

"You spoil me." And she liked it. She'd never been spoiled before.

"Listen, before we go, I want to talk to you about something."

"Ugh, really? Am I going to want to punch you in the throat after you tell me?"

He laughed and led her to the couch where he pulled her to sit with him. "I hope not. But it's been on my mind. Up front, I'm telling you this not because I did anything wrong, but because if you heard about it from someone else you might get hurt and I can't have that." He brushed a fingertip over her heart, against the curve of her breast. His fingers sought the cool metal of the choker she always wore. For him.

"You better tell me because now I'm getting worried."

"At the Halloween thing at Gillian's, Levi asked me if I wanted him to do a background check on you."

Was that it? She'd frankly expected him to have done it already anyway. "Oh. Well, what did you find out?"

He shook his head. "I said no. Or rather, look, as he was talking Erin overheard and she was really pissed off. She tore a strip off both of us. Her anger was righteous. She did it to defend you. And you deserved defending. But I was about to tell him no, thanks, when she came down and got in my face."

Erin hadn't said a word. Still, it made her smile to imagine what Erin had been like. Her usually laid-back and happy friend could really get scary when people she cared about got threatened.

"I expect your brother was concerned about my lack of stability in the past. He's just trying to protect you. Though if Erin got that mad he probably made a gold digger comment." Which would hurt her feelings considering she'd never done anything like that, ever. She was used to being misjudged, but it still sucked.

"Charlotte has treated me like an ATM these last years. Hell, pretty much since day one. She came from money so I figured she was used to a certain level of comfort and as her husband it was my job to provide it. And then when she had Carrie she used to use that to get more from me. A few thousand here to go on spa trips. Plastic surgery. New wardrobes. Whatever. Even after the divorce she was like that. He's sensitive about it because he saw me get hurt by it. It doesn't excuse any hurt you'd have felt if it had happened in your earshot, and believe me when I tell you that when Erin was finished defending you, Levi felt like complete and utter shit. He likes you. He was just trying to protect me. Anyway, I'm not doing it and he's never asked again. I was going to let it be once I figured Erin hadn't told you, but I began to panic about how hurt you might be if you heard it from anyone else but me."

She shook her head. "I don't even know what to do with you. I mean, the sex stuff, sure. But the heart stuff? I don't know how to manage it. If you'd done the background check, you know you could have found out about whatever happened in my past. You'd have answers to your questions."

"I want to find out from you. Your past, the things you've endured and survived, aren't something I should hear from reports. They're yours. To go around you and find out when you've slowly been revealing yourself to me would be a rejection of what you mean to me. I admire you for how you survived. It's your story, you should tell it."

She looked up at the ceiling to hold back the tears, blinking quickly. "I don't know how to do this stuff. I've never been in a relationship before."

He took her hand, kissing her fingertips. "Sure you have. You're in a relationship with Erin, who is quite the defender, let me tell you. She loves you. You're in a relationship with Alexander. Hell, and Poppy and Martine. Rennie, who stares at you like you're a disco ball or something equally shiny and miraculous."

"That's not what I mean."

"I know. But you seem to think you can't do this simply because no one has really been worth it before. And I'm telling you, you *have* made a commitment to people and you've done it successfully. And you've made one to me. And that's pretty damned successful too. I love you, Raven. You make my heart beat faster, even when you're being particularly vexing. I want to be worth it for you, the way you are for me."

She swallowed past a knot of emotion. "You don't love me. You can't love me. I'm a novelty, nothing more."

"You really make me angry when you say stuff like that. I'm not twenty, or a fucking cat. I can tell the difference between novelty and love. I've loved you since the start."

"I'm sorry. I'm not trying to hurt your feelings or offend you. But see how I am? I do it without even trying. I can't fit into your world of benefits and swanky dinners and people with names everyone knows. I'm not that girl."

"You're *my* girl. That's what counts. Can't you see that? I had a wife who looked good on my arm at parties and was nothing more. You're so much more than that. Can't you see yourself? Hm? You're here in Seattle for Erin and Brody. And Alexander. You do for other people all the time. They don't even need to ask, you just do it. You're something so special."

"And you."

He cocked his head.

"I'm in Seattle for you."

He smiled. "Yeah?"

She nodded, not knowing what else to say, so she just kept quiet.

He pulled her close, kissing her temple. "I'm sorry I didn't tell you sooner. About the whole background-check thing."

"You didn't tell me to spare my feelings. I get it, Jonah. You're rich. Good god, I'd be such a liar if I pretended I didn't know that. Levi wanted to protect that, and given the women you all married, well, I get it. If you want to run a check, I won't be hurt. I don't have an arrest record. I have five figures in the bank. I own this condo and my car.

Well, I pretty much own the condo; I only have a year of payments left. The point is, I don't have any real debt. Mainly because I didn't really stay in any place for very long to accrue it. I live simply except for my addiction to travel and panties. I do like nice underwear. Probably comes from wearing hand-me-downs and garage-sale stuff for most of my childhood. I don't want your money, but I love the presents you give me. I'm with you because of who you are to me, not to everyone else."

"You say you don't know how to do this, but you're doing just fine."

He was so glad he'd told her. He'd been worrying over the last month about it. Vacillating between wanting to let it go and wanting to tell her so it wouldn't pop up to hurt her.

A weight was off his shoulders and after their conversation, she never ceased to touch and surprise him. Things felt good. Better than ever.

And now he watched her move. Goddamn. They'd done a little dancing when he'd taken her to the big band club the month before. But this . . .

A distinctly Latin remix played in the club and she switched her hips back and forth in time with the beat, her tits moving just right, enough to render him so hard it nearly hurt. Of course, knowing she wore the chain helped too.

He just stood there and let her make him look good. He'd confessed he wasn't much for club dancing and that's what she'd told him.

She backed up to him, whipping her hair back. He slid his hands over her shoulders and then down to her hips. Her head was turned to the side, her gaze locked with his as she brushed that luscious ass against his cock and then dropped it low, stood, bent at the waist and pressed back as she slowly stood again when the song ended and something else came on.

Her hands went up and he held her waist as she stayed against him.

This was his woman. Oh, he saw the glances. Saw that some of the people knew her. One or two of them actually got near enough for her to shake her head no and turn back to him. Far from feeling jealous, it made him hot all over. Others may have wanted her, but she was his. Totally and utterly.

That was fucking sexy.

Finally after a while she turned to him, encircling his neck with her arms. "I need a drink. I'm hot."

He bent to kiss her. "You sure are. I think I can buy you a drink in thanks for all the entertainment your ass has given me all night long."

He walked in front of her, keeping her behind him, one arm reached back to keep her against him and to take the bulk of the crowd so she wouldn't get bumped.

"What would you like?" he asked when they finally reached the table where their group had set up.

"A water and a cosmo. Please."

She scooted in next to Erin and he followed. The waitress caught his eye and came over. He indicated a reorder of what everyone already had at the table and got his and Raven's drinks.

It was loud, though thankfully not so thick with smoke he could barely breathe like it had been in his premarriage days. The lights flickered all around them as he took her hand. Levi and Daisy came over and sat with them as well.

It was good. He was too old to want to do this on a regular basis. But dancing with Raven when she was all sensual and moved the way she did? Well, that was totally worth the crowd and the noise.

They stayed for several more hours before making their way back to his place. She still slept in his guest room and that was . . . all right. He hoped that one day she'd move to his bed. But he got it. And he would let her make those steps herself. He knew her well enough to understand just spending the night in his house was a big step for her. So he'd continue to be patient because she was worth it.

She changed into the pajamas she seemed to own in every possible combination from sexy silky vixen stuff to what she wore then, flannel with her ever-present socks.

They snuggled in his living room listening to music and drinking tea.

"Erin told me to invite you to pool and karaoke when Carrie goes back to Italy and you're free for social stuff again. They used to go once a week but now that everyone has babies they go once a month. Sometimes it's at Adrian and Gillian's place because they have a game room and a pretty nifty karaoke machine."

He hadn't really been part of a social group since he'd been married. Most of them had been Charlotte's friends and had chosen her after the divorce. He did hang out with his brothers, but now that he and Levi had girlfriends in the same circle he saw his brother more than he had in some time. He liked that too.

"Sounds good. Listen, Erin invited me to Thanksgiving. I said no because there's a big thing at my parents' place. My grandparents will be there. All my brothers and Carrie too. I know you're busy with dinner with them and with Alexander's party and stuff. But after. You know if you were done, I mean. We won't eat dinner until eight. I want you to meet Carrie. I've told her about you so that's not a problem. She wants to meet you too. Daisy and Levi will be there, and you know Mal will be there, but not Gwen since they've split and all."

"I don't know. I barely want to go to Gillian's for Thanksgiving. I'm not really cut out for dinners with the family. You know? It's not . . . I'm not good at it. I'm going to say something offensive. And I don't want to put you in that position."

"I think you're better at it than you let yourself believe."

She laughed. "I nearly got into a fistfight with your brother's wife!"

"She deserved it. And she started it. My grandfather will tell you stories about Korea and my grandmother will drink wine and make my mother uncomfortable all day. It's really the only day of the year we get to see my mother on the other side of the way she often treats others."

"Oh. Well, that *is* alluring."

"Look, I know this is new. But I would like you to be with me. I haven't had anyone at a holiday dinner with me since Charlotte."

"So no pressure or anything,"

He squeezed her hand. "No pressure. I just want to be with you. Nothing more."

She sighed but he could tell she was seriously thinking it over.

"You don't have to say yes for sure at this point."

"I'll be there. Dinner at Gillian and Adrian's will be at noon. They'll do the cake for Alexander just after that. Erin is very low key for his birthday parties. Just family and cake."

"No unicorns or anything? Gift bags with diamond rings and a pony?"

"She doesn't want to spoil him. Well, with material stuff. They're going to Disneyland in the spring with Brody and Elise and their kids."

"I like that. I'm the same way with Carrie. I mean, yes, she's studying abroad and stuff, but a lot of girls her age in her crowd got BMWs for their sixteenth birthdays. I just couldn't see that sort of extravagance. I got her a car, I can't lie. But it was used. Safe though, of course."

"I wouldn't imagine anything else. So I should be done by five or so."

"If you want to come to my house, you can ride over with me and Carrie. That way you can meet her before we get to my parents' house. Might be a little easier that way."

She blew out a breath. "Yeah, no pressure."

He tipped her chin. "No pressure. You're part of my life, I want them to know that. I want them to know you and for you to know them. People do this all the time. You can do this with one eye closed."

"That might make it easier."

He grinned.

18

She pulled up in Jonah's driveway and tried to stay calm. Gillian had given her a pep talk. Erin had said everything would be fine. Daisy had said Carrie was a really nice young woman. Alexander had given her a hug and smeared frosting on her shirt, but the hug had been worth the price and she was going to change anyway.

She ran home to change, choosing the dress Gillian had given her just a week before. She'd said, when she handed it over, that she'd seen it in a shop window and it had called out to be owned by Raven. Gillian wasn't a clotheshorse at all. She didn't love shopping the way Erin did. So Raven had taken it as a great compliment. And when she'd put the dress on she'd agreed it was something perfect for her.

That and she'd known Gillian knew how nervous Raven had been about this dinner and wanted her to be at least a little more comfortable. Gillian, an outsider as well, in her own way, got that about Raven better than most anyone.

It had a boatneck; the top piece sort of looked as if it were a separate thing, falling to her hips. Then a skirt with two color blocks, falling to just above her knees. The top part was purple, the middle block was a sandy beige and the bottom was two or so shades lighter. It was something she'd never have chosen on her own. But it made her feel beautiful. And that was a lot.

Neutral-toned heels completed the look. She'd kept her hair down but pulled back from her face with a band. A cardigan would keep her warm and also hide her ink. She wasn't ashamed of it or anything, but there was no use showing it off the first time she met most of his family.

She got out and headed to the front door and knocked. He answered with a smile. "You're here." He kissed her, turning to put an arm around her shoulder and guide her into the house. "I like that dress."

"Gillian gave it to me a week ago. Everyone says hello. Daisy and Levi said they'd see you later tonight."

A lovely young woman came downstairs.

She looked Raven over and then smiled. "You're Raven." She held her hand out. "I'm Carrie. My dad talks about you all the time."

Raven shook her hand. "Does he? He talks about you all the time too. You make him very proud." She'd practiced that one a few times. She meant it so she hoped it sounded genuine.

She had great teeth. Holy cow, that smile was big and bright. Her hair was long. Dark like her father's. The cut was perfection. It fell around her face just right, emphasizing her eyes, more green than brown. This girl's mother must have been stunning. Correct, must *be* stunning. Raven tried not to think about Charlotte, but damn, if this child was any reflection on her, Raven was going to develop an even bigger complex.

"My dad showed me the tattoo you're doing on his back. It's amazing. I said I was going to ask you to do one for me."

Raven laughed as she allowed herself to imagine Jonah's look of horror when his kid sprung that on him. "I'm going to guess he gave you a lecture about how you should be older before you made such a permanent choice for yourself and your skin."

Jonah made a little sound and suddenly Raven was all right. His kid was all right. She could have been snooty and spoiled, but she wasn't.

"That's pretty much exactly what he said. So I told him I'd catch you in the summer before I went off to college. I'll be eighteen then."

Raven put her hands up in surrender. "I tend to agree with the being-older-and-really-think-hard-about-how-you're-permanently-changing-your-skin viewpoint. Plus, I'm afraid he might send your grandmother to rough me up if I did that without his okay."

Carrie's eyes widened, lit with amusement. "I heard you met her. She's something else, isn't she? She is a good person most of the time. She's really old school and sometimes she forgets her manners."

"I just figured she was bossy and powerful and liked it that way." Oh, for god's sake, did she say that out loud? She winced, but Jonah just squeezed her shoulders.

"That too. Are we ready?"

"I have something to take along with me. Jules, she's a pretty talented pastry chef. She makes these cherry walnut things. I brought some. Don't worry, Gillian put them on some fancy plate she said would be a nice gift. And in case someone was allergic to nuts, I have an apple cranberry tart too."

"We'll get them on the way out. Oh, you left your coat here. It's in the hall closet. Carrie, get the stuff you brought back for your grandparents."

Carrie ran upstairs and Raven turned to him. "I didn't leave my coat here." She gave him a raised brow. "Maybe one of your other girlfriends did."

"I know. I didn't want you to be uncomfortable. I bought you one."

"You did what? I don't need a coat. I have a parka thing I got when I agreed to go snowboarding a few years back."

"Yes, you do. Your *parka thing* is too heavy and not pretty for events like this. Plus that sweater you have on is lovely, but not warm enough."

"It's not fur, is it? Because I don't wear fur."

He fought a smile, turning to pull the coat from the closet. He was charming. Far too charming for her peace of mind because she had trouble saying no to the man. This was nothing she'd encountered before. She loved saying no. It was a favorite. But not with this guy.

"Not fur. Cashmere."

It was a simple but beautiful black coat, and when she put it on, she nearly moaned. He'd clearly thought about what she'd like and what would look good on her. Another reason she was helpless against him. He gave presents, yes, but he put effort into everything he surprised her with. The material was soft and very warm, the hem had movement—she thought they called it a swing coat. Daisy would know that sort of thing.

"Thank you. It's gorgeous."

"Any time. I don't like to see you shiver."

"I usually go south or west in the late fall and winter. I hate the heat, but I really love to be somewhere balmy and sunny when it's cold here."

"We'll go to Maui soon."

"Dude. You spoil me. The coat is plenty."

He kissed her temple. "It's my job to spoil you. Anyway, you like to travel and I like the idea of you in a bikini. That's a win/win for me. Now, come on. Time to have dinner at the Warner household."

She sucked in a breath and staved off the panic. "If you say so."

She had an idea the Warner house would be pretty swank. But what greeted her when they got to the end of the drive was of course swank, but also understated and elegant. Sort of a Cape Cod, maybe? She didn't really know what the real name for it was, but this seemed to be a more historic part of Seattle so several in this style had dotted their way here, though other big, clearly newer modern homes had been erected in the place of the older house that came with the lot.

The front of the house had a smallish yard, but it was well mani-
cured with big trees dotting the area.

Other cars were already there. Plenty of BMWs and Mercedes. She
saw the truck though, but pressed her lips together hard to keep from
commenting.

"Uncle Toby is here already." Carrie, who insisted on riding in the
back rather than Raven, who'd wanted to. She'd said Raven was her
dad's girlfriend and could ride in the front. Jonah had sealed it when
he put an arm around Raven's waist and opened the door for his daughter to slide into the back. Raven had given him a look but he smiled
and kissed her nose.

Carrie had chattered on as they'd made their way the short distance
to the neighborhood where Jonah's parents lived. Raven had asked
many questions and Carrie had answered with the openness only kids
who were as happy and well loved as this one had. She appeared to be
thrilled with the program, with the choice of college she'd made, with
Italy and the other parts of Europe she'd seen. She was well spoken,
intelligent and gracious.

Jonah had done a good job with her.

"Toby is an architect. His is the truck. He's got a really nice car
too, but he drives this one here to agitate my grandmother." Carrie
shook her head, grinning as they headed for the front door.

"I think I'm going to like Toby," she muttered, and Jonah barked a
laugh.

"You will. Everyone does."

Jonah carried flowers for his mother and grandmother, Carrie
helped Raven, holding the apple cranberry tart, and Raven had the
plate with the cherry things. She was so nervous she was afraid she'd
break the plate she held on so tightly to. So she concentrated on not
squeezing so tight and that seemed to make things a tiny bit better.

An older man who was so clearly Jonah's father answered, his gaze
going straight to Carrie. "Hello, sweetheart."

"Grandfather." Carrie went to him, giving him a big hug and kiss on the cheek.

"Glad you're here. Come in, come in." He looked to Jonah and then Raven. "You're Raven." He kept an arm around Carrie, but held a free hand to Raven. "I'm John Warner, Jonah's father. Welcome."

He was much less frosty than his wife, Raven gave him that. She smiled and shook his hand.

Jonah steered her into the house. The outside may have been under-stated, but the inside was punctuated by the wall of glass overlooking Lake Washington. Views to the Eastside were clear, even on a cloudy day. There was a dock with a boat and the back lawn sloped down to the water with little clusters of tables and chairs.

"Wow."

John smiled at her again. "We looked at houses for six months. Liesl is very particular, and to top it off, she was pregnant with Jonah so the hormones and the nesting thing only accentuated that. Must have seen three dozen homes. But when we walked in and stood here, looking out at that view, she simply turned to me and said, 'This is the one, John.' And that was it. We've lived here ever since. Raised five boys and it's still standing, so that's a testament to the architecture of the late twenties when it was originally built."

"For heaven's sake! Don't just leave them standing in the hallway. They still have coats on and are holding things."

"This is my mother, Beth. Mom, this is Jonah's lady friend, Raven." John indicated Raven, and the older woman, who was maybe five feet tall, gave her an imperious look from head to toe.

"I see where Jonah gets it," Raven said.

Whoops, starting early on the offensive stuff. *Go me.*

Raven held her hand out, hoping to get past the statement. Beth took it and shook.

"Gets what?"

Jonah didn't say a single thing, the jerk.

Oh well, in for a penny. She could have said good looks, but he didn't much resemble his grandmother at all.

"The imperious-look thing. He does it too."

John tried not to laugh, and barely succeeded. His eyes lit with amusement and Carrie didn't bother hiding it; she laughed full out.

"He really does."

Beth narrowed her eyes long enough that Raven started to apologize, and then longer so she didn't because what the hell, it wasn't that offensive after all.

Instead Beth nodded. "He does. I got it from my mother. It's a good tool when you're a bigshot like he is. Me? It keeps everyone on their toes because they're scared of me. What is it you've got in your hands?"

"Walnut cherry bars. Oh, and an apple cranberry tart."

"Bring them through to the kitchen. John, get the flowers. Jonah, for goodness' sake, get their coats."

The kitchen was nice, but it was also clear actual cooking happened there. Smelled good too.

Liesl came out and smiled at the sight of her granddaughter. "Hello, darling."

Carrie hugged her. "Hey, Grandmother."

Still smiling, Liesl looked to Raven. "Hello, Raven. I'm pleased you were able to come today."

It was a genuine statement. Liesl was cool, like pale blue, and white carpets. But she clearly loved her family, and that made her all right in Raven's book.

"Thank you for inviting me."

"Oh, you brought dessert." She cast an eye at the food, but must have found it acceptable. "We have pies and things, but thank you."

Also, she had very few filters. Raven knew it was sort of rude, but she suffered the same problem, and so on some levels she wasn't bothered, though she knew it was sort of a slap. But it was pretty half-hearted, so she must have liked Raven well enough or there'd have been more said.

"I, for one, always appreciate more dessert." Another clearly Warner son came into the kitchen wearing a smile that looked a great deal like Jonah's. "You're Raven and I'm Toby. Nice to meet you at last. I've been hearing a lot about you." He stuck a hand out and she took it.

"You can all leave the kitchen. You're underfoot."

"Don't mind her," Toby said of his mother, "she has trouble speaking her mind. It's very sad."

Carrie laughed and hugged her uncle, who kissed the top of her head and set her back from him, assessing her. "Christ, kid, you have to stop being so beautiful. Jonah's uptight enough, he's going to have a stroke when the boys come around."

Carrie blushed and Toby tipped his chin in Jonah's direction. "We're watching the game in the other room. Eli just finished making up a few batches of sidecars if you're parched. Soda for you, missy."

The living room was just beyond and also had a fabulous view of the water, along with comfortable couches and a large television some football game or other played on. She wasn't a football person, though most everyone else she knew was.

Carrie went in and her uncles all cheered to see her, standing up to give her hugs and exclaim over how lovely she looked and how amazing her grades had been.

Raven hung back at the entry and Jonah turned to her. "You all right? I know it's overwhelming. I'm sorry about the weirdness over what you brought. I promise you she was happy you did. She'd have thought you rude if you hadn't. She likes a no-win." He shrugged.

"It's fine. I've got it. With your mother, I mean. I'll give her leeway. If she takes too much, I'll let her know in a hopefully appropriate manner."

He grinned. "You're so sexy." He said it so that no one could hear and it warmed her insides that he'd see what most thought of as her biggest flaw as being sexy.

"Still, should I offer to help your mother in the kitchen?"

Jonah shook his head. "She and my grandmother are in there, battling with cutting words and stuff. I don't want you anywhere near that."

"Seems to me your dad should step in and take her side."

"He does when my grandmother goes too far. It's good for my mother to get a little of what she dishes out so regularly."

Raven shrugged. "Or maybe she's that way regularly because her mother-in-law is a mean-spirited harpy."

He laughed then and people looked over.

"Guys, this is Raven." He then indicated the men in the room. "Raven, you know Levi and Daisy and you met Toby in the kitchen. The guy with his arm around Carrie is Eli, he's Toby's fraternal twin. And you, um, know Mal."

"Sort of." He'd been too busy essentially calling her a lying whore at the time to really be formally introduced. Raven was proud she'd kept that last bit in her head.

"Yeah, about that. I'm sorry. My manners were atrocious." He stepped forward and held a hand out. "I'm Malachi. Jonah talks of you often. I'm pleased to meet you and I apologize for what went down last month."

"Apology accepted." Was she supposed to apologize for his divorce? Congratulate him? She had no idea so she just kept quiet.

"And the guy in the recliner over there is my grandfather. His name is also John, but everyone calls him Jack."

She nodded, waving. He grinned and waved back. "Come over here, girl. Jonah, get her a drink. Carrie, come give me a kiss."

Raven did as he'd asked. He patted the couch next to the recliner. "Sit here. Those pretty shoes have to hurt and I figure you need a drink after meeting my wife and seeing Liesl too."

She tried not to smile, but it was impossible.

"I'm old," he said jovially. "It means I get to say whatever I like and people chalk it up to that. I figure it makes up for actually being old, which is a bucket of garbage. Nose hairs. That's what will happen to Jonah when he's my age."

Jonah handed her a drink and sat next to her on the couch. "Thanks, Grandpa Jack."

"Girl should know what she's getting into with this family. She's already met your mother and grandmother and she's still here. I figure some nose hairs are the least of it."

Raven smiled brightly at Jonah, who rolled his eyes.

She took a sip and tried not to cough. "What on earth is this?"

Eli grinned. "That, gorgeous, is a sidecar. Cognac, Cointreau, some lemon juice, sugar and a cherry."

Her eyes watered. "It's, um, hearty."

"You've met everyone, right? Tell me after two of these if things don't get just a little easier."

She laughed then. "Two? I'm sort of a lightweight. Let's see if I can finish this one."

It was a nice afternoon, and yes, it certainly seemed easier after she'd finished the first drink. Jonah sat with his arm around her shoulders, laughing and talking easily with his brothers. Daisy seemed to get along with them too. But really it was pretty much impossible not to like Daisy, who'd cleverly avoided the sidecars.

"Time to eat." Beth came in and everyone got up immediately. Mal discreetly helped his grandfather up from the recliner and they all made their way to the dining room.

"I changed the cards earlier to put you at our end of the table," Daisy said in an undertone.

"But that's Liesl's end."

"Dude, it's not Beth's end. Please trust me on this."

Jonah pulled her chair out and she sat. Grace was said and the food began to make its way around the table. There was no shortage of it, that was for sure. A turkey, a ham and a beef tenderloin, three different kinds of potatoes, creamed spinach, corn, sweet potatoes, bread. It was a huge feast.

"I can't see why we needed the beef. But I hope you all like it." Beth sent a look to Liesl, who took a deep breath. Raven pushed her wineglass toward Liesl.

"It's quite delicious." Levi smiled at his mother.

"Tenderloin is my favorite. She makes it for me every year," John lifted his glass in his wife's direction.

"There'll be leftovers. She makes too much every year so she has to send food home with everyone."

Jeez. Who thought that was a bad thing? Turkey sandwiches the next day was like part of the whole thing. Hell, Raven hadn't even grown up with regular Thanksgiving dinners and she knew that.

Everyone talked around it and soon enough it died down, but it agitated Raven because it wasn't something without filters, it was meant to make Liesl feel bad.

"Oh man, I think I have a mashed potato baby." She rubbed her belly as she said it in an undertone to Jonah, who laughed.

Of course Beth had to speak up. "What was that? It's rude to speak in whispers."

She blinked several times and Jonah put a hand on hers, which enabled her to keep her comments on the non-napalm side of the spectrum.

"I wasn't aware I was whispering." Raven smiled and went back to eating.

"Well, you were."

Good god, this old woman was a sharp-tongued bitch. It was admirable to a point.

Jonah reached for his glass and raised it. "To mother and grandmother for all this delicious food."

Everyone raised their glasses for the toast.

"I did most of it. Liesl's strong point isn't cooking."

Raven leaned closer to Liesl once the conversation had started again. "Wow, so here's the thing. I was sort of annoyed at you for the dessert comment you made, but now that I see what you have to deal with I'm giving you a pass. Feel free to insult my cherry walnut bars to your heart's content. That offer is only open for today."

Liesl laughed, nearly choking.

"More whispering?"

Raven smiled sweetly. "Don't worry, it's all about you."

The entire table got very quiet until Liesl just kept laughing.

Beth's eyes widened and then Jack started to chuckle. "She's got your number, duckie. Jonah, your lady will fit in here just fine."

Jonah took her hand, kissing it. "Yes, I agree."

The rest of the dinner was fine. The ease of conversation returned. Dessert was really good and served with hot coffee and brandy, though she skipped the latter.

But she was really ready to go by eleven when Jonah finally signaled it. Everyone shook her hand. His brothers all kissed her cheek. His grandfather, who'd told her some awesome stories about Korea, had taken her hands and told her it had been his pleasure to meet her. Even Beth deigned to kiss her cheek and say it had been nice to meet her and seemed pretty genuine about it. The woman had been a little nicer since dinner, not totally of course—there'd been a few remarks, but they hadn't been as cutting.

Liesl took her aside as they were preparing to leave. "No one has ever taken her on like that for me. John defends me of course, but over the years it's become an elaborate game."

"Jeez. I'd suggest you try Monopoly or backgammon or something. Pick-your-family-apart seems like a sucky game to me."

Liesl jerked just a little. "Charlotte never would have said anything like that."

"Yeah, well, aside from Carrie, I can't see much good in anything that money-grubbing skank has done, so forgive me if I decline to aspire to her level of behavior. My flaws are legion, but I'm not like her, nor do I ever plan to be. I can't see the point in sitting around a table and cutting people apart. Unless I was a surgeon or something."

"As it happens, I agree with you when it comes to Charlotte. Honesty is refreshing. I appreciate it. I do hope you come back to dinner soon."

Raven lifted a brow and Liesl laughed. Jonah saw it and hurried to get free of his grandparents to make his way over.

"He's worried I'm being mean to you."

"I can handle you. I like your son a great deal. I respect his life and his need to lead it however he feels necessary. But I don't think it's a game to hurt people. It's tiring enough to have to keep from blurting out everything I think. I don't want to combine that with a meal. I like food too much to ruin it with this sort of thing. I'm not good at it."

"Yes, I do believe you can handle me. How about if I promise to not make a game out of insulting you? Will you come to a Sunday dinner here next month? My son is in love with you. He's satisfied with his life since you came into it. It's been rough for him since that bitch ran off. You're not the running-off type of bitch."

"No. A different kind of bitch though."

Liesl nodded, satisfied. "Yes, but that's all right. You'll be in good company."

"I'll work out schedules with Jonah about dinner." She knew he wanted it and that meant a lot, even if Liesl hadn't just sort of gone out of her way to give her the seal of approval.

"Everything all right here?" Jonah eased up, putting an arm around Raven's shoulders.

"Yes, darling. I was just inviting Raven to Sunday dinner next month."

He gave a sideways glance to Raven, who nodded.

He kissed his mother's cheek and Carrie caught up with them, her coat in hand. "I'll see you tomorrow, Grandmother."

"All right, darling. Sleep well."

Raven could dig a lady who got softhearted for her grandkid.

19

"So how did it go? At Jonah's place, I mean." Brody worked, chatting to her as was their usual rhythm.

"Most of it was fine. His kid is pretty awesome. I liked his brothers and his father and grandfather. But there were aspects of the evening that were like fucking Thunderdome. His mother and grandmother were all artfully cutting at each other. Mainly the grandmother. That part was not fun. But Liesl, the mother? She invited me to Sunday dinner, which I take it is the seal of approval. I may have to have a drink before I go over there. The stress of keeping my mouth shut probably takes years off my life."

Brody laughed. "You really dig this guy. I like it on you."

"He's not like anything I've ever experienced before." She paused. "Which sounds weird talking to you, but you have that with Elise so I figure you get what I mean."

"I do. So he's decent? I mean, he seems to make you happy. Seems to treat you well. Adrian even commented on that."

She sent a raised brow to him at that comment. "Really?" Many years before, Adrian had seen her with another man at a club in Los Angeles. She'd been with Brody then. And though she'd always been up front with Brody about the fact that she wasn't monogamous, Adrian had hated her pretty much ever since. She'd never lied, but that hadn't mattered to Adrian, who loved his siblings fiercely.

"What happened, what he saw, well, that was between you and me. And he gets it. He's protective of me. But he sees what you're like with Gillian. And with Poppy too. He's mellowing as he ages."

"Hm."

"Raven?"

She looked up from her client at Maggie's hail of her name. Maggie stood at the front counter where she usually dealt with walk-ins and clients.

Raven stood, knocking the stool back and nearly losing her balance at the sight of the man standing there. It had been nearly twenty years since the last time she saw Mike Thompson, and he looked pretty much the same as he had then.

Brody was at her side immediately. Two other people were also working in the shop and they'd stood as well, looking back and forth between Raven and the man at the door.

"Mr. Thompson? What . . . Why are you here?" Sick dread filled her as the memories nearly suffocated.

"Raven? Are you all right?" Brody stood between her and Mike.

"He . . . That's . . . I'm . . . I don't know."

Brody examined her face. "Sweetheart, do I need to call the cops? Do I need to beat this guy's ass? What's happening? You're scaring the hell out of me."

"I know Raven from Happy Bend."

"Well, I know enough to understand that's not a good thing," Brody called back over his shoulder.

"It's fine." No. It wasn't fine. But she didn't want to get the guy beaten up by three burly tattoo artists. And Maggie held the phone in her hand like she was about to swing it into Mike's face.

She pulled herself together. It was in the past. She had a future. She wasn't going to let this harm her.

She managed to walk to the front counter as everyone got back to work, though they all kept an eye on the situation. That made her feel better. Brody was at her back, refusing to leave. That made her feel better too.

"I'm sorry, I didn't mean to make a scene." Mike licked his lips nervously. He had gray in his hair and in his beard. A bit of belly, though he would have been sixty or so by now, so she figured that was normal.

"Why are you here?"

"Is there somewhere we can talk in private?"

"Why are you here?" Raven repeated.

"It's about your mother."

She physically recoiled, moving back a step and hitting Brody. He took her shoulder in his hand, reassuring.

"Why don't you use my office?" He spoke softly.

She nodded. "I need to finish my client."

Arvin, who'd just cashed out his latest client, paused. "It's a simple one, right? I can finish it for you if your client is okay with it."

"Thanks. Mr. Thompson, I can talk to you in Brody's office. Come on back."

Her legs worked, which sort of surprised her.

Brody paused at the door, after she'd waved Mike to sit. "You want some company? Who is that?"

"My foster father. One of them." She'd never told anyone the whole story of just who he was and she wasn't going to do it then either. "I'll be okay." She touched his arm. "Thank you."

"Bang on the wall if you need me. Or call out. I'm just right here."

She nodded and turned, closing the door.

She walked to the desk and sat behind it. The familiar furniture, the pictures of Brody's women, Marti and Rennie, Elise, joined with others of Erin and Adrian. The room smelled like him. His jacket hung on a peg in the corner. This was her turf. It was her turf and it was nearly twenty years after her dealings with the Thompsons.

"I've upset you. Seems I've done enough of that and I'm truly sorry." He spread his hands out, letting them drop to his lap.

"You said you were here about my mother?" She turned her emotions off. She had to or she'd suffocate.

"About ten years ago I went to therapy. After we lost Missy . . . after Bonnie and I split and you . . ."

"Were dumped back on the state," she supplied.

He winced but it didn't make her feel better.

"Yes, after we failed you. Anyway, I spent a lot of years in the bottom of a bottle. I lost one job after the next. I hit rock bottom and then Bonnie came to see me in jail. I finally got some help. Therapy. It was either that or lose everything. Bonnie and I had been talking again. I wanted her back, you see, and she said she wouldn't consider it until we got counseling. So I went. She went. We both had it. I worked through stuff and faced the grief. Not just over Missy, but how we'd abandoned you like all the others had."

She had her hands folded in her lap, her nails digging into her palms as she struggled to hold it together and keep a straight face.

"If you're here for old home week, Mr. Thompson, I'm sorry to disappoint you. I got over Happy Bend a long time ago."

He simply went on. "Bonnie and I, we started looking for you. To reconnect and see if we could make amends. Your kin, they weren't much help. But we kept our ears open. Last year, one of Bonnie's patients was a retired police officer who did private investigation as a hobby. We asked him to see if he could track you down. He eventually found you; we figured out you'd changed your name. But first, well . . . we found your momma."

"Her grave?" Though she'd known her mother had died of an over-dose, no one had known where her grave was. She had no plans to go leave flowers either.

"Raven, your mother isn't dead. She's in a mental institution where she's been for the last eighteen years. Before that she'd been in another institution in Louisiana."

Icy cold washed over her. "You're telling me my mother isn't dead?"

"I'm telling you your mother is alive. She's . . . well, she's not in the best shape, but she's alive. In her lucid times, they told her . . . well, they did to her what they did to you I guess. She thought you were dead. They used the news about Missy—" His mouth wobbled a moment and then forged ahead. "They told her you'd been murdered. For the last nearly twenty years she thought you were dead. She tried to kill herself after that. That's when they moved her to a different institution in Oklahoma City. She didn't abandon you, darlin'. She had a psychotic break. Apparently she's had mental problems most of her life. She's been diagnosed with schizophrenia. It's resistant to most treatment. She's a threat to herself more than anyone else."

"Who is *they?*" *Hold on, hold on, hold on.* "Who told her I was dead?"

"Your aunt. She wouldn't speak to us when we went to see her. We tried many times. We tried to talk to cousins and they wouldn't say much. One of them asked us for money to tell us and sent us on a wild-goose chase. He didn't know, not really."

"You saw her? My mother?"

He nodded. "She knows you're alive. We told her we were trying to find you. I promised her when we did, I'd tell you about her. Raven, I know we did you wrong. It tears me and Bonnie up to know how wrong we did you."

"Your daughter was murdered. You had enough to deal with." Intellectually she understood it. Believed it. But her heart had broken just the same. She'd lost *everything*. For a time she'd had everything she'd ever wanted. A family at last. Her own room. A sister. Safety and stability.

"She was kidnapped, raped, tortured and murdered. It's taken me years of therapy to be able to say that out loud. But we fell apart and we tossed you back like you were an animal we took to the pound. We took a horrible moment in our lives and we betrayed you. We made a promise to you. We made you believe we were making a home for you and we didn't. I will regret that for the rest of my days. We loved you, Raven. Bonnie and me. Missy too. You were meant to be our daughter and we failed you as surely as we failed Missy. We want you to know about your momma because we'll be damned if we fail you again."

For so long she had wanted them to seek her out. To know that what they'd done to her had devastated her entire life. She'd felt selfish even thinking it. Missy had died. And Raven hadn't. Things had been bad, yes, but she was sitting there and Missy wasn't.

Worse, this business with her mother was beyond confusing. Why would they have told her she was dead? She'd been all alone all these years in an institution and no one ever told her?

Everything she'd ever believed about her life crashed down around her ears. She hadn't been tossed away by her junkie mother. Her mother hadn't been able to take care of her. Worse, her family *knew* and didn't tell her.

"Why would they do that to me? I don't understand." And then it fell away. All the energy she'd put into holding back her emotions simply wasn't there anymore. There was nothing left but her emotions.

She started to cry, putting her head down on the desk. The sounds she made came from someplace so deep inside she didn't know how to stop. The door slammed open and Brody bellowed at Mike to step back from where he'd moved to comfort her.

"No. Don't." She held a hand out.

Brody stared at her, never having seen her fall apart. He moved to the desk, picking her up and sitting, holding her in his lap, rocking her back and forth as she wept.

"Everyone get back to work."

"Should I call someone?" Maggie asked from the doorway.

"Erin."

She shook her head no, but Brody just grumbled and held on, rubbing a hand back and forth on her back.

Erin rushed in just a few seconds later. That day was one she staffed the café in the mornings. "What's going on? Oh! What's wrong? Who is this guy? What did you do to her?"

Raven lifted her head. "It's not him."

Erin came to her knees in front of where Brody had been holding her. She put her arms around Raven and held on tight. "What can I do? Tell me and I'll make it happen. Do you want me to call Jonah?"

"I need a plane ticket to Oklahoma City."

"I'll go with you, Raven. Bonnie and I will be with you, right at your side. If you want us." Mike spoke from where he'd sat, watching helplessly on the other side of the desk.

"You're not going anywhere until you tell us what's going on." Erin handed her a wad of tissues.

"My mother is alive and in a mental institution. She's not dead. They lied to me."

"Oh my god."

He'd left several messages and she hadn't called back. He'd stopped by her building but she wasn't there. For the last several days he'd tried. They'd both been busy. She'd been pulling long days at the shop and he'd been working and spending time with Carrie before she'd had to go back to school.

But his general annoyance that they hadn't connected had shifted to discomfort. Something was wrong.

He dropped Carrie at the airport and headed to Written On The Body to see what was up.

But it wasn't open yet so he went into the café. Erin wasn't there. But he knew where she lived, having gone there a time or two with Raven, so he headed there. If all else failed, he'd go to Bainbridge and to Gillian.

But he didn't have to. Erin told the doorman to send him up and she met him at the door with a concerned look on her face.

"Where is she?"

"Come in. I'm going to have a cup of coffee. Want one?"

The place was quiet.

"Alexander is in preschool for a few hours today. That's why it's so quiet. Odd. I guess you'd know that too."

"Carrie is always running up and down the stairs, on the phone, listening to music or watching television. It's unnatural when she's gone."

He took the proffered cup of coffee.

"You're here about Raven. I knew you'd come."

"What is going on? I'm really alarmed now."

"I've thought about what I'd say. I bounced ideas off Brody. Off Todd and Ben. You love her. She deserves that love and I know she's told you some of her past, which says so much more about how she feels about you than you probably understand."

He blew out a breath. "It's hard enough to hear. I can't imagine having to live through it. She's gone for something to do with that? Why didn't she tell me?"

"Two days ago she got a visit at the shop from a former foster father. He told her that her mother was still alive. In a mental institution in Oklahoma City."

He sat, stunned. "Oh my god. She must be gutted. Why didn't she tell me?"

"Because your daughter was here. Raven wanted you to have that time with Carrie." Erin smiled at him like he was a little slow. And he supposed he was. Of course she'd done it for that reason.

"She's in Oklahoma City all by herself?"

"I offered to go. Brody offered to go. She refused. We have children who need us and she wouldn't take us away from that. The foster parents offered to meet her and go. I don't know if she took them up on it. She wouldn't tell me anything about them. Something happened to her when she was fifteen. She's mentioned it a few times, but never has told me exactly what happened. Maybe she's told you."

He shook his head. "She's mentioned it. I asked but she said she doesn't speak of it, ever. She's told me a lot of other stuff. I know why she doesn't sleep over. I'm trying to be patient and let her share as she can."

Erin nodded. "But she sleeps in your house. That's huge. She trusts you and she needs you. She needs you now more than ever." Erin turned and dug out a piece of paper, sliding it across the counter. "She's here. Go get her or I'll hate you forever."

He stood, draining the cup. "On it. Thank you, Erin."

"Don't be mad at her. She does the best she can."

He shook his head. "I'm not mad at her." He was frantic to get to her.

He rushed out, making a call to his assistant to get him on the next possible flight and a suite at the hotel Raven was staying at. One with a bedroom that had a lock on the door.

20

She'd finally been able to get permission to visit her mother the following day. It had been harder than she'd thought, getting that permission. One of her doctors wanted to meet with Raven first, so she'd do
that first thing. They'd done a check on her as well.

Bonnie and Mike had offered to come back to be with her when
she visited. They only lived an hour from the hospital and had invited
her to stay awhile when she was ready.

She might do it.

She did decline their offer to be with her when she visited her
mother. She needed to do it alone. She had enough baggage with Mike
and Bonnie that she wanted all her energy to be on her mother first.
Then she'd deal with them.

She picked up her phone and dialed Jonah before she talked herself
out of it. He'd left several messages for her. At first she'd been too busy
to reply, and then Mike had come in and turned everything on its ear.
But Carrie had still been visiting and she'd be damned if she messed
up the visit with all this stuff.

But she knew Carrie was due to go back that day. And God help her, she'd become used to him in her life. Needed him.

She got his voice mail this time though.

"I'm sorry I haven't called you back. I hope you got Carrie to the airport and she's back in Italy already. I'm away right now. I found out . . . I found out my mother is still alive. I know, right? I can't . . . I don't know much more than that right now. I'm in Oklahoma City now. They're letting me see her tomorrow. I don't know if I'll have any more information after I see her. She's mentally ill. After this, I'm heading to Happy Bend to confront my aunt about everything. About why they lied. I'll call you when I can. Please don't worry. I miss you."

She hung up and watched television aimlessly for a while as she huddled under the covers. Finally, she headed into the shower to warm up.

She was drying her hair when she heard a knock on the door. She needed to eat, but she hadn't called room service yet.

Pulling her robe on, she headed to the door and looked through the peephole.

Her heart stopped as she yanked the door open and Jonah came into the room, pulling her into a hug, kicking the door closed in his wake.

He smelled good. Familiar. Safe. He held her tight, reminding her she was all right. Everything was fine and she would make it through. He was there for her. Because he loved her.

"I don't deserve you," she said as she buried her nose in his neck.

"Says you. I think you deserve me just fine. Why didn't you tell me, baby? You've been alone for two days dealing with this?"

"Not entirely alone. Erin and Brody know some of it. I flew here with Mike Thompson. Anyway, I didn't want to bug you while Carrie was here. She's your first priority and that's how it should be. I left a message for you a few hours ago."

"I know. I came straight from the airport. Come on. Let's get you packed up. I have a bigger room for us on a higher floor. It's got a separate bedroom with a lock on the door. I can sleep on the couch. But there's no way we're not being together tonight."

She swallowed hard. "You don't have to sleep on the couch. I want to try. I want you with me. I've missed you so much."

"No pressure. We'll take it slow and if you have a problem, we'll do what we normally do."

He helped as she tossed her clothes back into her suitcase. He'd expected her to argue about it, but she didn't. She looked small and sad and it tore at him. She tossed all her toiletries in the bag as well, which he then took from her.

"Leave the robe on, we're only going up a few floors."

She nodded and allowed him to shuffle her out, holding his hand.

He nearly drowned in the emotion of seeing her need him so much. The way she'd held on so tight, his strong, independent Raven. Pride filled him that he made her feel better. Guilt that she'd not come to him, out of her need to protect him and his daughter.

It was he who didn't deserve her. But he wasn't giving her back so that was that. On their floor, he opened the door and ushered her in. The room wasn't bad and he'd turned the heat on, knowing she tended to get cold. Outside it was sleeting. He'd white-knuckled it on the way from the airport, praying it would hold off until he'd arrived. Thankfully it started just as he'd made his way off the highway.

"Get some socks on." He put her bags in the bedroom and her toiletries in the bathroom. When he came out he saw she'd snuggled up on the couch in the main room.

"How about some hot chocolate? Or tea? Have you been sleeping well? Stupid question."

She took a deep breath and blurted out, "Do you want to know? The story, I mean?"

He sat with her. Saw the strain on her features. He wanted to know so very much, but he knew it was stressful for her to relive it too. "Yes. But first, have you eaten? You look pale and a little thin."

"It's only been two days."

"Don't get peevish with me, missy. It's been four since we con-nected and two before that since I actually saw you. I'm agitated that you've been alone dealing with this as it is. Now, you look pale and if I know you, you've been running yourself ragged. Have you eaten?"

She smiled and it made him feel better. "I was getting ready to order food up when you came. *You came.*" She blinked away tears and he pulled her legs up into his lap.

"I did. I will always be here for you. Get that through your head right now." He leaned to grab the room service menu and flip through it. She needed taking care of and he was going to do just that.

"Anything good?"

She nodded. "Get the pie. I had the lemon meringue last night."

He grinned. "All right. What else?"

"I want the chicken and potatoes. They're real, not that powdered stuff. A bowl of soup, whatever they have is fine. And pie."

He called it all up, adding the French dip for himself with some extras and a few beers.

"They said about half an hour."

"Erin said to me, when she dropped me at the airport, that secrets hurt. And that it was time I let go of the stuff that was hurting me. You've been patient, letting me tell you on my own terms. You can't know what that means to me."

"I love you. There's nothing else I can do. It means so much that you'd share. I know it's not easy." He took her hand.

"It's not pretty either."

"It's not on you. You understand that, right? The stuff that hap-pened to you when you were growing up was not your fault. I don't think that and I want you to stop it too."

"I'm trying. So when I was ten or so, my mom came back to town and we made a go of it for a while. She had a job at the grocery store.

We had a little one-bedroom apartment over the hardware store. It wasn't fancy, but she was with me.

"And then she just wasn't. She didn't come home. Two days later she hadn't come home and we were out of food and her boss came over and saw I was on my own and they called child services. Again. They put me in foster care, this time in the next town over, Harperville. A few months later my aunt, my mom's sister, came to the school and told me my mother had overdosed and died. I didn't know enough then to ask any real questions. I just knew for sure that I'd never have a home. My great-grandmother was too sick to take me in and as I said, my other relatives wouldn't. Later, when I was sixteen or so, I confronted her— my aunt, I mean. I wanted details. It had been a . . . rough time for me. She told me my mother had died after selling herself for a dirty bag of heroin. That they'd found her body in the gutter where she'd belonged."

He sucked in a breath, trying hard not to let his rage show. She didn't need that.

"So you know, I came out to L.A. that next year after I'd saved up every cent I could, believing my mother had abandoned me. Believing no one wanted me." Emotion made her voice thick. He squeezed her hand tight. *He* wanted her.

"So two days ago one of my foster fathers came into the shop. He'd been looking for me—and I'll tell you that story after we eat. Anyway, he and his wife had been looking for me. But first, they found my mother. Who wasn't dead at all, but in a mental institution where she'd been for years."

Her voice broke.

"I thought I'd cried it all out of my system. God knows I've probably gotten dehydrated from it since I found out. Anyway, she's had a lifetime of trouble. They knew it, Jonah. My family knew she was alive and they told me she was dead and had abandoned me. I don't

understand why. Anyway, Mike and Bonnie visited her a few weeks
ago. They had told her I was dead too. Back when I was fifteen. I can't
even tell you. She tried to kill herself then. And several times since.
That's why she's here. She's a self-harm risk and I guess the usual treat-
ments don't work on her. She asked them to find me and tell me she
was alive and wanted to see me."

He blew out a breath. "Wow. That's some soap opera shit right
there."

"I know. I've been reeling. Everything I thought about my childhood, well, it's not the same. None of it is what I thought and I don't
know how to process it. So I've been avoiding processing it. I feel like
if I really face it I'm going to fall the fuck apart. What if *I'm* crazy too?
Schizophrenia runs in families. I've got a family full of addicts and
fuckups. What if it's in me right now, just waiting?"

"Have you talked with a doctor about it?" He kept his voice calm,
knowing she was scared.

"Not yet. I had to go through a background check to see her. I'm
meeting with her doctor first, before they let me meet with her. But I
don't know that it'll be the right time to ask about that. Or even if I'm
ready to know yet."

A knock sounded the arrival of the food, which was set up quickly.
He pointed a finger at the table and she rolled her eyes, but got up and
moved over, settling as she sipped the tea and began to eat.

"When I was fourteen I'd been placed, temporarily, in a far-removed
family member's home. It was through family court. They really only
wanted me for the money and, well, apparently for other things. That's
where . . . well, the place I got the worst of the bad dreams from."

"Where you were raped."

She flinched but nodded. "A teacher at school noticed the big
change in my behavior and called my case worker. They removed me
the next day and put me in a halfway house."

He knew enough about the system to know quite often halfway

houses were the last resort placements for older kids who had been in the system long term and for kids with criminal and severe behavioral issues.

"And then the Thompsons came along. I was sent there and they gave me my own room. They had a daughter who was nearly two years older than I was. They were so good to me. Bonnie—that's Mrs. Thompson—was a nurse. She had this way about her. They left me alone when I needed it. Let me lock my door when I went to bed. After eight months there, the longest placement I'd ever had, they asked me if I wanted to live with them permanently. I was going to have a family. My god. You have no idea what that felt like. I had a family. People who wanted me. So they started the process. My biological family were pretty much like yeah whatever, take her off our hands. But it's a long process. My grades improved. I made friends. I had a cat named Ginger. For the first time in my entire life I was happy every single day."

She ate for a while as dread tore at his insides.

"You don't have to say anything else."

"Yes, yes, I do. So Missy, that was their daughter, she was a cheerleader and had convinced them to let her go to cheerleading camp at a nearby private college. It was a summer program, the students slept in the dorms with their teammates. She had classes and stuff on tumbling and that cheerleadery jazz.

"And one day she didn't come back from dinner. They ate in the residential dining halls but it wasn't that far from their dorms or practice field.

"For two weeks they combed the area. They waited for a ransom call. They went on television begging for her safe return. They found her body. It was bad. She'd been tortured." She had to stop, putting her fork down and mopping her face with her napkin. "What had been done to her, well, no one should have to have endured it. The Thompsons just sort of checked out. One day, a month after they found her, Mrs. Thompson picked me up from school, took me to the hospital's social worker and said the state had to take me back. They weren't going to adopt me. They weren't going to keep me as a foster placement. She gave me all the money in her wallet, hugged me and walked away."

He had to stand, the rage pulsing through him was nearly too much. He clenched and unclenched his fists.

"These people are scum, Raven. They had no right!"

"No, they didn't. But they lost a child. I heard over the next year that their marriage had broken up and they'd lost their home and had moved away. I'd heard here and there that Mike had developed a problem with alcohol. That next placement was my last. I'd been saving up money since I got my first job at fifteen. I was going to buy a car with it. Such a normal thing and something else that I'd never have in Happy Bend or anywhere else in Arkansas. A few months later I packed up everything I owned, which filled one suitcase. I left my sketchbooks in my great-grandmother's garage and she sent them to me a year later. I never looked back. Except for when I came back to her funeral. When my aunt told my mother I was dead, she used the story of Missy's death. She didn't just tell my mother I was dead, Jonah, she told her I'd been tortured, raped and murdered. I will not rest until that's been dealt with."

"Jesus, baby. I'm so sorry."

She shrugged. "I've never told that story to anyone. It's been like a sore in my belly for so long it's been what I thought was normal. But Mike Thompson came to me at the shop. He apologized. He and Bonnie have been looking for me for ages. I have closure on that. I needed that. And I have it and it's been important. He flew out here with me. They live just about an hour away. They invited me to stay with them. But I had to do it without them. But thank God I don't have to do it without you. That is if you're still, you know, if you still want to be with me after I told you all that stuff."

He knelt in front of her chair and hugged her, his face buried in her chest. "I love you so fucking much it should be scary. I wanted to be with you before I knew this. I want to be with you now. I want to make this better for you and I can't. I want to punch people and sue them and make them sorry they treated you so poorly."

She hugged him back, her heart pounding against where he laid his head on her chest. "I'm a terrible person, but that makes me feel better. Jonah?"

He pulled back and looked up into her face. "Yes, baby?"

She smiled. "I love it when you use endearments. If you tell anyone, I'll only deny it. I love you too. I don't know that you're getting as good a deal as I am. But there is it. I'm so weary. You make me less so."

He grinned. "That's a pretty damned good deal. I'll take it."

They talked for a while longer. He watched her while she ate, making sure she cleaned her plate. Though she was nauseated from the telling, she had been letting herself get run down and she needed the energy and calories. It also made her feel better that he was there to frown at her and tip his chin at the next bite to be taken.

"I'm going to take a shower. Why don't you get snuggled into bed?"

"Sadly, these showers are of the very small variety or I'd offer to get your back."

"You're here. I'm here. That's what matters. I'll let you get my back when we get home. I'll join you for a snuggle when I'm done."

She went into the bedroom adjoining the smaller common space and pulled the blankets back. Two weeks ago, while staying at his house, she'd stopped locking the door. The first night she'd been awake pretty much the whole time. Dreams intruded when she did get to sleep. But the next night she was there, she tried it again and that time she slept.

She hadn't told him because she didn't want to get his hopes up that she'd be able to transition into his room soon. And she was tired of it. Tired of the things that had sort of frozen her life into a ball of anxiety. She wanted to be with him and so she pushed herself bit by bit, and the last time she'd stayed at his house, right before Carrie had come, she'd slept with her door open a crack.

And she'd slept all night long.

So when he came out of the shower, she patted the mattress as she drank in the sight of him. So masculine, even in sleep pants and a T-shirt. He smiled and slid in with her, pulling her close.

"Thank you for coming. I know I said it before, but I want to say it again. It means so much to me."

"I'm here for you. Carrie would have wanted me to come to you, you know. She likes you. She'd be heartbroken to imagine you were here alone all so I could have taken her out to dinner and a movie or whatever."

"Family is important, Jonah. Carrie doesn't need to know about this. All she ever needs to know about me is that I value your commitment to her and that I will always expect you to put her first. That's your job. And memories are made from dinners and movies. That's more important and you can't say a damned thing that would make me disagree."

"Stubborn." He ran his fingertips over her collar.

"I have to be to keep up with you. I had to take it off. At the airport I mean."

"The collar?"

"Yes. I'm sorry."

He laughed, pulling her even closer, which was just fine with her. He gave off heat like a furnace and he made her feel safe. Plus he smelled good.

"Don't apologize. It's not because I think you need it to remember what we have. Also it's the airport, you have to do it and I certainly don't expect you to do otherwise."

"It helped. The collar, I mean. When I felt alone or overwhelmed I'd touch it. Or when I was lost, it would be there against my skin. Reassuring. Strong. Like you."

He hummed, kissing the top of her head. "I like that. You should sleep. I'll leave when you fall asleep and lock the door. There's a bed in the couch. I'll be fine."

"The last eight times I slept at your house I started experimenting. At first I'd unlock the door when I woke in the middle of the night. Then I left it unlocked, which was hard, I admit. But then I left it unlocked and slept just fine. The last time I left the door open a crack. I want you in here with me. I can't promise I'll be able to do it, but I want to try. I want to sleep next to you. I need that. Especially tonight."

He moved so that she was on her back and he loomed over her. "Really?" He kissed her softly.

"Yeah."

"Then I'll have to make you nice and tired, good and relaxed, so you'll sleep well." The flash of that grin made things tighten up. Her nipples, her clit. Her skin was extra sensitive with him so close.

"Yay."

He kissed her again. A slow, deep, meandering kiss. His tongue slid over her bottom lip just before he nipped it. She moaned and wrapped her arms around his shoulders. Holding on.

He slowly unbuttoned her shirt, petting over her skin, bringing her to life in a way only he could. She gave over to him immediately because things were better when she did. Because he took away all the anxiety and worry and he made it all right.

"Love these tits." He pinched her nipples, tugged at the hoops in them until she writhed into his touch.

She managed to get the muscle control to grab the hem of his shirt and pull it off, tossing it away somewhere. She hissed when she rose up and they were skin to skin. The heat of him was so good.

She licked over his chest. "I can pierce you. If you like." She ran the edge of her teeth over his left nipple, the one he favored. The one that made his cock jump in her hand where she'd shoved it down the front of his sleep pants.

"Yeah?"

"Mm. Yes."

She ran her nails down his sides. She still had one last session to do on his back to finish up the shading and he'd be done. She was careful not to dig her nails into the muscles there, though she wanted to. Though he made a rather delightful groan when she did. He needed to be totally healed first.

Then she'd scratch her nails down his back so he'd know he was all hers.

"That smile you're wearing strikes fear in my heart."

She laughed, her head tipping back, exposing her throat to his hot, openmouthed kisses. "I was just thinking about how I'm going to mark your back up with my nails so no other ladies can get a taste. You're all mine."

He laughed, nipping the delicate skin of her neck. "I'm all yours already. Not like any other ladies will be around me with my shirt off to see anyway."

"Oh, well done. I like that answer."

"It's true." He reared up long enough to pull her pants and underwear off and kick his own free as well. When he returned he lay on her, all his weight for a short period of time. Skin to skin. Both groaned at how good it was.

"I never understood what it was to be like this with anyone. I heard people talk about the deep connection they had while they were having sex and I thought it was bullshit. Sex is great and you can feel close to your partner, sure, but this? What I feel every time I touch you? Nothing else compares."

He kissed her long and slow again, seducing her as she let herself fall under his spell. She was safe with him. No matter how much he excited her or stoked her desire, she could trust him with the barest parts of herself.

He licked her nipples and she sucked a breath, arching into his mouth as his hands found her hips and held her just where he wanted her to be.

He nibbled and licked as she was helpless to do anything but hold on. So she did.

"I need you a whole lot right now," she managed to say. "I want you inside."

He pulled back enough to look into her face. "Hands and knees."

She rolled and got into position. Once he got behind her, she leaned into his thighs because that's how he liked it. He thrust into her pussy so fast she nearly choked when she sucked in a breath.

He kept a pace that pleased him. He wanted to pull out and make her suck his cock before he let her come. He wanted to come on her tits and make her finger herself to orgasm. So much. But she'd opened herself up, told him some things that left him sure he needed to keep those things on deck for another time. That night he wanted to possess her, to let her know she was his to protect and cherish. It's what they both needed.

She was so tight and wet around him as she thrust back in the small amount of space the position allowed. She essentially bounced back on his cock, her ass against his thighs.

"You're so sexy." He ran his hands all over her back and hips before he reached around to take her breasts in his hands. Pulling and pinching those nipples wearing the hoops he'd given her.

"Mmmm."

He smiled as he leaned forward to kiss her shoulder. "Make yourself come around my cock," he whispered against her skin.

She whimpered, changing her balance to slide a hand between her legs. He felt the brush of her fingertips where he thrust into her cunt. A feather of a touch before her hand moved up to her clit. She tightened around him, making him see stars for a brief moment.

He nibbled over her back. Nipping here and here. Hard enough to leave a mark where only he would see. Their secret. She arched on an indrawn breath.

"Greedy."

She raced to climax as he tried to hold his own back. He wanted a long slow fuck but she took it to a frenzy because he needed her with such an intensity he couldn't see straight. He sped up his thrusts and she pressed back against him, taking him even deeper.

Her inner walls began to ripple around him, her cunt squeezing, super heating, so fucking wet as she finally exploded. There was nothing he could do but go with her, follow her into climax as he whispered her name and took her to the bed, wrapping his arms around her and whispering that he loved her.

21

She hated the way the hospital smelled. It was more than the general antiseptic of a regular hospital. There was something else. It made her sad.

They had gone through two doors, acquired special visitor passes, had emptied their pockets and their belongings had been placed in a plastic bag to be kept at the nurse's station. They'd told her the day before to leave her purse at home, so she had.

Her hands shook, but Jonah just reached out and took one. "You okay?"

Raven shook her head. "No. But I'm better off than she is."

They went through another set of doors and were led into a room with a few pieces of furniture. There were big windows, but they were safety glass and bars held anyone several inches away from their surface.

"I'm going to go get Lena. Do you have any questions before I go?" The orderly who'd accompanied them was a pretty big guy, probably in his forties.

"Is there something I should avoid talking about? I don't know what to say."

He smiled. "You're her daughter. She's been talking about it all day long. She's having a good day today. Just tell her about your life. Everything will be all right. I'll be here the whole time. Over in that corner. If she gets excitable, and I don't think she will, but if she does, I'll step in and if we can't get her calm again, I'll take her back to her room." He paused. "The medications she's been on . . . she'll most likely be heavier than you last remember her. She also has some tremors in her face. Namely her mouth. The older drugs had more side effects than they do now. I just wanted to let you know. She's not in pain or anything."

They sat at a table, Jonah at her side, and they waited.

It wasn't long before the door on the far side of the room opened and the orderly led her mother in. Raven hoped she hid her shock well. Her mother was still recognizable, but she was heavier, yes. Her once glorious deep black hair was short now, shot with gray.

Raven stood and moved toward her mother.

"Beautiful Raven-Haired Baby Girl." Her mother used Raven's full, given name and then she opened her arms. "Got a hug for your momma?"

She went into the hug and tried very hard not to cry. And failed.

"Shhh. Everything's gonna be all right now." Lena patted her arm and they walked over to the table together. "Sit now and introduce me to your young man."

Jonah stood and took Lena's hand, kissing it in chivalrous fashion. Lena blushed.

"Ma'am, I'm Jonah Warner. Not so young, but certainly Raven's. I'm very pleased to meet you."

"You're alive. My lord, girl. For so long." Her mother had to stop speaking, dabbing her eyes with a handkerchief. Raven made a mental note to buy her mother some more and send them. They had said she could send care packages.

"I know. But I'm here now. I missed you so much."

"Dolly, I'm sorry. So very sorry I wasn't there. I've been sick a long time. I kept losing my way. Heard voices. I was afraid I'd hurt you. I got arrested and they put me in a mental ward. That's when they finally found out about the schizophrenia. And then I tried to get better. Sometimes the pills worked. But before they'd let me out, they wouldn't work no more. And then my sister Lorene came and told me you were dead! I lost myself for a long time. Can't say I cared much about getting better then. And those nice people came. Mike and Bonnie. They told me you was alive and that my sister lied. I can't imagine why she did that, Raven. My goodness, you're a beauty. Like Mama Eula in her day."

Eula was Raven's great-grandmother. "She sure did love you. I think they lied to her too, Momma. I don't know why they did it either. But I'm going to go down there and find out. Lorene is still alive and living in Happy Bend." And she was due a reckoning.

"She ain't worth your time. Don't you let her get you all worked up."

"Answers need to be had. But never you mind. Now that I got you back, I'm not getting worked up."

Lena looked to Jonah. "You be sure of that. I don't want her down there near my people alone."

Jonah nodded, solemn. "Yes, ma'am."

They talked for the entire hour allotted for the visit and Raven promised to return the following day for another visit. She could stay a week or so and she planned on it. And on her way back home she was going to pay a visit to her aunt in Happy Bend.

Jonah walked her out, an arm around her shoulder.

"I figure I can visit her once every two months or so. Write her. They said I could. I've been without her a really long time. It's strange to think I have a mother. I was so used to being alone. And now I have her. And you. God, next thing I'll start being nice."

He laughed, pulling her closer. "Well, let's not get ahead of our-selves."

"I know you need to get back to Seattle." She moved around their suite, putting things away, organizing them. He'd figured out some time before that it had to be connected with a childhood of total chaos. She liked things where she knew they'd be. Wanted to know they were in their place.

So he tried to make that easy for her, though he had to admit to being messy at times to watch her get grumpy and then smooth out as she worked. It made them both feel better, to click. She needed to fix things just like he did. So he gave her things to fix and when she did, it fixed him too.

"I have the time. I'm not leaving you here." He worked at his lap-top at a makeshift office space he'd created at the table. He could totally work from there and so it wasn't necessary for him to leave until two days from then. After they'd gone to Happy Bend to deal with her bitch of an aunt.

Even if he'd had to back out of his cases, he would have rather done that than have her face any of this on her own. The week with her mother had strengthened her in several ways, but it wore on her. Her mother was not okay. Her medications were stabilized, yes, but she'd lived a long time with a great deal of upheaval and it had taken a toll. Her physical health was also in bad shape. Her liver was shot from having been exposed to years of the medications she'd been on. Her heart was bad. Raven wanted to move her up to Seattle, to a private facility. He'd secretly looked it up and would take care of the costs himself, though he knew it would be a big fight. That kind of care was ridiculously expensive. But if that's what she wanted and if the doctors approved it, he'd make it happen.

Raven had endured enough heartbreak for multiple lifetimes. He'd do his damndest to spare her any more. Even if she got testy.

But he didn't think it would come to that anyway. Lena had a life there in Oklahoma City, such as it was. She had physicians who knew her and who she knew and trusted. She had relationships with some of the other patients and the orderlies and other staff she dealt with. It was her life and he knew, deep down, that Raven knew it too.

He'd let her work it through and be there every step of the way.

His mother had checked in several times. The way Raven had backed Liesl at Thanksgiving had forged a bond between the two. He was grateful for it and Raven seemed to be as well. He had only given a small bit of information to his family, not wanting to share until Raven was ready. They knew she was dealing with a family health crisis here, but not anything more specific.

"You have a law practice, Jonah. It's not like you can just up and take a week off without batting an eye. I don't want you blowing off work for me."

"We've gone over this. I'm not blowing anything off. I'm working several hours a day here remotely. I don't have any appearances for two weeks anyway. The motions I needed filed are easily filed through my staff. That's why I have a staff. My father is a far better attorney than I am; if there's any problem, he'll handle it."

"Have you noticed how you argue with me as easily as breathing now? Think of all the color and adventure I've added to your life."

He looked up from his screen and smiled at her, often surprised at the things she said. At how she got him and teased. Her way of connecting.

"I've told you many times, you're beyond awesome. And you have a nice rack."

"Always a plus." Her phone rang and she answered.

"Hey, Brody." She went to sit near the sliding glass doors, staring out into the gray.

"How are things? How's your mom?"

"I'm fine. She's okay. She's tired a lot. They say it's normal for her though. How's the shop?"

"Fine. We had three people call in this week to volunteer to fill in for you. You have a lot of friends."

She started to cry. She sort of hated that part. After not crying for years and years, she couldn't seem to find a way to get all her emotions in check. The day before she burst into tears when they were in a diner and they ran out of cherry pie.

"Aw, sweetheart, it's okay. I told you to make you happy, not upset you."

Jonah moved nearer, his laptop on his legs. He worked to be close to her, understanding she didn't want to be petted right then, but needed his nearness.

"It's not you. It's all this stuff going on. My mother's doctor said it was normal for people who are dealing with this stuff be emotional. I'm glad you're covered. I feel terrible leaving you in the lurch."

"You shut up. Jesus. It's a fucking tattoo shop. I can limit hours or hire extra help, which I have. What you're dealing with is way more important, so stop or I'll be mad and sic Erin on you."

She smiled, taking the tissue Jonah handed her.

"She okay? Alexander? Martine? Rennie? Poppy?"

"Everyone is fine. The kids miss you a lot. They've all gotten used to having you around so don't go running off."

"I won't. Seems I've sort of hooked up with a dude there and I have a mortgage and a life and all."

Jonah made a grumbly sound of assent and it soothed her. He was good at that. Soothing.

"We'll be back day after tomorrow."

"Don't you dare come back to work for another two days after that. You got me? Can we do anything to help? All you need to do is ask."

"I know, which is really all I need. Thank you."

"You got it. You know where we are. I'll see you soon."

He hung up and she did too before putting her phone on the table and leaning back, tucking her feet beneath her. She needed to get a decent night's sleep. They were waking up early and driving to Happy Bend first thing. She was going to confront her aunt and get some answers.

22

She was up long before dawn. She'd tried to go back to sleep, but that hadn't worked so she'd carefully gotten out of bed and moved into the main room. The hotel had a perfunctory gym so she got dressed, dashed off a note to Jonah in case he woke up, and headed down.

The nice thing about hotels at four in the morning is that they're deserted. So she didn't have to share the machines with anyone as she warmed up or even when she set the treadmill. She hated running. With all her heart. But it was a good way to deal with all this shit in her head.

That's where he found her. Her hair in a ponytail, swinging back and forth. Sweating. She wore headphones as she ran. He used to not know what from. But now that he did, it hurt him to see her this way, even as he knew it was necessary.

He got on the one next to hers and started slow. She ignored him awhile, starting and then relaxing when she saw it was him. Her gaze had been blurred. Most likely in the past where she was a helpless kid with no one to protect her.

The entire trip had been hard on her. When they got back home he planned to help her through with lots of sex, pampering, and a trip to Maui in January after Carrie went back to school. He'd have taken her off right then, but she was anxious to get back to the shop.

He'd spoken briefly to Brody and Erin a few days prior. Erin asked if Raven had gone to any counseling at all and he'd said no, though the doctor had suggested it quite strongly and had given her some basic coping advice. Raven didn't trust authority. And he understood why. But goddamnit, she needed someone to listen to her in a situation where she didn't have to worry over burdening someone with her past. He knew she held back with him, trying to protect him.

When he'd first met her he'd thought she was the strongest, most vibrant kick-ass bitch he'd ever laid eyes on. He *knew* that for sure now. So much pain to have shouldered, and she had, mostly alone for nearly all her life. Christ, if all she took away from that was a bitchy exterior and a habit of speaking before she thought about it, the world was lucky. He wasn't sure how she kept from going nuclear.

He saw on the monitor that she'd run eight miles. Jesus.

He'd only run two, but that was enough. He wanted her to stop. They had a day ahead of them. He turned his machine off and stepped to the rails and down.

She waved and he rolled his eyes, pulling her headphones off. "Come on. We have to check out and then stop and get breakfast before we get on the road."

She scowled and he grinned. "Oh the first scowl of the day and it's only five. We may just break records today."

She took her shower first, coming back out looking marginally better. She'd said her good-byes to her mother the day before so they could leave first thing.

"You're looking a little scruffy." She examined him, running her fingertips through the ends of his hair and then over his chin.

"I've been short on time to go to the barber."

She laughed. "Go. Sit over there. Let me take care of you for a change."

She fiddled around in the bathroom for a while, gathering things until she came out where he'd been waiting.

A bowl of steaming hot water, scissors, his razor, shaving cream and a healthy supply of towels and washcloths were what she placed on the table next to him.

"Don't worry, I'm a professional."

He raised a brow and she leaned forward to kiss his forehead. "I learned how to cut hair when I was eight. My aunt has a salon." She laughed. "'Salon' is not really the word for it. It's in her garage. She does it on the side and the cops ignore it because there are better things to do than roust an old bitch trying to make a buck."

"My delicate flower."

"Anyway, so I actually got a job at a real salon when I was fifteen." She ran her fingers through his hair, which was still wet. "I used to do the men's side of stuff. Which was practically nonexistent because you must know dudes in small towns like Harperville and Happy Bend go to the barber or let their wives or mothers get out the clippers. But occasionally I'd do a shave and a trim."

She draped a towel around his neck and massaged his scalp first, making him groan at how good it felt. "I can't believe you haven't done this yet. My god, this is fantastic."

"Less pain than three hours of me jabbing you with ink and needles, hm?"

"You have many talents."

She continued on, taking up the scissors and a comb. He heard the snip from time to time as she worked, moving around his body easily.

"You're going to be with me at Christmas."

"Um, that's an interesting thing to say while getting a haircut. That's a first."

"You're staying with me and we'll have dinner at my house. Just me, you and Carrie. On Christmas Eve anyway. Then my parents have a thing on Christmas Day. A buffet. There are card games and all that sort of thing."

"Oh delightful. Will Beth be there? I haven't been kicked in the face in ages."

He laughed. "I think she's afraid of you. Or maybe she respects you. Anyway, I promise to keep myself between you."

"For a lady like her, I think fear and respect are closely tied. You know I hate this stuff, right? All this family stuff and I have to be nice and not say the F word. It sucks."

"But I'm there. That's good right?"

"Maybe. Depends on how you compensate me later. I'm going to have to do something with Erin too. I try to avoid it by leaving town that week, but she sees blood in the water. Like a shark. She's not going to let go until I agree to go eat turkey or whatever. Probably sing carols and make crafts."

"You should stop acting like you hate it. I see how you are with those kids."

She tousled his hair, brushing the hairs away from his forehead. "You'll have to jump back in the shower to really get rid of all the little hairs. Now you need a shave."

She put a pillow back and he rested against it. "Tip your head back." And then she placed the warm towels on his face. "Relax, they're not hot enough to do you any real damage. You have very nice shaving gear. It's rare. Most dudes use electric shavers or soap."

"The shaving stuff was a gift from Carrie. I think she liked the brush so much she got the rest for that."

It felt good to be pampered and so he relaxed, his eyes closed, listening to the sound of her moving nearby. Then her fingers were back in his hair and against his scalp.

"It's the oil I use. It doesn't have a girly smell, I promise. It's good for you."

Like he'd argue? It felt so damned fabulous, her firm, strong knead-
ing touch against his scalp. He'd nearly fallen back to sleep by the
time she stepped back, removing the towel from his face.

"Now."

She climbed into his lap, wrapping her legs around his waist. "This
wasn't part of what I learned. Just in case you were worried. I like
being close and since we're all alone, I can get *really* close." Her smile
did wonders for his cock. Nearly as much as her pussy being so close
and her weight in his lap.

She lathered up the brush and made small circles on his face to
distribute it. Then she would shave a bit, clean off the razor in the bowl
of hot water, use another hot towel to clean him up and start again.
Over and over until he relaxed again, letting her minister to him.

He wasn't sure how long it lasted, only that when she managed to
get off his lap, he opened his eyes to find her smiling down at him.

"All done."

He moved to the bathroom to admire his haircut and the shave.
He did look much better and it was special because she'd done it
for him.

"I think you need to be my personal barber."

"Certainly the benefits would be better than the person down at
Gene Juarez. Or they'd better be." She smiled at his reflection and then
she got that look he loved so much. "Before you shower again, I should
make you extra dirty." She let her robe slip down off her shoulders to
pool at her feet and he was on her in two steps. He grabbed her, moving back to the bed quickly, falling to it still holding her.

He kissed her hungrily, taking in her taste, never getting enough.

She let him lead, though she wrapped her thighs around his waist
to hold him close. He had zero complaints with that. Then again, he
rarely did when it came to Raven.

"I want you to ride my cock awhile," he spoke, lips against her neck.
"And then, because I've wanted it for a while, you're going to suck me off."

She shivered and he pulled away to look into her face, needing to see if he'd pushed her too far. If it was too soon.

Clearly it wasn't either of those things. Her eyes had gone half-lidded and her mouth parted just slightly, lips wet from his kisses.

He rolled and she shimmied down. "I don't want you suited up." She slid her pussy over his cock. She'd very seriously asked him to take care of getting tested and he had. She had as well. The world had changed since he'd dated, before Charlotte. But it had been the right thing to do. "I'm on the pill and I want to feel you."

He nodded and she got to her knees to guide his cock to her pussy and slide down, achingly slow, onto him. Hot. So hot he nearly lost his mind and came right then. He got his control back as he held her, his fingers digging into the flesh and muscle at her hips.

He watched as she licked her fingers and played them against her nipples and then down to her cunt, spreading her labia open with one hand to expose her clit and that hoop.

"So fucking sexy."

She smiled, so open and beautiful, even as it was carnal.

And his.

"I love to see you like this. So sexy it blows my mind. There's never been anyone like you." He reached up, grabbing her breasts and tugging on her nipples. They'd left the chain behind, along with all his favorite toys. The last week had been exhausting for both of them. But they'd recharged each time they came back to this room and closed the door.

He learned more about her than how wet she got when he used the paddle or how she squirmed and sort of squealed when he plumped her clit between his fingertips while he fucked her from behind. This week she'd let him help. This week he'd learned about the spine of steel that made up the core of the woman he loved.

He didn't need chains or paddles for that part. But he sure as hell planned to use them when they got back home.

"Can I come?" Her voice halted a few times before she got all the words out. From the way her inner muscles fluttered he knew she was close.

"Yes."

She kept her gaze on his face but he alternated between her eyes and her fingers on her pussy. When she climaxed, her head tipped back as she groaned. A pretty flush worked up her body from her thighs, over her breasts, up her neck. Her nipples hardened impossibly more, darkened.

In one move he grabbed her hips and pulled her up, off his cock. "Suck me."

She lay on her back as he knelt next to her, running his cock over her mouth. She opened her eyes. Lazy, pleasure-stunned. Her tongue darted out, slid against his skin.

"Hands above your head. I'll put my cock where I want it to go."

She whimpered and obeyed, her gaze still on his face.

"Yes, like that." He tapped his cock against her lips and she opened, taking him inside. Christ, that was good. He pulled out again and tapped; she opened, repeating her last move. This time she turned her head a little to the side, taking him in deeper as he fucked her mouth in earnest.

Her fingers gripped the blankets as she moaned around him, bringing him right up to the edge. He let himself stay in her mouth a few strokes more before pulling back, chest heaving.

"Open your legs."

She did and he found his way to her cunt again, sliding into that glorious, slick heat. She wrapped those long legs around him again, holding on, rolling her hips to meet his thrusts.

He wasn't long for it and he dipped down to kiss her, tasting that combination of his skin and her honey. He groaned and came so hard his teeth seemed to tingle.

"We both need to shower now." He winked, kissing her again, helping her to stand.

"It's worth it."

23

He was used to her now, he realized. Used to her in his bed in the mornings. Used to her in his car as he drove. She was all slow sensuality, and now that they were back on her home turf, her accent had deepened, which he really found hot.

She'd pointed out that she knew the way to her tiny little hometown better than he would. And then he pointed out that she drove like a maniac and he liked being alive, thankyouverymuch. She'd snorted but got into the passenger side of the rental and curled up in her seat.

"Fine, but I get to control the music."

Which wasn't a hardship.

She hooked her iPod into the car stereo system and hit shuffle. Ahh, Frank Ocean. Just the thing as they hurtled down the road toward a childhood she'd packed away and left at the back of her closet nearly twenty years ago.

He didn't talk to fill the silence, instead he relaxed into the driver's seat and headed in the right direction. He'd been so patient with her it had been a total miracle to her. He didn't want anything from her but everything. As opposed to men and women wanting her body, or to control her choices, or to demand she unload her whys and why-nots on their schedule.

Jonah Warner wanted her totally and utterly. And that included her past. But he trusted her to reveal it in her time. A gift from this pushy, bossy man who drove, not because he was worried about how she drove, but because he liked to be in control. And she didn't care about driving one way or the other enough to tussle with him over it. It was most likely the sex chemicals still pulsing through her system. But whatever worked.

She hugged her coffee to her chest and sat back. Telling him things was good. For so long she'd held on to the details of her life because she hadn't trusted anyone to hear them and not judge her. Hell, they judged her before they heard the story, so why bother? The telling made her vulnerable and she'd never wanted to be at anyone's mercy ever again.

But with him there was an unburdening of sorts. He wanted to know her with such an intense hunger that was patient at the same time. And when she spoke the words, they had less power over her.

"My first vacation I didn't know what to do."

He kept his gaze on the road, but she knew he was listening.

"I had settled in Los Angeles enough to have rented a small mother-in-law apartment over a friend's garage. He and his wife were nice people. She, the wife, left me things on the porch. Bread sometimes. Extra fruit and vegetables from their backyard garden. They took a week's vacation every six months. To the Grand Canyon or to Glacier National Park. So I thought, why not me? I planned a road trip to San Francisco. Just a weekend's stay. I loved it. So I started doing them all the time. I loved all the places to stop. I loved all the pictures I could take. I'd stop at those stands . . . Have you been on the 5 from Los Angeles to the Bay Area?"

"Yes. I know which ones you mean."

"So I'd stop there and buy stuff and then when I got to San Francisco I'd have food for a while. I'd wander down to whatever part of the city I was staying in and I'd eat locally. And then I met Brody and Erin and I decided to road trip up to Seattle. Brody and I . . . well, you know. Anyway, I managed to house-sit and live in places before escrow closed and after the owners had moved out. Always in my own place. But I liked it up there."

"What did you think when you flew the first time?"

"I'm not a fan of airplanes. Enclosed spaces for really long periods of time when I can't stop and stretch my legs or whatever, it makes me nervous. Plus you know they're always watching you and so I have to be so careful and it takes the fun out of it. But I have to get on planes to go to Hawaii, so I deal. I just remember seeing all these families and wondering if they realized how awesome it was that they were giving their kids memories."

"Clearly you've never been on a road trip with a kid in the car." He chuckled.

"Oh, I know it's a pain sometimes and there's a lot of 'are we there yet' and stuff. But every time you go on vacation you're putting your energy onto your family or the people you travel with. You're stepping from your everyday life with these other people. Like now. I mean, this isn't a vacation, but I'm going to remember the time I've spent here with you. The way you look when you wake up in the mornings. How you talk to waitresses at diners. You're a flirt."

"Hey, my flirting got you pie when they thought they were out."

"That's true. You do make the ladies go googly-eyed. Anyway, travel is my way of saying a big old fuck-you to my childhood and all the people in that town who told me over and over again I'd never be anything."

She'd wondered for most of her life why they'd all treated her the way they had. What she'd done to them to engender such nastiness. She told herself it didn't matter, and by that point it didn't because she'd made something out of herself. Maybe because they were so shitty to her and she had to make a point.

Travel taught you things. Travel exposed you to new people and other perspectives. It broadened your life and helped you cope when things got complicated. It was one of her favorite things.

"Only now you don't travel to run away."

She paused for a long time, thinking about it. She'd wanted to deny it immediately. But really, he was right. Her lifestyle had been one of never staying in one place for very long. It had kept her from putting down roots and from getting run over by people.

"You're very smart."

"I am. I'm also really good at eating pussy."

She laughed, reaching out to run her hand down his arm. To reassure herself that he was really there. That he'd come for her. Because he loved her.

They stopped for lunch an hour or so out of Happy Bend and he noticed she only picked at her food. He'd considered suggesting she just leave it all alone. After all, she had a good life now. She knew where her mother was. What did it matter that her aunt had lied?

But it did matter and he understood that she needed the closure. She had a lot of rage inside. She'd dealt with a lot of the hurt and disappointment. Though he supported her getting therapy when they returned to process more. But the anger? He knew it was there. The questions regarding why they'd not only lied, but why they'd been so harsh with how they'd done it. All that remained and she needed to be an adult woman confronting her aunt about it.

"You're going to . . . The town isn't like a television small town." She'd gotten very quiet when they'd approached Happy Bend.

"I'm going to what?"

"Be horrified. I am. It was a shithole then; I imagine it's worse of a shithole now."

"Be that as it may, it has nothing to do with you. You have nothing to be ashamed of."

"Says the guy who grew up with a view of Lake Washington out his window every morning before he went to private school."

"Yes, I did have those things and I'm grateful for them. And yet, it has no bearing on you, or how I feel about you."

"I hate when you're calm when I'm being a dick."

He laughed. "I know, beautiful, that's why I'm doing it."

"I knew it! Needling me to get me riled up."

"You're hot when you're riled up." And she wasn't thinking too much on the mess they were about to face.

"Get off here. Head east when you get to those railroad tracks."

He followed her directions, getting farther and farther from the main roads.

"Pretty countryside around here." Lots of trees and green stuff.

"Yeah, that's one thing."

"Hey, it's going to be fine. I'm here. Always. Okay?"

She blew out a breath. "It's been a long time since I've been here."

"You have a home now. In Seattle. This is just a place you did some shitty years of your life when you had no other choice. It formed who you are now, but it doesn't need to have any more power over you than it already does. I know this is easy for me to say. But I believe in you, Raven. I know you better than any of these assholes ever will. You're worth a thousand of them. No matter how hard they tried to fuck you over. No matter why."

"Don't make me cry again or I'll be mad."

He turned his attention back to the road.

"About two miles or so. There'll be, or there used to be, a gas station at a crossroads. Country Road Fourteen. Go right."

She hadn't lied about how horrible the place was. Rusted-out cars and farm equipment overgrown by weeds and berry bramble. The houses were run-down. It was more than poverty; he'd seen plenty of that. It was that the place seemed to have a dearth of hope.

"Go up to Copperhead and take a right."

There was a tiny grocery store with a few cars in the parking lot. A post office.

"One stoplight. But we have a post office."

He followed the directions.

"Up there. The white house with the blue truck in the driveway. That's my aunt's place."

He turned around and parked so they could easily leave when the time came. She was pale, but otherwise holding it together.

"You don't have to do this, you know."

"I do. Now come around and open my door like a gentleman."

He grinned and kissed her quickly. "I love you."

She shook her head, wearing a confused smile. "I know and I really don't know why. But I love you too. So there's that."

He got out and opened her door. She wore jeans and a sweater with some sneakers. Nothing fancy. She'd said if she'd worn a dress her aunt would have accused her of putting on airs or thinking she was too good.

He kept a hand on the small of her back as they walked up to the front porch. A woman appeared there, one who bore a strong resemblance to Lena.

"What do you want?"

"Hello, Aunt Lorene."

The older woman peered through the screen door with a start. "Raven?"

"Yes. This is Jonah. I'd like to talk to you."

Suspicion was already on her face and it only doubled. She didn't open the door.

"You do? What about then?"

"Wouldn't you rather take this inside instead of on the porch?" Jonah asked smoothly.

Raven wanted to laugh because the situation was so ridiculous she had to. But she kept it together.

"You're just fine where you are. Why are you here?"

"I've been to Oklahoma City. To see my mother."

Even through the screen door Raven noted how much more pale her aunt got.

"Why did you lie? To me and to her?"

"I don't know what you're talking about."

"Sure you do. You told me she had died. Of a drug overdose. You told me she died in the gutter."

She clenched her fists and reminded herself she was better than her instincts. Better than the desire to rip that door off the rusty hinges and beat the hell out of this woman who'd harmed her so much. "And then you told her I'd been murdered. Me, instead of poor Missy Thompson. She tried to kill herself multiple times after that. I know you know that. Why?"

"I don't have to say anything to you."

Raven took a step closer. "No, you don't. But you will because you owe me that much. You made this mess and you'll tell me why."

"I did it for your own good." Lorene's voice was small, petulant.

"Come again?"

"She couldn't take care of you. She done left you how many times? It was best that you just stopped believing she'd come back and save you. You needed to accept your place in life and you wouldn't until you had no other options."

Jonah put an arm around her, restraining her, but also comforting her.

"My place in life? What place is that?"

"She thought she could go off to the city and be something else.

But she was a country girl born and bred. She thought she was better than all her kin and look where it got her!"

"Look where your behavior got me! I never lived in a single place longer than six months from the time I was three until I was fourteen years old. I was raped. I was beaten up. Not a single person but Mama Eula ever told me I was loved. How is that my place?"

"Reaching above yourself would only bring you heartache."

"I ate heartache breakfast, lunch and dinner for years of my life. Years."

"I didn't know about your cousin. I didn't know he'd hurt you. I just . . . Do you want to be like her? Like me?"

Raven scrubbed her hands over her face. "Like her how?"

"You ran off too."

"I did, and by God, it was hard. It was lonely and hard. It's been lonely and hard for a long time. But I got away and things did get better."

"She never could take care of you. All she did was make you sad."

"It wasn't her fault! She's mentally ill. Chemicals in her brain. What's your excuse?"

Lorene stepped back like Raven had slapped her. "I never had any kids. I saw it with my aunt too. With my sister. With our momma. I think, when I was about seventeen and I had a burst appendix, they tied my tubes. It was for the best. So I couldn't pass it on."

None of this was what she'd expected.

"You're telling me you were sterilized without your permission because mental illness runs in the family?"

"Your precious Mama Eula! She knew it could happen to me like it happened to your mom. So she agreed to have it done. She told me later it was for my own good."

"How long, Lorene? How long are we going to keep secrets? No one should have done that to you. You were seventeen."

"Couldn't have afforded any babies no how. Never did find myself a decent husband. What did I have to offer any kid? Look what I did to you."

"You didn't have to! You could have taken me in. You didn't have to tell me my mother had died. You didn't have to tell her I'd died. I don't understand. Why do you hate me so much? What have I ever done to make you all hate me so much?"

It was only Jonah's arm around her shoulders that kept her from crying. That kept her from falling to her knees and weeping for all the lies, for all everyone had lost, and for what?

"I don't hate you, child. I never did. You was a beautiful little girl. Smart. But that sort of thing gets a woman picked on in our world. Toughening you up was a favor. Can't you see that? You get to be eighteen and you're a tough old bitch and you won't get beaten up by life. You won't get pregnant at fourteen like your momma did. This is a hard life we got here. Pretty girls don't last long. I did what I knew to do.

"I told your momma you was dead for the same reason. She'd done enough damage to you. She needed to let go and stop messin' up your life. I knew she wouldn't unless she thought she had nothing to go back to. I talked to Mama Eula and she agreed."

Raven gripped her stomach. "Mama Eula knew? She knew my mother was alive? Knew you'd told her I had died?"

Lorene's laugh was rueful. "I hate to go burstin' your bubble, girl, but where did you think we got to be the way we are now? She mighta softened up some in her later years, but your great-grandma was just as nasty as your grandmama was. Our women ain't no good. Not a one of us."

"*I'm* good. Did any of you ever stop to think about that? About how maybe I could have broken that cycle and made things better for all of us?"

"I'm sorry. I really truly am. I did all I knew how to do."

Raven stepped back on the creaky old porch. She had no words left, so she turned after pulling all the cash she had on her out of her pocket and placing it on a nearby chair.

"I don't need your charity!"

"Yes, you do. Take it."

She walked away, knowing she'd never be back again.

24

She walked back into the shop and everyone looked up, smiling at the sight of her. She didn't quite know what to do with it so she ignored it, waving and pretending it was any other day.

"Back to work, losers." She turned back to Maggie, who was the appointment book mistress. "What's on my schedule today?"

"I didn't know you were back today. Everything okay?"

"If you figure out the answer to that one, let me know. However, I'm good to ink some people up."

"All righty then. You're wide open, schedule wise. You can take walk-ins if you like. Been pretty quiet though."

"I know I told you not to come back until tomorrow." Brody approached and gave her a hug. "It's good to see you."

"Good to be seen, my man. I was bored at home. I've been in a hotel room for a week. I needed to get out."

"Where's Jonah?"

"Off rattling people and being bossy with the law, I wager. He had a week off and all his control-freaky ways got backed up."

"That doesn't sound like a complaint."

"Yes, well. He's all right. Enough mushy stuff. I'm back and I figured you might need some help around here."

"Which is good because I am starving and was just about to escape for lunch." Erin walked up to her and gave her a hug. "You're back. And you didn't tell me. I would frown at you, but you were gone for a week so my frowning muscles are all out of practice."

Seeing Erin filled Raven with joy. She smiled. "Pizza?"

"Yes, that'll do nicely."

"All right, well, I'm back and now I'm going out for a two-hour lunch."

Brody snorted. "Good. You have appointments. *Tomorrow.* I want to catch up though."

She nodded. "We will. Thank you, Brody."

He tipped his chin. "Any time."

Funny thing was, she knew he was telling the truth.

They headed off to Zeek's, a local favorite. Once they'd ordered and gotten settled, Erin's expression turned serious.

"So?"

"I don't know if I can even answer that. My mother . . . well, she's messed up. Her physical health is worse than her mental health. I want her here, but she's better off there. All her internal organs are crap from the meds and from her alcohol abuse to self-medicate. She has doctors she trusts there. She's hooked into a system that can help her."

Raven sighed. "My coming to visit her was good and all, but it upset her too on many levels." She blew out a breath. "She feels guilty when she's lucid. I don't want that. You know? It's too late for that. She did what she did and it sucked, but it's not like she did it on purpose. So guilt is wasted. I tried to talk with her about that and I think she might forgive herself someday. But I don't know how many somedays she has left."

She sipped her soda, the sugary caffeine helping a little.

"And I feel guilty too. I wasn't there all these years. Having me probably made things worse for her. I don't know what to do. I can't walk away. I can't bring her here. I feel like I should move there."

"For what? I get it, she's your mother and if you were close and if you could help her, then I could understand it. But your life is here. You just put down roots here. I don't want you to go. I know that's selfish. But I love you. You're my best friend and you're finally here to be with me and my kid and damn it." Erin tried not to cry, and it made Raven feel so much better.

"I'm terrible for wanting to stay here. But I do."

"No, you're not. Don't you dare feel guilty for finally building a life! You'll visit her often. As often as you can without upsetting her schedule."

"It's like five and half hours if I can keep the connections close. That means I can visit her once every few weeks. Jonah said he'd come with me as often as I liked if we did it over a weekend." She shrugged. "I want to do the right thing, Erin."

"Oh, sweetie, you are. Don't you see that? Just at least see how things go over the next few months. See how she adjusts. See how *you* adjust. You deserve some good mental health for a change too."

"Maybe."

"I'm glad Jonah was there."

Raven looked to Erin. "He saved me. I can't even begin to tell you how much his being there just made it easier, better. I could take that next step. Open that next door. He managed me like the bossy guy he is, but he also protected me. Let me work shit out on my own when I needed to. He's changed everything. I never thought . . . ever that there'd be what he is to me."

Erin smiled. "Yeah. I so totally understand."

"He's so good to me. He leaves me alone when I need it and when I don't, well, he's all up in my face, poking around, making me confront stuff. Aggravating but . . . he gets me. He doesn't judge me. I never anticipated him. He was awesome with all the medical stuff. He did all this research about the system. It's so complicated and if I take her out of the place there, she loses so much. I don't want that. But I wouldn't have known really, not if he hadn't done all the heavy lifting."

"No one's ever done it for you before, have they? I mean, I had Brody and Adrian before Todd and Ben. I had help, but for so very long I was on my own and I did my heavy lifting. I needed to, to get through stuff. But sometimes when I feel like this stuff will never end and my arms are so tired, well, Todd or Ben come in and take over. They make it all right. Alexander is growing up with them as examples of what it means to be a man. I'm so lucky for that."

"I never had a lot of men around, you know? The ones I did were assholes. Or so distant and distracted they weren't really a factor. My mother never had boyfriends and the ones my other relatives had were utter cockbags. And then Brody of course, and I knew there were guys out there who were good. But he wasn't mine. He was never mine. Jonah is mine. More than that? I'm his. I've never belonged to anyone before. I'm not a burden. Or a responsibility. I never knew I could feel this way."

She dabbed her eyes quickly. "Also, I cry a lot lately. Just warning you. They say it's because I'm dealing with all this stuff at once after pushing it aside for so long. Her doctor—my mom's doctor, I mean— he gave me a few names of people up here who have specialty practices. You know with people who have dealt with what I have. I may call one of them."

Erin reached out to squeeze her hand. "Do whatever you need to do. You are surrounded by people who love you and will help however they can. I'm so happy to see you like this. Vulnerable. Not hiding it, but accepting it. This shit you've endured hurts and you can admit it. It's odd to say that makes me happy, but you know what I mean. What happened with your aunt?"

Raven told her about the visit.

Erin sat back in her seat, eyes wide. "I'm astounded."

"You and me both. I don't know what to think. I'm still angry, but she's a victim too. Clearly I have mental health issues in my DNA and that freaks me out too. But the doctors were pretty good about talking to me regarding risk factors. Her doctor told me I was the most all-right person he'd met who dealt with all the stuff I had. Of course he's surrounded by mental patients, so."

"It runs in families, right?"

Raven nodded. "Yeah. The risk factor is right about one percent. If one parent has it, your risk goes up to about six percent. I'm scared. I'm scared I'll end up like her."

"But you haven't. I did some research while you were gone. You know, so I could understand. It says most people have onset of symptoms in their late teens or early twenties. You're an old hag. Knocking on forty."

Raven took a deep breath, relaxing a little more. "Yes. That's true. They have this screening test thing. I mean they can't do a blood test or anything, but there are warning signs. I'm a crazy bitch, but not like that, they don't think. Anyway. Jonah is gently pushing me to see someone. Just to talk it through. He's probably right. He usually is. Hell, this schizophrenia thing is at the bottom of my worry list at this point. All this stuff with my family, with my past . . ."

She began to eat once the pizza arrived.

"I used to have it all in my head. Who I blamed. Who was right, who was wrong. But that's all jumbled up now. My great-grandmother, who was this rock to me, well, she's not so pure now. And what, if anything, does that mean? My aunt isn't a villain, or rather she is, but not solely. I don't know. I don't know if I ever will. And I have to figure out if I can be all right with never knowing."

"Jesus. You never do anything halfway, do you?"

"Poor Jonah, he thought he was getting a hot chick in bed and he got all this extra shit. It's a good thing I'm so genteel and fascinating."

Erin giggled. "He's a lucky man, either way. Well, Beautiful Raven-Haired Baby Girl, I'm glad you're home."

"I never really had a home until now. I'm glad to be back too."

25

She'd put her hair up so the earrings he'd given her sparkled in the light. Her collar necklace accented the neckline of the dress she wore and filled him with heat every time he looked at it.

Christmas had arrived and they were at his parents' annual mixer. People he'd known most of his life moved around the house, glasses in hand, smiles on their faces. Toby stood in front of her, grinning as she tried to appear stern but failed. Jonah had been pretty happy about how his family had taken to Raven and she to them.

Carrie moved to Raven's side and Raven turned a big smile her way. His women there together. Raven might have been off-putting and socially awkward in some situations, but she was good to his daughter. Kind.

Perhaps it was that her own mother had failed so terribly and she saw some of herself in Carrie. Perhaps it was that Carrie belonged to Jonah so she extended that caring because of that connection. But regardless, though she was still totally unique in the way she dealt with Carrie, his daughter had taken to Raven. She'd even suggested Jonah ask Raven to move in.

They'd come a long way since that first meeting. In the weeks since they'd returned from Oklahoma City they'd gotten a great deal closer. Raven trusted him enough to lean on him when she needed to. He kept finding out things about her that made him love her even more.

She slept in his bed now without hesitation, though it had been rocky the first few times. There were nightmares from time to time but she didn't speak of them. He simply put his arms around her, letting her snuggle back against him and fall back to sleep.

He was totally and utterly satisfied with his life and ass over tea-kettle in love with the funky, bitchy, inked-up gorgeous dame across the room.

One of the waitstaff approached him quietly. "There's someone at the door asking for you. They weren't on the guest list."

"Thank you." He headed toward the front entry to find Charlotte standing there. "What are you doing here?"

She once had belonged there. Had been welcomed by his family. Her beauty turned heads. Still did, he'd wager. She was pale and fragile and knew exactly what to wear to accentuate it. But she left him cold and had worn out that welcome years before.

"Carrie told me you were seeing someone."

He shook his head, trying to figure her out. "What?"

"Carrie told me you were serious about someone. She said you were in love."

"As it happens, I am. But that doesn't answer the question of why you're here."

"Isn't it obvious?" Raven came into the entry. For all Charlotte's regal, fragile femininity, Raven was all fire and sensuality. And, he could easily see, some anger.

He put an arm around her waist, partly because he loved to touch her and partly to keep her away from Charlotte.

Charlotte curled her lip. "This? Jonah, she's your midlife crisis. I'm the mother of your child."

Then it hit him and he barked a laugh. "Are you shitting me?" He looked to Raven. "Gorgeous, I had no idea."

"Hm."

He kissed her, still laughing.

"Jonah, you're her ATM. Your daughter is nearly eighteen. Her ability to control you through Carrie will be lessened then. She's here to play the understanding and yet wounded woman. Jeez, how can you be so smart about everything but not have seen this a mile away?"

Raven then focused on Charlotte, losing the amused smile she'd had for Jonah. "You don't deserve that girl. How dare you come here and try to put her in the middle? What kind of person are you?"

"Oh please. You think you're just going to walk into my life?"

Raven snorted. "As if I'd want it? I have my own life. You have your life and it sucks. My life on the other hand includes Jonah. I should feel sorry for you that you only see Jonah's worth in his wallet. Frankly the other side of his pants has a lot more appeal."

Jonah guffawed a moment and tried to be serious again. It made Raven feel even stronger about her point. "Now, you need to go before Carrie hears you're here and you upset her."

"Don't you tell me how to be a mother."

"I'm telling you how to be a human being. You already failed at mothering."

"Charlotte, I really don't know what you thought you'd gain here. I'm not interested. You're not interested. This is insulting to both of us. You need to go now. You weren't invited. Carrie tells me you informed her you were in Gstaad for the rest of the year anyway."

"I'm staying with my parents for a few days. You can't stop me from seeing my daughter."

"Jonah, Raven, people are asking for you." Liesl came into the room and Charlotte took a step back.

Jonah turned, holding an arm out for Raven. She patted him.

"Just a moment. Charlotte, I'd like a word. Outside."

Liesl gave him a glare when he began to argue.

He looked nervous, but he sighed and clearly gave in. "I'll be here waiting. Don't get the police called out on such a cold night." He kissed her cheek and then put his suit jacket on her shoulders.

"I'll try not to ruin your clothes." Raven opened the front door and turned her attention to Charlotte. "It's me or her." She jerked her head in Liesl's direction.

Charlotte paled further and scurried out. "I can't believe you'd just give up on us, Jonah."

Raven shut the door in their wake. "Yeah, yeah. Of course you can. Now, you and I need to have a chat."

Charlotte rounded, her tiny little fists balled up around ridiculous nails. Raven found it hard to imagine her and Jonah together.

"I know who you are. I know what you are. White trash. Mother in an institution. Tattoo parlor? You had several relationships with women." She sneered. "You're a whore, a *lesbian*, and a temporary fling. Once he hears what you are he'll dump you so fast your head will spin."

Raven rolled her eyes. "Honey, I'm going to be totally honest with you. Mainly because I don't have the energy to blunt the truth and I don't like you. I'm *totally* white trash. I lived in more than one shitty little trailer growing up. My mother is schizophrenic and living in an institution, and Jonah has met her. I can't imagine why I should be ashamed of her mental illness, but you're fucked up, so there you go."

Charlotte began to speak again and Raven made a quick movement with her hand. "No. Not your turn. I'm many things. Since you're name-calling and all, you should get your terminology straight. I'm not actually a lesbian because I like men too. They call that bisexual. I call it not your business. I work in a tattoo parlor. Which means two things. First, unlike you, I have an actual job. Second, it's not a secret. In fact I just finished a full back piece on Jonah. It's amazing. He's got a great body, as I'm sure you remember. As to temporary?" She shrugged.

"Time will tell. One thing that isn't temporary is your divorce." Raven bared her teeth in a feral smile.

"However, I am not a whore. You see, I have more dignity and class than to ever sell my pussy. Not to a biker, and not to a rich guy who I plan to cheat on and divorce and hit up for money when my latest loser boyfriend strands me in whatever country I'm in instead of raising my kid."

She took a step closer, seeing all the women she'd met before and since Jonah who projected their own misdeeds onto her. "There's a whore out here, but I'm not it. You're not even a good whore! Instead of finding yourself a new rich guy you keep hooking up with losers. Oh? You thought you were the only one capable of doing a background check? I didn't even need to waste money. I just looked up your stupid ass online."

Raven let that settle in. This bitch and her little private investigator. So scandalized over a bunch of crap Jonah already knew. And she was there with him and his family at Christmas. It had taken her a long time to admit she was worth it, that she should open up and let Jonah in and let him love her. But she had and she would fight until she was bloody to keep what she had. *Take that, Charlotte.*

"So here's how it goes. You aren't getting Jonah back. Not ever."

"I could if I wanted."

"Really?" Raven looked all around. "Where is he? Hm? Please, you're embarrassing yourself. See, your mistake, one of many, was to assume I was a stupid useless twat like you. I have a job. I pay my own bills. I'd never use a man like that. I can see Jonah's value and you can't. He's a smart man. He knows what you are. He's only tossed cash your way to protect Carrie. But that's over too.

"You can't have him back. He hasn't been yours in a long time. You blew it. I'd urge you to put some effort into your relationship with Carrie. She's an amazing girl. You have so much to be proud of. But we both know you're a shitty mother. A failure. A heartless, conniving bitch. The best thing you ever did was to give birth to her and you can't even see that. But *he* can. She's got a wonderful father and a family who adores her. A great education and lots of opportunities will ensure she's nothing like you. Be proud of that and back off."

"Or what?"

She got right in Charlotte's face then, nose to nose. "Or I will make you. I didn't grow up in your world. I can't make a game out of clever insults. I'll end you. I love Jonah and I have no plans to have you messing around in my relationship. Back. Off. He's not yours. He's mine. I'm not giving him up. This isn't a game to me. This is my life and the man I love. Don't make this any worse than it is because I won't lose and we both know it. I love your daughter too. But I'm fairly sure that if you continue your little games, it's Liesl you'll have to watch over your shoulder for, and God help you. Now, take your high-class-hooker ass out of here before I let Liesl call the police and you once again hurt your daughter."

She turned and walked away, leaving Charlotte gaping in the driveway.

Jonah looked worried, but relaxed when she appeared to have no blood on her clothes. She decided to take it easy on him. "I believe your mother said we had people looking for us?"

He grinned and pulled her to him, hugging her tight. "I'm sorry. You know there's nothing—"

She made a dismissive sound. "Of course I know that. You'd be limping for the rest of your life if I thought otherwise. I'm not going to let her continue to mess with you. She needed to know that." An interesting thing, as she'd never actually felt the need to mark her territory or defend her man before. Oh, that Jonah, still making her break her rules.

Carrie came over, looking worried. "I heard my mother was here. I told her about you, but not in the way you think."

Raven took Carrie's hands. "It's all right."

"I told her because I wanted her to know Dad was happy. I thought it would help her let go."

"Jonah, can you please get me some cider?" Raven motioned toward the back deck where warming stations had been set up with seating. "Carrie and I are going to be out there a while."

Jonah kissed Carrie's temple. "Be right back with two ciders and probably some pie."

Carrie grinned and followed Raven outside. "This way he can watch us without hovering and feeling guilty. Carrie, I'm not mad that you told your mom your dad was dating."

"I didn't say that. I told her he was in love and that I figured you two would be married by this time next year. And I'm *glad* of it. She's just . . . I feel bad for her. But I didn't tell her because I think she and my dad should get back together."

"Look, kid, I promise you, I'm not mad. Even if you had done it that way, I wouldn't be mad. He's your dad, you have the right to feel any way you choose about him and me."

"I never pictured him with anyone like you."

Raven couldn't help it, she laughed. "I bet!"

"No. I mean, you're different than the women in this world. The ones he dated before were like my mom. Do you think I'm like my mom?"

"That's like making me tell you if your butt looks big in that dress." Carrie snorted, one brow going up in a very fine imitation of her father. Raven shrugged. "Well, okay, so I have to admit I have trouble not being really frank. But, the truth is, I don't know her. But I know you. And I know your dad and I know he's beyond proud of you. And from what I can see he's got reason. You're smart and successful and independent. Those are all good things. If your mom has those qualities, then I guess you are."

"Wow, you were working really hard there."

Raven snickered. "Your dad has had a good influence on me. Don't tell him that though. I like to keep him on his toes and perpetually concerned I'm going to say something rude."

Carrie giggled.

"It's really not in my best interest, nor is it my place, to say anything negative about your mom. She made you and really, right there that's all I need to know."

"She was awful, wasn't she?"

Raven took a deep breath. She'd tried diplomacy and it was damned hard. Carrie was a smart girl; she knew the truth. "Yes. But it was about me. Not about you. So that's something you don't need to be concerned over. She's in charge of herself. Like you're in charge of yourself."

"She's my mom. She's supposed to not be like that."

"My mom is in a mental institution after repeatedly abandoning me and leaving me at the mercies of her horrible family and foster care. Perspective is important."

Carrie's eyes widened. "I'm sorry."

"Don't be. I don't want you to be. Thing is, she's the way she is. Your mom, I mean. Now she's not eighty or anything. She could change. But chances are? She won't. You, on the other hand? You're seventeen and on the verge of everything. *Everything.* You come from a great home. Your family adores you. You will fall in love for the first time and get your heart broken terribly. So terribly your father will growl and snarl and buy you things to make it better. And possibly punch the boy responsible in the nose. You will go to college and have roommates. You will graduate and get a real job. You will make friends who will be at your side for the rest of your life and you will find that very right person. You have the chance to walk into your future with your eyes open and arms wide. What your mother is or isn't can't hurt you now. Not unless you let it. She's who she is and what she is. But that doesn't mean you can't make better choices. And, I speak from experience when I say it is absolutely one hundred percent all right to build a deep moat around yourself to keep out the people who will harm you either on purpose or because they are not fully formed human beings and only see themselves."

"I guess I keep waiting for her to snap out of it."

Raven shrugged, unsure what else she could say. Charlotte wasn't going to change because she was a spoiled bitch.

Jonah came out holding a tray with cider and pie. She grinned at him, enjoying his anxiety for a brief moment before she smoothed her grin into a smile to let him know everything was fine.

"I'm sorry, Dad."

He shook his head. "It's not your fault, honey. You warm enough out here? I think your grandmother is looking for you, and Levi and Daisy have an announcement so I'm supposed to round people up."

"You should assure him I didn't say anything scary."

He rolled his eyes at her. "I trust you with my most precious thing." He tipped his chin in Carrie's direction. That made Raven nearly tear up, but she wrestled it back by thinking of his dumb ex-wife instead.

They filed back inside, moving to sit on one of the long couches.

"I'm eating this pie." She spoke in an undertone after putting the cider down.

He placed a hand on her knee, making her tingly. The rogue. "Gorgeous, that's what it's there for. I enjoy watching you eat pie."

Well, given the swank level that night she wondered if the food wasn't for decoration. But it was pie and she loved pie. So.

A tray with champagne glasses passed through. He grabbed one for her. "Keep eating that pie." He leaned very close. "I'm just going to imagine licking it off your belly."

Guh.

"You're going to make me choke."

"Not on pie."

That one made her laugh and people turned to look. Jeez.

Levi and Daisy came in and waited for everyone to quiet down.

"As most of you know, we got engaged some time ago. Daisy has been busily creating art people have been busily buying. We set up house together. I've continued to build the Bainbridge Island office of the firm, taking on a new associate this summer. So we've been busy and the wedding kept being put on the back burner."

Liesl frowned and Raven held back a smile. She knew via Daisy that Liesl had been sending many *helpful* suggestions to them after they'd passed the year mark of being engaged. Daisy was feeling panicked and trapped by all the expectations placed on her for some big giant wedding.

"So it was sort of a surprise to find out we'll be parents in a little over six months from now."

The room erupted with applause and well wishes.

"We'd better get on that planning then." Liesl managed a smile and made Raven believe it. The woman did adore her granddaughter so it wasn't so hard to believe she'd be thrilled with another one.

"Well, as it happens, we snuck off to Las Vegas day before yesterday and got married. Just the two of us. We haven't told anyone yet." Levi looked to Jonah. "Sorry. I wanted you to stand up for me, but it was a whim."

"I'm thrilled for you both. You can make it up to me by letting me throw you a reception dinner."

He took Raven's hand and she squeezed it.

There was a toast or three made. Lots of happy hugs and well wishes, and at last things mellowed a little. Enough that Raven thought she'd make her escape. But Liesl pinned her with her gaze and made her way over.

"Damn."

Jonah, who'd been talking with Toby, turned and saw his mother on the way over. "Welcome to the family. Sink or swim, gorgeous." And then he scampered off with Toby like a naughty little boy.

Liesl glided to a stop at Raven's side. "He believes I didn't notice that. Now I'm going to have to think up something to make him do."

"You move me to tears sometimes, Liesl. You're like a total Jedi Master."

Liesl tried not to smile but it didn't work. "Yes. Well. Would you be willing to talk to me and my board of Created Families? About your experience in the foster care system?"

"I don't know."

"I know your experiences were not all good. But it's good to hear from someone who has a unique perspective. We want to make things better. We'd like to know how. Jonah didn't tell me much, if that's your concern. He's honored your privacy."

Raven nodded. "I know. You did a good job with him, you know. He's a good man. The best I've ever known."

Liesl softened. "Thank you. I'm proud of the men my sons have become." She paused. "I'd like to hear your story. If you'd like to tell it. I know I can be . . . difficult at times. But I've gotten to know Daisy, who is delightful. And I'd like the same opportunity with you. My son loves you. You're good for him and for Carrie too."

Raven laughed. "I'm *not* delightful."

Liesl sniffed. "I'm aware."

"All right. I'll let you take me to lunch. I'll tell you my story and you can decide whether or not you want me to address your charity board."

Liesl smiled, victorious. As if there'd been any doubt. "I'll be in touch. I hear you're off to Maui next week."

"Your son knows how to give a Christmas present. I'll give him that."

26

She sat on the chaise, a drink in one hand, her sunglasses perched on her face. The ocean roared just feet away from where he stood, watching her.

She was different on vacation. Different a thousand miles away from home and halfway across the ocean. Relaxed. Playful even. Her hair had been caught in two braids, exposing the beauty of the ink on her back.

She knew he was there, a smile on her face. "Would you like your drink freshened up, Sir?"

When it was just them she'd taken to calling him that. It made him so fucking hot and hard he wanted to bend her over and fuck her right there. It was a gift, freely given. He didn't require it. Didn't need it. It wasn't role-play. It was the way she submitted, in her own fashion. In a way she knew would get to him.

He slid onto the chaise next to hers. "I would. Thank you."

She got up, padding over to the bar he was doubly glad he'd had installed the year before. She mixed him a fresh Blue Hawaiian. Normally he was prone to simple drinks like martinis. But here? Well with the breeze and the clean salt smell on the air he let himself enjoy drinks that captured that sprit. And she was good at making them too.

She handed him a drink and sat again. "This house is pretty spectacular."

"I know. I bought it on a whim. An expensive whim. Four years ago. After the divorce and I wanted something far away from home."

"The real estate agent was hot, wasn't she?"

He laughed. "It was a he, as it happened." She was the only woman he'd ever had here other than Carrie.

"Hm."

He wanted to ask her to marry him. But it was too soon. He wanted to ask her to move into his house. But it was too soon. It had only been four months since he'd first met her, after all. He knew, without a doubt, that she was meant to be his. That this woman beside him was the one he'd spend the rest of his days with.

And he knew she felt the same, though she wasn't as generous with her words as she was with her deeds. In the end, that she showed him how much she loved him, what a gift she thought he was, meant far more than a million words.

She would let him know when she was ready to move in. When she was ready to stop relying on her place as her little bolt hole. He was an exceedingly patient man and she knew he was waiting.

"I was thinking of taking you to dinner tonight."

"You were?"

"Yes. You know how much I like to show you off."

And he did. Shamelessly so. She was so beautiful and vivid. And all his.

"There's a place. Just up the road. Right on the water. A dance floor. I want to dance with you with the breeze in your hair and my hands on your bare skin. I brought a dress I think will be perfect."

"I bet you did." She smiled, her eyes closed behind her sunglasses.

He liked to buy her things. He liked to see the dresses and other clothing he chose on her skin. Liked to know she allowed him to spoil her. It wasn't overly exorbitant. He knew she had limits and he didn't want to make her feel uncomfortable.

But he liked her in sexy clothing and she wore it all so well.

"Perhaps some shoes too."

She laughed then, reaching out to tangle her fingers with his.

"I'm a kept woman, Sir. My goodness."

He liked the fantasy of keeping her at home just for him. Waiting for him to get home, naked and willing. But the reality was nice too. Independent and creative. Bawdy and totally capable of pushing him back when he crossed lines. He'd never imagined finding that attractive. But oh, how he did.

Being at his side was her choice. One she made freely. Which made it all the sweeter.

She turned her head, pulling her glasses down her nose. "You're trouble. You know that?"

"I hope so."

"Dinner it is. But remember, you promised to try Hawaii my way too. I know just the place to have lunch tomorrow."

"Anything for you."

When he stepped from the shower he saw her note.

I'll meet you at the restaurant—R

Well now.

He got dressed and headed out. She'd worn the dress he'd laid out for her, and the shoes. Things were looking up.

She must have taken a cab because his car was in the garage. Once there he headed inside, looking around. It was then he saw her at the bar.

Stunning. Her hair was a tousle around her face, held back with a flower to one side. The side that said she was taken. Her lips were glossy and red, eyes dramatic, lined to accent how big and sexy they were.

He walked around to catch sight of her from behind. Her entire back was exposed. The dress had a halter neck and dipped to the small of her back. She had her legs crossed, slowly kicking the delicate strapped high heel back and forth.

He wasn't the only one staring.

He slid onto the seat next to hers. She gave a slow, sensual look his way. "Hello."

"Hello."

"You should buy me a drink."

"Should I?"

"You should. Or he might." She tipped her chin toward one of the men who'd been staring at her.

"Can't have that." He got the server's attention. "Another for her and the same for me."

She held a hand out. "I'm Raven."

Oh. A game. Well.

He took her hand. "Jonah."

Their drinks arrived and he clinked his against hers. "You should have dinner with me."

"Should I?"

"You should." He tipped his chin at a woman on the other side of the bar. "Or she might."

Raven leaned in close enough for him to catch the scent of her skin. "I think she's more my type than yours."

Christ. She was going to kill him.

She put a hand on his knee. "I'd love to have dinner with you, Jonah."

He checked in with the hostess and she led them to a table.

The view was gorgeous. The sky was on fire from sunset, but soon enough it would be the kind of dark it only got out in the middle of the ocean. The moon would hang overhead and shine silver on her skin.

They chatted as if they were strangers and he got harder and harder as the night drew on. He knew he'd have her in any way he wanted her. The real her.

This was fun and titillating, but the real Raven was special.

He took her hand after dessert had been cleared off and he'd watched her lick her spoon like she did his cock. He pressed a kiss to her palm. She shivered.

"I don't want to dance with you."

"You don't? I'm a very good dancer, Jonah. I may be insulted."

"I want to take you back to my house and strip you naked. I want to lick you from head to toe and then I want you to suck my cock. I'll fuck you."

"Naturally."

"Naturally. And then we'll nap. Then I'm going to wake you up and you're going to get on top so I can watch you while I fuck you again."

One corner of her mouth lifted. "I think I can find that amenable."

He paid the bill and led her to the car.

He put a hand on her thigh as they drove. Making little circles with his middle finger just on the inside.

"Don't get into an accident or you'll never get to see me naked."

He swore under his breath but kept his attention on the road. Just three or so miles more.

"Oh and Jonah?"

"Hmm?"

"I'm not wearing any underwear."

Once he was in the garage he turned to her and inched her hem up, revealing her neatly trimmed pussy.

"Touch me."

Heart pounding in his chest, he reached out with a fingertip and slid it along her labia.

"Wet." He pressed, immediately greeted by hot, slick flesh. "All for me?"

"Yes. I had to go into the bathroom and make myself come."

"You did?"

She licked her fingertips. "I did."

"I don't think I gave you permission to do that."

One brow went up and he leaned in to kiss it, and then her fingertips.

"What did you think about?"

"The way your tongue feels on my clit, with your fingers inside me. The way you say my name right before you come. The way you feel when I want you so bad and you finally put your cock in me. My fingers are never as good as that."

"Go in the house and get naked. I want you on the bed. You know how I like you."

She swung those long legs from the car and sashayed into the house as he got his breath and control back.

Raven smiled as she let the dress slide from her body. She knew she'd gotten him all worked up. Which was good as she was worked up too. All evening as they'd teased she'd known they'd come back here. She wanted his hands on her. Wanted all of him all at once.

She decided to leave the shoes on as she settled on the bed, on her knees, her hands behind her back.

He came in some minutes later, standing in the doorway, staring.

He was going to make her work for this one, she knew by the look on his face. And that was totally okay with her.

He left the room again for a few minutes and came back, his hands full. She shivered at the sight of the things he held.

"You've gotten me in quite a state, Raven. What are you going to do to make that right?"

"Whatever you want me to, Sir."

He cupped her throat around her choker, tipping her head back. He kissed her hard, a gnash of teeth and tongue. Need, like fire, licked at her skin. When he handled her like that it did something to her. Flipped an internal switch of some sort. That they'd built the sort of trust for him to touch her that way without fear he'd harm her or scare her, that he *did* touch her that way and only turn her on, it meant so much to her.

Made her want to do anything he asked. Anything he demanded.

He pulled back, his eyes burning, and a thrill slid through her. She made him like this. What they had wasn't temporary. Or a fling. This was bone-deep connection. No one else had ever made her feel this way.

She'd stopped questioning it. Stopped letting herself panic over whether he was the real deal. He'd proved it to her every time he touched her. Every time he looked at her—even knowing all he did about her past—not with pity but with love. He adored her. No one had ever adored her before. It was not overrated.

"You're the most beautiful thing I've ever seen."

He bent and straightened, holding the blindfold. She hummed her pleasure and he allowed himself a smile. "Do you like this?"

"Yes."

He tied it in place and her skin came to life.

He brushed something against her shoulder. She stilled, trying to figure out what it was.

"Something new I've been working on. Practicing so I'd use it just right."

His voice was taut with desire and it hardened her nipples. She tried to squeeze her thighs together but it wasn't nearly enough.

Then he struck. Hot and fast, tails of what she figured out was a flogger licked at her belly, just above her pussy. She gasped at how amazing it felt, the heat of pain that dissolved into fingers of desire in its wake.

He paused, she knew, to gauge whether her gasp was good or bad. After a few moments he did it again, this time against her ass.

"Hands high above your head. I want at that ass."

She obeyed quickly. More and more, the leather tails of the flogger scorched heat and then pleasure against her ass, leaving her panting. He pinched her nipples. Right and left and then the flogger hit them too.

"Ohgod," she gasped.

"You should see the color of your skin right now. Pink. The prettiest pink. Your nipples are so fucking hard. Do you like it when I use the flogger on them?"

"Yes," she managed to say.

"Does it hurt?"

"Yes." And this time it was a moan as he struck several times in quick succession. She was so fucking wet she ached with her need to come. "In a good way."

"Jesus, you're so hot." She heard the flogger hit the mattress as he tossed it down. Then his mouth was on hers, taking her pleasure, feeding it back as he left her drunk with his taste. With how much he wanted her. With how much she affected him.

Then he kissed down her neck to her nipples, licking them until she writhed. Her hands still high because he hadn't said she could move them.

"Please, please, please," she begged.

"Please what?" He breathed the words against her mound, now on his knees. "I can smell your cunt. I know how much you want me."

"I want you. I want your mouth on me. Please let me come."

He parted her with his thumbs and sucked her clit between his lips. There was no slow buildup, just climax so hard it nearly hurt as it shot through her body. He didn't stop. His fingers slid up inside as he continued to suck at her clit over and over, pushing her into another climax right on the heels of the first. Leaving her sensitive and raw.

He helped her to stand. "I'm going to walk you over to the chair where I'm going to sit. Then you're going to get on your knees and I'm going to fuck that pretty mouth of yours until I come."

She nodded, walking carefully as he guided her.

He let go of her, leaving her standing as he undressed. He was weak in the knees at how she looked. Her taste lived in his system, the feel of her skin on his fingertips. She stood there, waiting. Waiting for him to tell her what to do next. It nearly drowned him, how ridiculously alluring it was to see her that way.

He'd been careful with the flogger at first, waiting to see, wanting to be sure she was on board, but oh, how she was. Her scent hung in the air, she was so wet, and she nearly sobbed when she came all over his lips, shocking him with how fast it happened.

Once he was totally naked he pulled her close, hissing at how good it felt, her skin against his. His woman right there.

"On your knees." One hand on her shoulder, the other holding her forearm, he sat as he helped her to her knees and onto the pillow he'd put down for her. "Now." He pulled her hair, bringing her closer. Her mouth opened, seeking. He swallowed hard as she licked her lips.

Her hands were behind her back. "You can move your hands to my thighs to keep your balance. I'm going to be fucking that gorgeous mouth, so you'll need to brace yourself."

She licked her lips again and he groaned.

She braced, moving closer on the pillow as she did.

First she kissed his knee. Then up one thigh and down the other.

He ran his fingers through her hair, wrapping it around his fist as he pulled her to his cock. "Now."

The air gusted from her lips as she found his cock with her tongue, licking up the length of him. She grabbed him at the root and then in one movement she swallowed him deep.

"Christ," he gasped.

She hummed her pleasure and all his control began to unravel. Each time she took him deep he needed her more until he flexed his hips, taking his pleasure from her, fucking into her mouth over and over.

The mask made it hotter. The way she seemed to love what he did to her made it hotter. This woman, so strong and bold on her knees as he fucked her face, as she gave herself over to him, was more than his heart could take. His balls crawled up close to his body. He was torn between the need to blow down that pretty throat and to fuck her cunt. Indecision left him a breath or two from climax.

He pulled her back and she was slow to rouse from that sleepy, desire-warm place he took her when he was this dominant. She found herself being picked up and unceremoniously brought down on his lap, his cock sliding into her hard and fast

She grabbed his shoulders, still blindfolded, his taste still on her tongue.

He was speaking to her, low and dark. Telling her how beautiful she was in raw terms. How hot and slick her cunt was. The dirtier he got, the more his control slipped and that *GQ* mask fell away and he went into a rut. It made her feel gloriously beautiful and desirable.

"You're so fucking tight and slick, goddamn." He nearly snarled it as he thrust so hard her tits bounced. She hung on, her nails digging into his shoulders. She was going to leave a mark and she didn't give one single fuck. She owned him as surely as he owned her.

"I want to come inside you. Fill you up with me, mark you, gorgeous. I want to bite you." He moved and his teeth sank into the side of her right breast. She cried out, her cunt rippling around him. God, she was going to come again.

"Tomorrow. Next week. Next month I want you to be at work and think of this. Of the way my cock feels inside you."

"Yes."

"Yes. Beautiful, beautiful Raven. All mine."

"Body and soul."

"You wreck me with your spine of steel. With your tight cunt and your big gorgeous tits. With the way you suck my cock and take me deep. There is no one like you."

She arched, undulating on him, brushing her clit against his pubic bone.

"Is this what you need?" He put his fingers in her mouth and she sucked, getting them wet. Those fingers found her clit moments later. "Hm? Should I play with your clit until you come?"

"Yes."

He did and it felt so good she thought she might die from it. But if she died, she'd miss the climax, so she held on, thrusting, taking him as deep as she could. He growled low in his throat and she knew he was coming. His cock moved inside her, jerked, right as she came, and there was nothing but the circuit of pleasure they made. Thrusting and moving as he fucked her, as she fucked him.

He stood and she managed to hold on. He pulled the blindfold off and kissed her as if his life depended on it.

"Good god."

He stumbled to the bed and they both fell to it, still wrapped around one another.

"Yeah."

"I'm so glad I needed to get a tattoo and saw you across the room at that engagement party." He kissed her again. "Damn, you fill every part of me."

She held on tight. "You fill parts of me I never thought would stop hurting. I love you, Jonah."

"Thank God, because I love you too."